Award-winning Lorraine Heath, the author of Never Love a Cowboy, *shares the remarkable story of a love and passion that is larger than life ...*

Never Marry a Cowboy

From the moment Kit Montgomery walked into Ashton Robertson's life, she knew her heart would always belong to the dashing English rogue. Years later, her brother is determined to see Ashton married to Kit in order to fulfill her greatest dream. And though Ashton knows that Kit will never love her, in his arms she finds the freedom that's been denied her all her life. But will a few days in paradise be enough to satisfy a lifetime of denial?

Kit was a man who lived every day in a hell of his own making, carrying the burden for a choice no man should have to make. But Ashton's gentle beauty and fiery spirit that allow her to find pure joy in every moment are slowly captivating the hardened rogue. Before long Kit finds himself devising opportunities to show Ashton the world and keep her close to his side. . . but will a man with no hope be able to let go of the only woman who might save his soul?

Other Avon Romances by
Lorraine Heath

NEVER LOVE A COWBOY
A ROGUE IN TEXAS

If You've Enjoyed This Book,
Be Sure to Read These Other
AVON ROMANTIC TREASURES

AFTER THE KISS *by Karen Ranney*
A DANGEROUS LOVE *by Sabrina Jeffries*
MARRYING WALKER MCKAY *by Lori Copeland*
NO MARRIAGE OF CONVENIENCE *by Elizabeth Boyle*
THE PRICE OF PASSION *by Susan Sizemore*

Coming Soon

A BREATH OF SCANDAL *by Connie Mason*

LORRAINE HEATH

Never Marry a Cowboy

An Avon Romantic Treasure

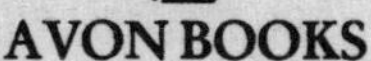

AVON BOOKS
An Imprint of HarperCollins*Publishers*

This is a work of fiction. Names, characters, places, and incidents are products of the author's imagination or are used fictitiously and are not to be construed as real. Any resemblance to actual events, locales, organizations, or persons, living or dead, is entirely coincidental.

AVON BOOKS
An Imprint of HarperCollins*Publishers*
10 East 53rd Street
New York, New York 10022-5299

ISBN: 0-380-80331-3
www.avonromance.com

First Avon Books paperback printing: February 2001

Printed in the U.S.A.

10 9 8 7 6 5 4 3 2 1

With each book I write, I'm amazed at the willingness of others to share their time, expertise, and support:

Mary Jo Putney held my hand beginning with *A Rogue in Texas,* patiently explaining the intricacies of the English nobility while I wrote three books that revolved around English heroes.

Peggy Moreland helped me place critical aspects of Kit's story into perspective.

My cousin, Karen Peterson, gladly researched her neighboring city of Galveston, saving me valuable time and effort.

Fay Robinson has served as mentor, sounding board, and confidante throughout my writing career. For this story, she trusted me with her rare copy of an 1837 medical book on consumption.

Ladies, I also want to thank you for sharing with me the gift of your friendship.

Lorraine Heath

Prologue

England
1865

He had made a pact with the devil and bargained away not only his soul, but his heart.

Gripping the intricately carved poster of the canopied bed, he grimly accepted the bittersweet luxury of gazing upon his love's delicate features as she slept. Like gossamer wings, her silken blond hair was spread across the massive pillow. She would soon be in death what she had been in life: an angel.

"My lord, I did not hear you come in," the physician said as he moved away from the bedside table.

"I entered quietly," he murmured. "I did not wish to disturb her."

"Your wife called for you earlier. She knows the end is near."

"How near?" he asked.

"That is difficult to say, my lord. Several more days at least, perhaps a week or more if she is fortunate."

He snapped his head around, unable to keep the bitterness from his voice. "You have a sadistic understanding of *fortunate*."

The physician's face turned red. "I meant no offense, my lord, but life is precious, every moment to be treasured."

"She is not yet twenty-five. Is there nothing you can do for her?" he asked, his frustration and anger growing at the incompetence surrounding him.

"Nothing but ease the pain."

"Then I damn you to hell."

The physician blanched. "You hardly seem yourself—"

"How should I seem? Clarisse hovers at death's door, and you expect me to accept her suffering docilely when I know heaven awaits her?"

"Humility may well be the better part of valor. Surely this illness is a test of your faith as well as hers."

He glared at the man. "Do not attempt to placate me with philosophy when you have no cures."

The physician tilted up his chin. "Very well, my lord. If you will excuse me, I must attend to other patients, but I have left the pain medication on the table beside the bed. Only a pinch of powder in a glass of water. More than that, and you risk killing her."

"Heaven forbid that her torment should end too soon."

"It would be a sin to take her life. That is God's decision, not ours."

"Then I rail against God."

"My lord, you speak blasphemy! I would expect

those words from your brother, not you."

"Ah, yes, my twin. There are those who cannot tell us apart."

The physician snorted. "Your facial features may be identical, but your actions separate you."

"So I've heard."

"Christopher," a soft voice called.

He waved the physician aside. "Be off with you and tend your other patients. I shall see to her needs."

"Remember my instructions regarding the pain medication. Only a pinch—"

He jerked up a hand. "I will do as you instructed."

He did not move until the physician had walked from the room and closed the oaken door. With a heavy heart, he stepped quietly to the head of the bed and smiled tenderly at the woman he had loved longer than he could remember.

"Christopher." Her voice seemed to come from such a great distance, as though she'd already begun her journey toward heaven.

He knelt and took her frail hand in his, cursing the pain that caused hers to tremble. "I am here, my love."

"I feared you would not come."

He brushed a soft kiss across her fingers. "I would not leave you to suffer alone. If only I could take this disease upon myself and spare you—"

Her hand clutched his weakly. "No, I would not wish this affliction upon my worst enemy."

"Are you in pain now?"

She nodded slightly, but her lovely blue eyes revealed the true extent of her agony. "It never ceases. Sometimes," she whispered, her breathing labored, "I wish for death, I wish the physician would leave the medication within my reach. I know it is a sin—"

He cradled her cheek and touched his thumb to her lips. "It is not a sin to wish."

Tears filled her eyes. "I wish I had given you a son, an heir to Ravenleigh."

"I never desired anything beyond your love."

She gripped his hand, breathing heavily, and he required no words to know that she suffered greatly.

"I'll ready your medication." He stood and turned to the table. With a steady hand and a throat tightening to the point of suffocation, he poured the cool water from the earthen pitcher into a glass. Following the physician's instructions, he added a pinch of powder—before adding more. Stirring briskly, he watched the liquid swirl like the sea during a tempest, like the storm of impotent anger raging through him. How could a disease eat from within and not be seen from without?

Gingerly, he sat on the edge of the bed, hating the thought of causing her the least discomfort. Gratitude softened the lines of her face as he gently lifted her head and brought the glass to her lips.

She took a sip and grimaced. "It is so bitter."

"But it will ease your suffering."

"Not completely," she admitted before finishing off the brew. She lay back. "I have missed your embrace."

He set the glass aside. "I do not wish to cause you further harm."

"I am beyond the stage where a bit more pain is noticeable. I need your comfort."

He slid beneath the covers. He lifted his arm, and she came to him as he had so often dreamed. Her head nestled within the crook of his shoulder, her small body pressed against his larger one, her delicate hand curled on his chest.

She sighed wistfully. "Oh, how I have longed to again know your warmth and the steady rhythm of your heart."

"I was a fool not to come sooner."

He felt the slight shake of her head. "I am torn between having you near and knowing that you must endure the sight of my sickly appearance."

He slipped a finger beneath her chin and angled her head until he held her gaze. "Through my eyes, you are as beautiful now as you were the first time I saw you, dressed in a gown of blue."

She smiled softly. "It was green. I wore blue when I met Christian."

He kissed her forehead. "Ah, yes. I remember now. He described you in such vivid detail I suppose his memory became mine."

"It is often like that with the two of you, isn't it? You always know each other's thoughts and feelings."

"It is a strange blessing, and at times, a curse."

She furrowed her brow. "I overheard the servants talking. They said your father is sending Christian to Texas."

"It seems his rakehell reputation does not sit well with Father."

"It is hardly his fault that women adore him. Incredibly handsome features and irresistible charm are lethal to a woman's good sense. As you proved with me. Still I worry about him."

"Do not concern yourself, my love. He wants to leave. Besides, Harry and Gray are going as well. I have no doubt that they will create enough trouble to keep themselves happy."

Her eyelashes fluttered. "I grow so . . . weary."

Fighting back the tears, he swallowed hard and drew her more closely against him. "Then sleep well, my love."

"I love you, Christopher."

"And I love you, more than I could ever tell you."

He held her near until she went limp and her final breath was but a whisper against his throat. The unbearable ache in his chest almost had him reaching for the last of the pain medication.

Carefully, he eased away from her. With tenderness, he arranged the blankets and folded her arms across her chest. Then he did what he'd never done before. Lightly, he touched his lips to hers. "God must have been in desperate need of angels, my love. He has surely acquired the finest."

He straightened and strode across the room, knowing his brother would want to see Clarisse before the warmth left her completely. He opened the door and stepped into the magnificent hallway.

Sitting on a bench, his brother snapped his head around and slowly came to his feet. "Has our vigil ended?"

He nodded. "She went peacefully, your name upon her lips."

He watched as Christopher's face crumpled and tears filled his eyes. "I know you think me an awful coward, but I loved my wife too much to watch her die."

"I loved Clarisse too much to allow her to die alone." He held up a hand to stay whatever protest his brother might make. "It matters not which is the greater love, Christopher. You are the one who held her heart."

Christopher took a step toward him. "I shall talk to Father. I know he feared Clarisse was a temptation you would be unable to resist, but now no reason exists for you to travel to Texas."

"Do not bother yourself on my account. It matters not where my body is, *I* shall be in hell."

Chapter 1

Fortune, Texas
1870

Christian Montgomery had no desire to be a hero, but it seemed Fate held little regard for his aspirations.

The crack of a gunshot echoed through the saloon. The young woman who sat on his lap twitched, and he tightened his hold on her as he slowly brought his glass of whiskey away from his lips.

Standing in front of the bar, a man badly in need of a shave and a bath released a hysterical guffaw before firing into the wooden floor again. The fellow before him hopped and jerked his gangly body, his arms flailing like those of a scarecrow caught in the wind. The cowboy with the pistol laughed louder and shot the floor again.

Christian thought he might never understand these Texans' sense of humor. He cast a quick glance at the faro dealer who owned the saloon. Behind his gaming table, Harrison Bainbridge reached for his cane. *Bloody hell.*

Tenderly, Christian guided Lorna off his lap. "Excuse me for a moment, sweetheart."

"Now don't go gettin' yourself kilt." She pushed her full lower lip into a pout that made him wonder if she might truly care.

He scraped back his chair, stood, and winked at her. "Not to worry."

He strode across the saloon as the cackling man shoved bullets into his gun before spitting a stream of tobacco juice, not even bothering to aim for the polished brass spittoon. Another disgusting habit many of these Texans possessed.

"Let's see some more dancin'," he ordered and pointed his gun between the feet of the poor fool who had been too frightened to move beyond harm's way.

"Excuse me," Christian murmured.

The man with the gun jerked his head around, his tobacco juice seeping between his lips. With the back of his hand, he wiped his mouth. "What'd you say?"

Imploringly Christian held out a hand. "You must forgive me, but I don't quite understand why shooting the floor would make you laugh like a lunatic."

The man darted a glance at the three men who'd accompanied him into the saloon, men who were alternately flexing their fingers and stroking their guns. Then he grinned, and the tobacco juice once again claimed its freedom. "It ain't the shootin'. It's the dancin'."

He fired a bullet into the floor between Christian's feet. Christian didn't flinch, although he heard Lorna's tiny screech and someone else's gasp.

"Hey, Jasper, the fella don't seem to know you was

aimin' for his toes," one of the cowboy's comrades shouted, grinning around the thin cigar clenched between his yellowed teeth.

Jasper wrinkled his pug-shaped nose. "I reckon he didn't at that." He aimed.

"Give me the gun," Christian ordered quietly. "I know the couple who own the saloon, and the wife is not going to be pleased that you have marred her floor."

"Think I give a damn?"

"You would if you knew her," he assured the man, but Jessye seldom worked in the saloon, now that she had children to keep her busy. He held out his hand. "Give me your pistol."

"Take it from me," Jasper dared with a steely glint in his brown eyes as he jerked up his chin.

Christian plowed his fist into the target the man had conveniently provided. The gun thudded to the floor a heartbeat before Jasper did.

Christian might not understand their humor, but he understood their pride. Cowboys settled everything with a gun. They seldom fought hand to hand because they considered it an embarrassment to take a punch. Bullets and blood they could fathom. Boxing baffled them.

Leaning down, Christian picked up the weapon while Jasper watched, stunned, his face burning a dull crimson.

"About time you took action, Marshal," Harrison Bainbridge said as he limped closer, leaning heavily on his cane.

Christian gave his friend a warning glare as he reached into his pocket and wrapped his fingers around his tin star. "I had planned to take the evening off."

He pinned the symbol of his authority onto the lapel of his jacket, right over his heart. Then he gave a pointed look to each man who had accompanied Jasper into the saloon. "Gentlemen, I'll take your firearms."

"You can't be the marshal. You ain't wearing a gun," the one with the cigar protested.

"I find them cumbersome." He pointed toward his fallen comrade. "But as you can see, I don't require one in order to enforce the law of this town, a law which prohibits the bearing of firearms in the saloon."

"You hit Jasper," another man said, his eyes blinking rapidly.

Christian nodded at the scruffy fellow's brilliant deduction. "Shall I hit you as well?"

"That ain't fair," the man pointed out.

"Little in life *is*. Now, give me your weapons or spend the remainder of the night within the confines of my jail."

Grudgingly, the men unfastened their gun belts and handed them over. Christian gave them a perfunctory nod. "You may retrieve these from my office when you leave Fortune, which I trust will be tomorrow morning after you've finished sanding and smoothing Mrs. Bainbridge's floor."

With long, confident strides, he returned to his table, set down the weapons, and sat.

Lorna grinned brightly. "Gawd, you are so brave."

She plopped onto his lap and flung her arms around his neck. He wrapped one arm around her tiny waist to support her precarious position. With his free hand, he removed his badge, slipped it into his pocket, picked up his glass, and smiled warmly. "Now where were we?"

"You was tellin' me naughty things you done in England." She lifted her bare shoulders to her tiny, delicate ears. "And how you might do 'em to me iffen I wanted."

"Ah, yes. I assure you, sweetheart, that you will want—"

He scowled as Harrison Bainbridge approached his table, dragged back a chair, and dropped into it with a heavy sigh.

"Lorna, get me a glass and a bottle of whiskey," Harry ordered.

Lorna cast a furtive glance at Christian. He patted her hip. "Go on, do as he says."

Christian watched her saunter to the bar, gather up Harry's request, and stroll back over. She placed the glass and bottle on the table before sidling toward Christian.

"Lorna, you need to see about serving drinks to our other customers," Harry said quietly without rebuke.

Lorna stuck out that lower lip that Christian had an urge to nibble on. "But them other fellas don't pay me two bits for every smile I give 'em like the marshal here does."

"I pay you to serve drinks, and if you want me to give you your wages for the evening, you will tend to the other customers' needs."

With a huff, she flounced away. Christian grinned with appreciation at her naturally seductive movements. "Ah, Harry, you do have a knack for hiring beautiful serving wenches."

"Jessye hires them, and she expects me to protect them from rakes like you." Harry opened the bottle and refilled Christian's glass before filling his own.

"That's rather like asking the fox to stand guard at the hen house, isn't it?"

"Not when the fox's mate is skilled with a gun and a knife. Besides, she gives me no reason to stray and every reason to remain faithful."

"Dear God, but you are well and truly married, aren't you?" Although his voice held the expected disgust, Kit took absolute joy in his friend's good fortune. He held a great deal of respect and admiration for Jessye. She had single-handedly lifted Harry from the depths of hell.

"Yes, and I ask that you take care with the girls that work for me. I've mended one broken heart in my life. I have no wish to mend others."

"I was only engaging in a little harmless flirtation."

"Which is the way you always begin. Then you conquer, and later abandon. Yet none of the women ever hates you."

"Because I leave them feeling as though the victory were theirs instead of mine."

Harry grinned. "They say you have the eyes of the devil."

"More like his soul." Kit picked up his glass and downed the whiskey. He'd thought he'd never grow accustomed to these Texans' strong drink. Tonight, it didn't seem powerful enough.

Harry poured more whiskey into the glass. "It's been a while since you've spent the evening here."

"I was feeling a bit restless."

"Care to expand?"

Leaning forward, he crossed his arms on the table. "I don't know if I can explain it. I watched you and Gray get married, build yourselves homes, have children, and I just thought perhaps I needed to stop my wandering and take root as well." He sighed and shifted back in his chair. "But I am not content."

"You seemed happier when we were herding cattle."

"I didn't enjoy working with the beasts, but I welcomed the opportunity to see the country. Still something was lacking, and a man can hardly make a living by simply traveling."

Harry shook his head in obvious bewilderment. "I don't understand, Kit. With the money we made off that initial trail drive—"

"I have very little of it left."

Harry's green eyes widened in disbelief. "What in the bloody hell did you do with it? I know you didn't gamble it away in here."

"What I did with it is my concern, not yours."

"The first year we were here, we picked cotton, and you wouldn't tell me then what you did with the money you earned. But it wasn't available when we decided to try our hand at herding cattle, so we were forced to take on an investor—"

"For which you should be eternally grateful, since you ended up marrying her," Kit pointed out in his own defense, although he'd never felt that he needed to justify the disappearance of his money.

Harry grinned, warmth reflected in his green eyes. "God, Jessye was something on that trail drive, wasn't she?"

"She was indeed. You weren't so bad yourself."

Harry's smile faded. "I would have liked to have seen it through to the end, but broken legs and a smashed hip do not a worthy cowboy make."

Kit glanced around the saloon that had over the years, in small ways, begun to take on the appearance of the gentleman's clubs they'd frequented in London. Nothing extravagant by any means, merely the shadow of their memories preserved here and there. "You've done well for yourself with the Texas Lady."

"I can't complain. Besides, I think we've all done rather well. Gray's farm is prospering. Your skill with a rifle became legendary and the citizens appointed you marshal. Can't say that I blame them. You saved my life more than once."

Kit felt the familiar ache of an ancient festering wound. No matter how many lives he saved, he had not managed to spare the one that had mattered most. He drained the remainder of the whiskey from his glass, not bothering to protest when Harry refilled it. "It's not enough."

Harry glanced up. "The whiskey?"

Kit shrugged. "My life."

"My Lord, but you are morose this evening. You must have received a letter from Christopher."

Kit nodded at his friend's perceptive deduction. "It

seems Father is arranging another marriage for him. Although he failed to mention his feelings on the matter in his letter, I sense he's not in favor of the match. However, obligations and duty will no doubt bind him to Father's demands. It's almost innate, isn't it?"

"Would we be here otherwise? We were rebellious, but when our fathers commanded us to leave, we left. Perhaps we were good sons after all."

"No goodness resides within me, Harry. I would not have done the things I have, otherwise."

Harry rubbed his thumb over the lion's head that adorned his cane. "You're thinking of Clarisse."

"She is constantly on my mind. Even when I seek solace with other women, they always leave me wanting because none is her."

"You've turned her into a saint. She wasn't one, you know."

Kit lifted his glass in a mock salute. "No, she was an angel." He took a long swallow of whiskey, relishing the final drop. "I must be off."

"Take the bottle with you."

Kit picked it up. "Gladly." He stood. "Give my best to Jessye and the girls."

"Always."

He grabbed the confiscated weapons, tucked them within the crook of his arm, and walked from the saloon, making a mental note to look over the wanted posters in his office. He could tell when a man was a fun-loving cowboy simply looking for a good time and when one had evil running through his soul. He suspected the latter of Jasper and his comrades.

Kit welcomed the cool night air hitting him, the

only natural thing in this state that ever reminded him of England. The stars he'd never noticed until he'd watched over a herd of cattle at midnight.

The desire to return to Ravenleigh plowed into him. After five years, he should no longer miss the place of his birth, but he had yet to find anything to replace it in his heart. He missed the grounds, the books, and the art. And he missed the people. He longed for conversations that weren't accentuated with crude swearing and spitting.

Discussions with Harry and Gray offered some respite, but he spent less time in their company. Once they'd been in hell together. Now, he alone remained, and with that admission, the loneliness deepened.

He often wondered if he'd accepted the position of marshal because it offered him the opportunity to meet death. Not that he would purposely seek it out, but he knew in his heart that he would welcome it.

Although they no longer herded cattle, he and his friends continued to invest in their ranching enterprise, hiring men to do the arduous work they abhorred. Just as he'd told Harry, he had retained little of the money from their first venture, but he had set aside a considerable amount since. He was not a wealthy man by any means, but he could provide for himself when needed. When no needs existed, he had other things upon which he preferred to spend his money.

He opened the door to his office and staggered to a halt. A dark-haired man turned away from the wanted posters lining the wall behind Kit's desk.

Kit smiled broadly, truly pleased to see his visitor.

"David Robertson! What an unexpected pleasure. When did you arrive in town?"

"Late this afternoon."

Kit closed the door and strode across the room. "Are Madeline and Mary Ellen with you?"

"No, I left my wife and daughter in Dallas."

Kit laid his burdens on the desk before extending a hand toward the Texan he'd met in England several years ago. "What brings you here, man?"

David looked uncomfortable as he shook Kit's hand. "I'm here to test the boundaries of your friendship."

"That has an ominous ring to it," Kit said as he studied the man speculatively. He had rekindled their friendship when he and Harry had herded their cattle north, but he hadn't seen David since Harry's wedding four years earlier.

David nodded toward the bottle. "Some whiskey might help to take the edge off my request."

Kit grabbed the two tin cups he used to take water to the prisoners the few times that he had them. He settled into the chair behind his desk and liberally poured whiskey into the cups. "Please, make yourself comfortable," he offered, indicating the chair across from him.

David sat and took the cup. Kit watched as his friend studied the contents as though he searched for an unfathomable answer. He would not classify David Robertson as a close friend, but he'd always enjoyed his company. The man was successful and well bred, with a wife and daughter who adored him.

Kit brought the cup to his lips. "Your request?" he prompted before drinking his whiskey.

David lifted his gaze. "I want you to marry my sister."

The whiskey burned its way into Kit's lungs. He sputtered and coughed, the fire spreading through his chest.

David bolted out of his chair and pounded Kit's back. "I'm sorry."

Gasping for breath, Kit shoved him aside and glared at him. "Are you out of your mind? I am a rake, a scoundrel, and a rogue. Besides I have a rule not to get involved with the sisters of friends."

"I don't care about your rules. In England, your reputation for luring women into your bed was legendary."

"Women to whom I was not married," Kit felt compelled to point out.

"But you did charm them, didn't you? Isn't that how you persuaded them that a night with you was worth the loss of their reputation?"

Ah, yes, he had charmed them, become obsessed with them, striving to forget the one woman he could never possess. A dismal failure, that undertaking had been. Nothing, no one, would ever allow him to forget Clarisse. He gulped the remaining whiskey from his cup and reached for the bottle. "Regardless of my charming nature, knowing my tarnished reputation, why in God's name would you want me to marry your sister?"

"Because she's dying."

Kit felt as though he'd been bludgeoned. He set aside the bottle and the cup that now carried the dented impression of his fingers. "Are you certain?"

David nodded and lowered his gaze to the floor as though the pain were too great to bear. Kit certainly understood that feeling.

"Ashton has always been frail," David said quietly. "So incredibly delicate. When our parents died, she came to live with Madeline and me. Her health began deteriorating. Madeline took her to the doctor. He diagnosed her with consumption. He gives her until Christmas."

Kit shot out of his chair, feeling as though the walls of the room were closing in on him, suffocating him. "Then why ask me to marry her?"

David shifted his stance and met Kit's gaze. "I discovered her in the attic one afternoon wearing the dress our mother had worn the day she married our father. Ashton was weeping because Fate would deny her the opportunity to become a bride. It seemed such a small thing to want. I'm not asking you to act as her husband, only her bridegroom, to give her one day in the sun."

"Why me?"

"Because you come from a country where marriages are still arranged, and you understand that vows can be spoken with feeling even when no love exists between the couple." He took a step forward. "And because when last we met, you told me that Christopher's wife had taken ill and died. I saw in your eyes that you suffered from her loss, so you know that death can be cruel."

Kit snatched the bottle off the desk and drank

greedily, relishing the unmerciful flames burning their way through him. He lowered the bottle. "I have watched one woman die. I will not watch another."

"I'm not asking you to watch her die. I'm only asking you to marry her. Charm her for one day, one evening. Allow her to be a bride. Then I'll take her back to Dallas."

Shaking his head, Kit laughed and dropped into his chair. He remembered being introduced to Ashton at a party David had hosted, but his recollection of the woman was vague and blurry. The image of a timid mouse hovering in a corner popped into his mind. "I hardly know her."

"How well did you know the other women you've charmed?"

All good humor fled. "I seriously doubt you want to put your sister in league with them."

"How many of them hated you?"

"As far as I know, none. I always managed to stay on good terms with my *conquests*."

"That's the reason I think this idea will work."

"You want your sister to become one of my many conquests?"

David placed his palms on the desk and leaned forward. "I do not want you to bed her. She is far too frail. I only want you to marry her, allow her to walk down the aisle, dance a bridal dance with her. She'll have her wish, and you'll have—"

"A wife! I shall have a wife until she dies."

"For six months. Is there someone in your life right now who would object, whom this act of charity would hurt?"

"I object. This insane notion of yours is ludicrous. I would be shackled to a woman I hardly know, a woman I don't want."

David straightened. "As I said when you greeted me, I was here to test the boundaries of our friendship."

"Ask anything else of me and I will grant it, but do not ask me to marry a dying woman."

David nodded, obviously accepting Kit's decision. "Madeline opposed the idea as well."

"I always knew your wife was remarkably intelligent."

"I hope I didn't damage our friendship with this request."

"No," Kit said somberly. "I know how difficult it is to watch someone you love die. At the time, you would do anything for her—even die in her place if you could."

Chapter 2

The morning after he'd finished off a bottle of whiskey always made Kit wonder why he bothered to carry the decanter to his lips in the first place. The dull ache pounding between his temples rolled to the back of his head.

Marry a dying woman. The thought had kept him tossing and turning on his narrow cot for the remainder of the night. What had ever possessed David to dream up such an incredibly insane scheme?

The answer came before he'd finished asking himself the question: love.

He knew the emotion too well to ever be lured by it again into doing something he would regret.

His mouth felt as though someone had stuffed the cotton he'd picked that first summer into it. That first summer. He stared at his reflection in the mirror as he shaved, finding it difficult to believe how quickly five years had passed. He had been the marshal of Fortune for three.

In the beginning, excitement had flourished when the trail drovers had begun driving their cattle through Fortune. Kit had needed to calm the rambunctious cowboys. They still passed through every spring, but with a bit more restraint. Even the younger men had heard the tales of the marshal who didn't wear a gun. Someone had written a dime novel about him. He would have to send a copy to his brother when he found one.

He lifted his chin to scrape the remaining lather from his face. His gaze fell on the shiny scar, a gift from his father, given to him moments after he was born so he would never be mistaken for the heir apparent. The room had been too dark for Clarisse to notice it the last time he'd seen her. As for the physician, he paid little enough attention to his patients, much less to those who were healthy.

Kit finished dressing in the back room of the jail that served as his home. Sometimes he laughed when he thought of the opulence that had surrounded him at Ravenleigh. Here his spartan existence suited him.

He shrugged into his jacket and walked into the front office. Through the grayish hue of dawn easing through the windows, dust motes waltzed above his immaculate desk. Felons glared at him from posters pinned to the wall. He glanced into the hallway that separated the two cells that were his dominion. Today, as usual, they were empty.

He grabbed his wide-brimmed hat from the peg beside the door and settled it on his head before stepping into the cool morning air of early May. His boot heels echoed over the planked walkway as he headed toward the boardinghouse at the south end of town. His salary from the township included room and board at that establishment, but he preferred his privacy. His stomach, however, preferred Mrs. Gurney's cooking to his own.

He stepped off the boardwalk, ducked beneath the whispery branches of a weeping willow, and came to an abrupt halt. A shawl draped over her narrow shoulders and tucked neatly beneath her crossed arms, a woman stood on the boardinghouse porch. Her gaze was latched on the sunrise.

Her profile to him, he could barely see one corner of her mouth, her soft lips tipped up slightly as though she were appreciating a fine work of art. A black ribbon held her hair in place, one long trail of golden strands that curled at the tiny dip within the curve at the small of her back.

Ethereal. Angelic. A thousand words tripped through his mind, but none did her justice. She was a work of art. He imagined an artist's brush outlining her shape with soft strokes that created delicate lines.

His stomach growled at his delay in getting to the breakfast table. The woman turned her head, her eyes a deep blue that reminded him of the sky.

Her smile blossomed. "Isn't it lovely?" she asked quietly as though she feared disturbing the day's beginning. She shifted her gaze back toward the dawn.

He walked over the dew-coated lawn, stepped onto the porch, and swept his hat from his head as though he'd come into a place of worship. "Beautiful," he whispered.

"I love the start of a new day. It holds so much promise, and each moment is a secret to be revealed."

She laughed lightly, as though embarrassed by her words. She cast a furtive glance his way. "I'm not usually so fanciful."

"Are you a writer?" he asked with a generous smile, more than intrigued by her frail beauty.

Her gaunt cheeks flushed pink. "You don't remember me."

His smile withered and his heart slammed against his ribs. The mouse in the corner. "You're David's sister. Ashton."

She bobbed her head and extended a hand that looked as fragile as the willow branches through which he'd just walked. "And you're Christian Montgomery."

He closed his hand around hers, expecting to feel the cold scepter of death. Instead, warmth greeted him. Holding her gaze, he bowed slightly and brought her fingers to his lips. "I apologize for not recognizing you."

"There's little about me to capture the attention of a man such as yourself, and many beautiful women were in attendance the night we met. Have you talked with David?"

Straightening, he released her hand and cleared his throat. "Yes, we spoke late last night. I take it you haven't seen him this morning."

"No, I was exhausted once the stagecoach arrived. I went to bed fairly early. He seems to be sleeping in." Stepping back, she reached into her pocket and withdrew a handkerchief. She pressed it to her mouth before giving several slight coughs.

Kit's stomach tightened at the sight of her curled

shoulders and the rasp of a chest that seemingly lacked air. She glanced at him, her eyes less bright. "Excuse me. You were saying?"

He swallowed hard. Why hadn't David told him that he had already brought his sister to Fortune, that she was at the boardinghouse, or that their paths might cross before David had a chance to talk with her? Kit preferred never to have set eyes upon her again, much less to have to explain his decision. "I think in spite of your brother's heartfelt motives and good intentions, our marriage would serve neither of us well in the end."

She blinked eyes that seemed too large for a face as delicate as hers. "Our marriage?"

"Yes. His notion that you and I should wed."

With horror sweeping over her lovely face, she gasped and stepped back until she rammed into the porch post. "He asked you to marry me?"

Kit felt as though he'd just learned that he was to be drawn and quartered. "You didn't know?" he asked quietly.

She shook her head vehemently. "No. He said he needed to talk with you about business. I'd never seen this part of the state, so he let me come along." She pressed trembling fingers to her lips and tears welled within her eyes. "Did he tell you *everything*?"

A rusty blade gouged into his gut could not have caused more anguish than he experienced at this moment, having to acknowledge the truth with such inadequacy. "Yes, and I am so incredibly sorry." He held out a hand imploringly. "Words fail me."

"How could he ask that of you?"

"His heart was in the right place."

"His head obviously wasn't. I am sorry, Mr. Montgomery. So sorry. Dear God, I wish I *were* already dead. Please excuse me."

She rushed past him, opened the door to the boardinghouse, and fled inside.

Her wish for death echoed through his head like a scream released within a cave from which there was no escape.

Breathing heavily, Ashton flung open the door to her brother's room. He shot up in bed, his eyes red, as though he'd had a grueling, sleepless night.

Too bad. She'd had an awful, embarrassing, mortifying morning. She slammed the door shut, and he jerked.

"What's wrong?" he asked groggily.

She crossed the room and wrapped her hands around the bedpost. She knew she had the advantage because he wouldn't get out of bed and expose her to his half-clothed—if he were clothed at all—body. Her entire life, everyone had sought to protect her. In death, they were doing the same. "You came here to ask Mr. Montgomery to marry me?"

He closed his eyes and dropped his head back. "Ah, God." He squinted at her. "You saw Kit?"

She nodded, unable to stop the images of Christian Montgomery from seeping into her mind. The sun easing over the horizon had toyed with his hair, turning it a burnished amber. And his eyes. Those pale blue eyes looked almost silver and seemed to pierce her soul.

When he spoke, his deep voice sent shivers of pleasure rippling through her. Only once had she ever experienced anything like it—the night he'd come to her brother's house and regaled the guests with tales of his adventures. She'd hung onto every word like a smitten schoolgirl.

This morning, his touch had been the gentlest she'd ever known, and yet his hand had also possessed strength. So much strength.

She released her death grip on the post and took a step toward him. "David, how could you ask a friend to marry your dying sister?"

She saw in his eyes that he wanted to deny that she was dying, but his words were honest. "Because he *is* a friend."

"That was an awful thing to ask."

"I know that now, but when I saw you in Mother's dress—" She watched him swallow. "There's so much I want to give you, and so little time to give it to you."

Suddenly drained from the turbulent emotions swirling within her, she sat on the edge of the mattress. "But a husband?"

He held up his hands. "No, just a bridegroom."

She furrowed her brow. "I don't understand."

"I only wanted him to make you a bride. You would go through the marriage ceremony, have a day like you dreamed of having, and then come back to Dallas with me."

"A pretend marriage? That's even worse." She would have shot off the bed if she'd had the strength.

"A pretend marriage, but a real ceremony. Kit is British. He understands that people get married for reasons other than love and that often husbands and wives don't live together. That's why I thought this idea would work."

She shook her head. "Ludicrous."

David smiled warmly. "He said the same thing."

"But why him? You know men in Dallas—" A horrible thought struck her mind. "You found my private journal."

He averted his gaze.

She slumped forward, tears burning her eyes. "You read my most intimate thoughts," she rasped in a hollow voice echoing betrayal.

"Not everything. I only know that you favored him."

"Did you tell him that?" How would she ever face the man again if David had told him what she'd written in her journal?

"No, of course not." David leaned forward and took her hand. "I only wanted to give you a dream."

"Instead, you've given me a nightmare."

Kit heard soft footfalls and lowered the newspaper he'd been staring at while Ashton's parting words continued to intrude on his thoughts. David walked down the stairs, Ashton clinging to his arm, her face a reflection of calm. Slowly Kit came to his feet.

"So you two have talked," David said, his smile mocking.

Kit felt the heat suffuse his face, his gaze darting between brother and sister. How different they looked. He had grown up with a sibling who was his mirror image. "I apologize for speaking out of place. I thought she knew."

David pulled out a chair for Ashton. "I decided against telling her until I'd tested your feelings on the matter. I didn't want her to be disappointed."

"David!" Ashton snapped.

Kit raised a brow. She might be ill, but she wasn't weak. Elegantly she sat, picked up a cloth napkin, and settled it across her lap. Images drifted through his mind of another time when she had sat across from him—at David's table. He had been too caught up in his own hell truly to notice her, to notice any of the women that night.

Kit took his seat as Mrs. Gurney bustled into the room, carrying platters laden with biscuits, eggs, and bacon.

"Good, everyone's here for breakfast. Nothin' worse than cold eggs lessen it's no eggs at all." She set the platters on the table. "You folks hear that our marshal was a hero last night?"

Grimacing, Kit reached for the plate of biscuits and extended it toward Ashton. "I simply prevented a few men from murdering a floor."

Laughing boisterously, Mrs. Gurney patted his back with her beefy hand. "You are too modest, Marshal. You stopped a man from havin' to dance to their tune, is what I heard."

"You shouldn't believe everything you hear, Mrs. Gurney, unless it's the rumble of my empty stomach."

"Well, then you eat up. All of you, eat up!" She hurried from the room.

Out of the corner of his eye, Kit watched Ashton place a small portion of eggs and one piece of bacon on her plate. He remembered how little Clarisse had eaten at the end. His throat constricted, and he wondered if he'd be able to swallow.

"I was surprised to hear you'd taken on the job of marshal," David said as he scooped up a large serving of eggs.

Kit shrugged. "It was something to do."

"Risking your life for others is a bit more than that, Mr. Montgomery," Ashton said softly.

He stilled, wondering how he could explain that everything he did was an attempt at retribution for the one life he had been unable to save. He couldn't. "You make too much of it, Miss Robertson. My main duty involves carting drunks to the jail so they can sleep off indulging in too much whiskey."

She met his gaze. "I believe Mrs. Gurney is right. You're too modest."

"I assure you that modesty has never been one of my character flaws."

"David told me you have no flaws."

He darted a quick glance at David, who shifted uncomfortably in his chair. "I spoke more of your virtues than your flaws," David explained.

"That must have been a short conversation," Kit said.

Ashton laughed so sweetly that Kit wanted to capture the sound and hold it deep within himself.

"Are you trying to convince me that I should be grateful you thought David's idea was as ludicrous as I did?" she asked.

He met and held her gaze. "I'm attempting to convince myself."

Her cheeks flushed, and she lowered her gaze to the small amount of food on her plate.

Bloody hell! What did he think he was doing? The last thing he needed to do was flirt with her, charm her, or give her cause for hope. He jerked his gaze to David, not surprised to see the man's eyes narrowed.

"When do you leave?" Kit asked.

"There's a stagecoach coming through tomorrow afternoon. Since my plans fell through here, I'll make arrangements today for us to take it."

"David, will you stop these uncalled for subtle rebukes? They grow wearisome," Ashton chastised, her gaze never wavering from her food.

Kit scraped his chair across the floor and stood. She lifted her gaze then, so fragile and incredibly innocent. She had yet to learn the ugliness of death. He had no desire to be near when life taught her that lesson. "I wish you both a safe journey."

She gave him a charitable smile. "It was a pleasure to see you again, Mr. Montgomery."

"The pleasure was mine, Miss Robertson." He turned to leave, stopped, and knew he would regret the words even before he spoke them. "Miss Robertson, you mentioned earlier that you had a desire to see this part of the state. Will you honor me with the privilege of escorting you through the area this afternoon?"

"You're too kind, Mr. Montgomery," she said softly.

"Hardly. But for one afternoon, I can pretend."

* * *

Kit. Kit. Kit. In her mind, Christian Montgomery was and would always be Kit. But the years since she'd first met him had created a chasm and a formality between them that caused her to now address him as "Mr. Montgomery" when she hadn't before.

She twirled around the room. Christian Montgomery had asked her on an outing. How many times over the years had she dreamed of him returning to Dallas because he'd been unable to forget her . . . ?

She came to an abrupt standstill. He had forgotten her. So easily. That knowledge had hurt but not nearly as much as knowing that he had refused David's offer of Ashton's hand for marriage. She didn't hold his decision against him. After all, he was strikingly handsome and cultured. Ashton had not been the only woman to admire him in Dallas.

With a sigh, she cautiously approached the cheval glass. At twenty-six, Ashton thought she should know how to dress for an afternoon outing with a gentleman. She'd certainly read an abundance of books, living through the written word a life that she had thought her poor health would forever keep her from experiencing. She'd been a sickly child, tutored at home, and sheltered from people who might bring disease into the house.

In the end, influenza had taken her parents when they'd feared it would take her. The only comfort she'd found in knowing her *own* death was near had resided in the knowledge that she would be with them again.

She shook away the melancholy thoughts. She was

going on an outing. She'd napped, bathed, and put on a white summer dress and a straw hat with daisies lining the brim. Critically she gazed at her reflection. White made her look like a ghost. She wished she had something a bit more flamboyant.

The unexpected knock on the door nearly had her leaping into the mirror. Taking a shallow breath, hoping to prevent a coughing seizure, she tucked one errant strand of hair beneath her hat and strolled across the room. She opened the door and smiled at David. With his dark hair and eyes, he hardly seemed related to her. Until she'd met Christian Montgomery, she hadn't realized men more handsome than her brother existed.

"He's here," David said.

Like a silly schoolgirl, she pressed her hand over her fluttering heart and tried to sound as though this moment wasn't the most exciting of her life. "Where all do you suppose he'll take us?"

David crooked his elbow, and she slipped her arm through his, drawing her shawl closely with the other hand, resenting the chill that never seemed to leave her.

"I doubt he'll take us far. I've already explained to him that you tire easily, and he's not to keep us out long."

Her heart stopped its fluttering, and the moment took on the gravity of reality. She could do none of the things she wanted: shout with joy, skip through flowered fields, and stay out until midnight.

But she held her silence because she would gain nothing by hurting David and condemning his good intentions. As her older brother, he would sway her with common sense.

Arriving in the foyer, she saw Kit, and what little breath she had nearly left her. This morning he had been dressed is a brown jacket, plain shirt, and trousers similar to those her brother often wore.

Now he wore dove gray trousers, a black jacket, a pristine white shirt, and a cravat. Tilting his head slightly, he smiled at her the way she'd often imagined a beau smiled at the woman he intended to woo into his bed.

"Miss Robertson." He offered her a solitary white rose.

She stepped away from David and accepted the flower, bringing it to her nose, and inhaling the delicate fragrance. He had whittled away the thorns. A bouquet could not have pleased her more. She peered up at him. "How lovely. Thank you."

He crooked his arm. "Shall we see what other secrets today's moments hold?"

The heat suffused her face. "You tease me, sir."

His smile deepened. "It is the rake in me. I cannot always control the impulse to be a bit devilish."

She slipped her arm through his. Such sturdiness. Confidence emanated from him. She knew he was accustomed to having his way, especially with the ladies.

They strolled outside, and the day suddenly seemed warmer. Perhaps she would be able to dispense with her shawl after all. She despised feeling like an ancient woman.

"The carriage will only hold two," David said, his

footsteps echoing behind her. "Am I to take the extra horse?"

She glanced at the waiting carriage. Two dappled gray horses were hitched to the front of the buggy. A large black beast was tethered behind it.

Kit stopped walking and glanced over his shoulder. "My invitation was for your sister only. I brought the gelding because I'll have need of him later."

Her heart patted against her ribs. She looked back to see that David had narrowed his eyes.

"You don't truly expect me to allow you to take her without a chaperone?"

Kit raised a brow. "You expected me to marry her."

"But I never envisioned the two of you being alone. Besides, as I explained, you were only to partake in the ceremony—"

"But not in the pleasures of marriage."

"Kit." David's voice carried a warning tone she'd never before heard. "If you take any liberties with her, I'll kill you."

"I told you last night that I have a policy of not trifling with the sisters of friends. She will be safe in my company."

Ashton didn't know why it hurt to *know* she would be safe. She had hoped, however unrealistically, that there was a slight chance Christian Montgomery might find her as attractive as she found him. An absurd thought, considering her gaunt features and sickly pallor. Of course she had no need of a chaperone. She imagined the man could have any woman he wanted, which made her briefly wonder why he didn't.

Pity had no doubt inspired Kit to offer to spend the afternoon in her company. A sobering realization. Still she could enjoy his presence and strive to keep the conversation away from morose thoughts.

She smiled brightly, falsely. "He's right, David. We're only going for a short ride. What sort of mischief can we get into?"

Almost reluctantly, David took a step back. "I don't want to see her hurt."

"If I wanted to harm her, I would have agreed to your insane notion that we wed. Think it through, man, and you'll see that I'm right. Now, if you'll excuse us, I wish to show the lady the sights."

"An hour," David said firmly. "She is not to be gone for more than an hour. She needs her rest."

Ashton clutched Kit's hand as he helped her into the carriage. The buggy rocked as he settled in beside her. He released the brake, lifted the reins, and with a quick flick of his wrist, set the horses into motion.

Clutching the rose he'd given her, she peered over at him. "I'm sorry you've gone to so much trouble for only an hour's outing."

He smiled at her with a mischievous glint in his eyes. "A pity that I forgot to bring my watch. Besides, where I plan to escort you will take much longer than an hour."

"Where are we going?"

"Camelot."

Chapter 3

Ashton had read tales of King Arthur, but none of the stories prepared her for the reality of Camelot.

In every color imaginable, flowers formed a thick carpet across the ground that stretched between trees lining one side and the creek that gurgled on the other. Above, the sky seemed bluer, the white billowy clouds more abundant.

And the people, the laughter, the yelling, the absolute joy . . . it was almost painful to witness. Hushed tones and frightening whispers had filled her youth. The low voices had always terrorized her because she knew she was not meant to hear the words, and their secrecy could only be a portent of bad tidings.

As Kit brought the buggy to a halt, she watched a boy sitting astride a brown horse, a lance tucked beneath one arm, gallop along a trail lined with poles that held metal rings.

Clunk as one ring was hit and knocked off its hook. *Clink* as one was swept onto the lance.

Shouts exploded. She saw a woman and a young

girl jump up and down, hugging each other and screaming. With their blond hair and slender figures, they had to be mother and daughter.

A man with golden hair smiled broadly as the cherub sitting on his shoulders clapped. Beside him an older boy with brown hair laughed.

A family. They could be nothing less than a family.

The boy whirled his horse around, his dark hair flopping against his forehead as he trotted the horse along the track with his lance sporting the single ring he'd managed to snag. Grinning from ear to ear, he shoved his spectacles up his nose and lifted the lance. "Uncle Kit, did you see? I got my first one all by my lonesome!"

"Indeed I did see, lad. Splendid job, Micah!" Kit yelled as he climbed out of the buggy. He walked around the horses, came to her side, and held a hand toward her. "I hope you don't mind, but since I needed to practice, I thought you might enjoy the scenery."

She slipped her hand into his and clambered out. "Practice?"

He smiled warmly. "The first summer we were here, we began a tradition of having a jousting event on the eve before the cotton was to be picked. The only year we didn't compete was the year we herded cattle. It was also the only year the Englishmen lost to the Texans."

"You don't see yourself as a Texan?"

"God, no, although I fear Harry and Gray are beginning to see themselves as more Texan than British. A true pity."

"Kit, I didn't hear you arrive," a man said as he strode toward them, the tiny boy still perched on his shoulders.

"I didn't want to distract the lad from his endeavors." He reached up and tickled the youngest child. "Colton, when are you going to start competing?"

"He's not yet four. Don't give him ideas," the man warned.

Kit slipped his arm around her and tucked her against his side. "Miss Robertson, allow me to introduce you to Grayson Rhodes, son to the Duke of Harrington."

Ashton felt her heart trip. "Am I supposed to curtsy?"

"No," Grayson Rhodes said with a gracious grin that left no doubt in her mind that he, too, had wooed his fair share of ladies. "Here I am but a farmer."

The woman sidled up to him and smiled in welcome. "I'm Abbie."

"Gray's wife," Kit added.

"I'm very happy to meet you," Ashton said sincerely. "You have a lovely family."

"We're proud of them."

Ashton turned at the whir of carriage wheels. A dark-haired man guided the buggy toward them. A woman with curling red hair held a young child in her arms while a small girl sat between her and the man. She remembered the man and woman from David's party: Harrison Bainbridge and Jessye Kane, although now they were married. Ashton had been too ill to attend their wedding, although David and his family had come.

After bringing the buggy to a halt, Harrison awkwardly got out and, with the aid of a cane, walked around the carriage to help his wife disembark.

"You know, we could get in more practice if you people would get here on time," Grayson said.

"Bloody hell, Gray," Harrison snapped. "It's your land. Of course, *you'll* be here promptly."

Jessye held up a hand. "It was my fault. I was bringin' up my breakfast most of the morning."

Habit had Ashton shrinking back until she felt the sturdiness of Kit behind her. Her parents had raised her to fear anyone with a sniffle, much less the inability to keep their food in place.

"You shouldn't have come if you're not well," Abbie told her.

"Oh, I'm not sick," Jessye said, beaming as she settled one girl on her hip and took the hand of the other. "We got another baby coming. Ought to be here a month or so after yours, Abbie."

"Are you saying you both have children on the way?" Kit asked.

The women blushed, and their husbands looked as though they might bust the buttons off their shirts. Ashton swallowed hard, trying not to think of all the things she would never experience. "Congratulations to you all," she offered quietly.

"You look familiar," Jessye said, "but I can't quite place—"

"She's Ashton Robertson," Kit said. "David's sister."

Jessye smiled brightly. "Ah, yes, I remember now. How is Mary Ellen?"

"Growing. As a matter of fact, Madeline gave me a small portrait to give to you," Ashton told her. David and Madeline had adopted Mary Ellen when she was an infant. She could now see a striking resemblance between Jessye and Mary Ellen, and she couldn't help but wonder if that likeness had any bearing on the closeness that had developed between Madeline and Jessye.

"I'll pick it up on my way to the saloon this evening," Harrison offered.

"Thank you, Mr. Bainbridge," Ashton said. "I'll let David know to expect you."

"We're all friends here, so you must call us Jessye and Harry," Jessye said.

Ashton felt overwhelmed. Friends had never played a role in her life.

"Actually, I saw David earlier," Harry said, grinning. "He wanted to know where I thought a rake might take a lady. Seems you were supposed to keep her out for only an hour."

"An unrealistic expectation. From town, it takes two hours to get to this spot," Kit explained.

"I don't suppose you mentioned that to him or told him where this spot was."

"Of course not. And you—"

"Pled ignorance, naturally. I know you well enough to know if your goal is to ruin a lady's reputation—"

"No one's reputation is gonna get tarnished today," Jessye said as she shifted the daughter on her hip. "You'll answer to me and my loaded pistol, Christian Montgomery, if that's what you've got on your mind."

"If that were my intent, I certainly would not have brought her here."

Ashton wondered briefly where he would have taken her. David had thought she'd be without a chaperone, and she had more than she wanted, women and children studying her with watchful eyes.

"It was a longer journey than Miss Robertson anticipated," he continued. "I think she could use a bit of rest in the shade."

"I have quilts spread out near the creek," Abbie said. "Along with plenty of food and lemonade."

Ashton glanced at Kit. His arm was still around her, and she wondered briefly if she'd be able to walk without his assistance. She was weary. As though reading her mind, he said, "I'll escort you to the quilts, then leave you to the women's tender mercies while I work with the lads."

"I'm surprised David trusted you alone with his sister," Harry said speculatively. "While he was in England, he must have heard about your reputation for beguiling women."

Kit tried to keep his attention on young Micah's riding style instead of on the woman sitting on the quilt beneath the branches of a towering oak tree. "My reputation is the very reason he brought her. He wanted someone skilled at charming ladies, someone who could make her feel special, someone willing to marry her before she died. Micah, lean to the right a bit more!"

He felt the silence descending around him, thick and heavy.

"Before she died?" Grayson finally asked. "Has he been to a gypsy fortune teller?"

"A physician. It seems she has consumption. Her time is limited and her one wish is to marry. David thought I would oblige."

"Surely, you're joking," Harry said quietly.

"I wish I were, but he remembered me telling him how Clarisse had taken ill and died, and so he thought I would be more compassionate than most, willing to grant Ashton's dying wish of being a bride."

"That seems a bit much to ask of a friend," Grayson said.

Kit nodded in agreement. "This day will be the extent of my compassion. A flower, a picnic, a bit of old English charm, and perhaps if I'm feeling generous by evening, a kiss. No more than that." He sighed deeply. "God knows I have nothing else to give."

Ashton had not meant to fall asleep. She despised the moments lost when she drifted into a shadowy world of dreams. Abbie had been telling her how Grayson, Kit, and Harry had worked her farm, picking cotton, when they had first arrived five years earlier. Ashton had wanted to hear the story, every detail she could glean about Kit, but a heaviness had settled over her and Abbie's gentle voice had lulled her into sleep.

Something soft and velvety tickled her nose. She brushed it away, but it returned more insistent than before. She squinted and was greeted by the sight of silvery blue eyes and a yellow flower.

"I came over here to get something to eat, but I'm

half tempted to nibble on you," Kit said in a low, seductive voice.

She widened her eyes and pushed herself to a sitting position. He sat beside her, one arm draped over his raised knee, while he feathered the flower over her face with his other hand. She was fully awake now, but her voice still seemed to be asleep.

"Have you eaten?" he asked.

She shook her head. "I have so little appetite of late, although I've never really been a hearty eater."

"I suspected as much." He reached across her, grabbed a wicker basket, and dragged it nearer. "Abbie always has something good to eat. Gray got the better end of the deal when he was selected to stay with her, although none of us thought so at the time."

"What are you talking about?"

He removed a piece of chicken from the basket, tore off a section of meat, and offered it to her. "Eat, and I shall explain."

Even though she wasn't hungry, she nibbled on his offering, anything to hear the rich timbre of his voice.

"Shortly after the war, we came here to work in the cotton fields. There were seven men altogether, and seven merry widows each agreed to take in one boarder. Abbie got Gray. Harry and I spent one evening looking the area over and decided we wanted to return to Galveston, where our ship from Liverpool had originally docked." He slipped another piece of chicken into her mouth before shrugging. "But Gray wanted to stay so stay, we did, and soon learned that picking cotton is a harsh undertaking."

She glanced toward the older boy who was galloping along the track, gathering rings. "So the three older children must be from Abbie's first marriage. How did the jousting get started?"

She wanted to protest that she was full when he teased her lips with another strip of chicken. Instead, she chewed because she could tell from the gleam in his eyes that without her acquiescence, he would not continue the story.

"Have you ever read *Ivanhoe*?"

"Yes—" He slipped another piece of chicken into her open mouth. The rascal. She nodded, his warm smile dousing any anger she might have felt at being manipulated.

"Gray had brought the book with him, and he read to the children every night. They were enthralled with the notion of knights and jousting, and he was enthralled with them, so we made poles, rings, and lances, and taught them what we knew of our ancestors' penchant for games."

"I think it's—" Another piece of chicken which she spoke around. "Wonderful." She swallowed and held up a hand. "I really can't eat anymore."

"Blackberries, then." He reached behind his back and brought forth a bowl filled with the tiny fruit. "Picked them myself especially for you."

"It's a good thing we're leaving tomorrow," she said as she plucked one from the bowl and popped it into her mouth.

"And why is that?"

"I think you could easily break my heart."

He tucked a stray strand of hair behind her ear. "Breaking hearts is not what I do."

"Do you deny that you charm women?"

"I don't deny that, but a woman's heart is like delicate hand-blown glass, and I treat it so."

She plucked another blackberry from the bowl, not wishing to know about all the women's hearts he had handled. "Tell me about Galveston."

"Have you never been?"

She shook her head. "I was hoping we might make it to the coast, but David is anxious to get back to Dallas. Madeline is expecting a child in the next month or so. So he not only misses her, he's worried."

"But he left her to bring you here."

"I could have saved him the trip if he'd told me his plans." She placed her hand over his. "I'm so sorry he put you in such an awkward position. He never should have asked of you what he did."

"I'm sorry I could not have obliged him and given you your wish."

"Uncle Kit, Pa says you need to git yourself over here," the oldest boy said.

"All right, Johnny, I'll be there in a moment." He held her gaze. "Actually, I didn't come over here to make you eat, but to gain a favor."

"What favor?"

"Your hair ribbon."

She touched the black silk that held her hair in place. What could he possibly want with it?

Then it dawned on her so clearly that she was almost giddy with delight. A joust, knights, a favor from a damsel. She removed the ribbon and handed it to him. "Sir knight, you honor me."

With devilment reflected in his eyes, he brought it to his lips. "The honor is mine, sweet lady." He tapped the bowl. "Finish these off so my efforts weren't wasted."

She watched with interest as he unfolded his body and strode toward the buggy. Sleek and powerful. She could not imagine why he didn't already have a wife of his own. Any woman would be a fool not to want him as a husband. David could not have selected a more enticing groom for her. A shame his idea held so little merit.

Her breath caught as Kit removed his cravat, jacket, and shirt, placing them carefully in the buggy. "Magnificent" was the only word to enter her head. Her heart thundered as though to announce the arrival of a storm.

He swung into the saddle, and the horse pranced around as confident as his master. The other two men had also removed their shirts, but they didn't hold her attention as Kit did. Bronzed flesh stretched taut across his chest and back. His hardened muscles rippled as he took the lance from the boy, tied her ribbon around one end, and tucked the long, thin pole beneath his arm.

With a brusque nod, he kicked his horse's flanks and barreled along the track, the lance snatching ring after ring from the poles. Six in all.

For a fleeting instant, she wasn't in Texas. She was in England, surrounded by pageantry and gallantry.

Little wonder David had chosen Christian Montgomery. In one afternoon, he had her heart beating as though it had never beaten before.

He trotted the horse toward her, victory emanating from him. To have such strength, such confidence.

"Impressed?" he asked.

She smiled brightly. "Very."

"Want to give it a go?"

The air backed up in her lungs. "I beg your pardon?"

"Would you like to try your hand at some tournament play?"

She shook her head. "I don't think I can."

"Why not?"

"If I were to fall, David would have a fit." She stared at him as comprehension dawned. "That's why you didn't let him come."

"I'm sure he means well, but he's suffocating you as much as your illness." He dismounted. "The horse is gentle and trained. I'll ride behind you to hold the lance steady."

She set the bowl aside and slowly rose to her feet. "I'm not properly dressed. If I sit astride, my skirt will hike up."

"You're among friends. They won't care. Or if you'd rather, I can send them on their way."

"No!" It was the craziest thing, but she wanted an audience. She wanted people to see her taking a chance when she'd never taken a chance for fear it would shorten her life.

She barely noticed her shawl falling from her shoulders as she swiped her damp palms over her skirt, trying not to focus on the sweat glistening over his chest. Surely he would put his shirt back on before he climbed on the horse behind her. "I'm willing to give it a try."

"Good." He removed the rings from the lance. "Johnny!" The boy loped over. "Put these back into place, will you, lad?"

Johnny grinned broadly. "She gonna do it?"

"Of course."

"Uncle Harry said you could talk an angel into sinnin'."

"He spoke out of turn."

"Maybe so, but he still won the wager." He grabbed the rings and ran off.

"What wager?" she asked.

"Who knows?" he mumbled as he took her hand and pulled her toward the gelding. "Harry would make a wager on whether or not the sun would come up if he could find a taker."

He hoisted her into the saddle as though she weighed no more than a petal on the flower he'd given her. Her skirt and petticoats rose to an indecent height. She was jerking them down when he wrapped his roughened palm around her calf. She froze.

"You have lovely legs, Miss Robertson." He eased her foot out of the stirrup. "But I need the stirrup."

He vaulted up behind her. She thought if she didn't fall from the saddle, she might expire from a heart that pounded with too much force. Her mouth went dry when his arms came around her.

"Grab the lance," he ordered, his breath skimming

along her ear, sending delicious shivers cascading over her body.

She did as he'd ordered, tucking the lance in close to her body. His hand covered hers, his arm brushing against hers, his chest pressing against her back. His bare chest. The warmth was enough to make her wonder how he survived the summers.

"Hold onto the pommel with your free hand, and I'll take charge of the reins and the horse. With my arms around you, I promise you won't fall. We'll lope, not gallop."

Nodding, she took a deep breath. His tanned hand was so much larger than hers, his fingers longer than hers. Her paleness stood out in stark contrast.

He guided the horse around and her body instinctively nestled against his.

"What's the horse's name?" she asked as they neared the start of the track.

"Lancelot. Relax, Miss Robertson, or the horse will shy away from his task."

"I am relaxed."

"Liar."

Before she could respond, he urged the horse into a trot. She tightened her fingers around the lance as though that insignificant action could hold her in place.

Kit's body curled around her in a protective gesture that caused all her fears to recede. The wind caressed her cheeks. With her ribbon dangling at the end of the lance, her loosened hair flew around her face with wild abandon. Her heart thundered in rhythm to the horse's pounding hooves.

She felt the lurch and heard the *ping* as the lance hit the first ring. Amazingly it spun toward her hand. She wanted to laugh. Instead she focused on the next ring. As it sang its way down the lance, she realized victory held a sweetness she'd never experienced. Until this moment, her only victories had been waking up to welcome the arrival of the dawn.

They missed the third ring, but she didn't care. The remaining rings found their way home.

Kit brought the horse around, and only then did she hear the cheers and clapping. She thought she could sail to the clouds on the joyous sound.

"Five rings. Not bad for a beginner," he said, his warm breath skimming along the nape of her neck.

Smiling brightly, she swung her head around. "Thank you. I've never been so happy."

Steadfast and sure, his light blue gaze dropped to her lips. For one insane beat of her heart, she thought he might kiss her.

Disappointment reeled through her as he shoved off the back of the horse, grabbed the reins, and led her toward the circle of admirers as though she were a princess just rescued from a dragon.

Chapter 4

"I hope you'll forgive me for barging in, but I couldn't wait for Harry to come home from the saloon," Jessye said as she held the portrait of Ashton's niece, Mary Ellen. "Oh, look how she's grown."

Sitting in Mrs. Gurney's parlor, Ashton was surprised to see tears shimmering in Jessye's eyes when she glanced up at David. "She's quite the young lady, isn't she?"

"Yes, she is," David replied from where he stood beside the fireplace, one arm resting on the mantel. "She'll be ten soon, but then, I suppose you know that."

Jessye nodded, smiling wistfully. "It's just hard to believe."

"Madeline and I thought we'd bring the family down next summer," David said.

"That'll be wonderful. We'll look forward to your visit. Now, I'd best get to the carriage so Harry and I can get our girls to bed."

"He doesn't have to avoid me just because he lied to me," David said.

Jessye angled her chin. "He's not avoiding you. Getting in and out of the buggy causes him a great deal of pain so I told him to wait. But if you got something that needs to be said, you can say it to me."

David straightened and cleared his throat. "I find it strange that Harry didn't know where I might find Kit this afternoon when I asked, and yet you all apparently spent the afternoon together."

"We didn't know for sure that Kit would be there," Jessye said, smiling brightly. "A wise man wouldn't even hint at the possibility that my husband lied."

David tilted his head in concession. "Now I know where Mary Ellen got her stubbornness." He held up a wrapped parcel that Jessye had given him earlier. "I'll see that she gets your gift."

"Thank you." Jessye crossed the room and hugged Ashton. "It was good to see you again. Take care of yourself."

Ashton watched her walk from the room. She had admired Jessye from the moment she first met her. She'd gone on an adventure, herding cattle with Kit and Harry four years before. To her shame, Ashton had even envied her. To have the courage and health to do anything she wanted.

She looked up at David. "What did you mean when you said that you know where Mary Ellen gets her stubbornness?"

David met her gaze. "She's Mary Ellen's mother."

Ashton felt her eyes widen. David's revelation certainly explained the similarities she'd noticed earlier between Jessye and Mary Ellen. "How did all that come about?" she asked.

"It's a long story. I'll tell you everything on our journey back to Dallas."

"I always thought Jessye was a remarkable woman."

"So she is, and you'll find her even more remarkable once you've heard the story. I'm grateful she was there to watch over you this afternoon."

Ashton rolled her eyes. "David, I did not need a chaperone. Kit has no interest in me."

He raised a brow. "Kit? Before you left on the outing, he was Mr. Montgomery."

"Saying such a long name all day would have worn me out," she snapped, losing patience with his protectiveness, even though she hadn't had the courage to call Kit anything other than Mr. Montgomery. Calling him "Kit" seemed so intimate. It hadn't bothered her when he was in Dallas, but that was before her imagination had created fantasies in which her feelings for him blossomed and he returned her interest in kind.

"Look at your face, Ashton. The sun burned it," David scolded.

She touched her fingers gently to her face. "Only my nose."

David sighed heavily.

"Oh, David, don't ruin my memory of the day. It was wonderful."

"Kit was a perfect gentleman?" he inquired.

"A perfect gentleman," she assured him. Unfortunately. She'd experienced moments when she'd hoped he wouldn't be.

David knelt before her and took her hands in his. "I just want you to take care. Consumption—"

"Consumption?" Mrs. Gurney said as she rounded the corner into the parlor carrying a tray of cookies and hot tea. "Who has consumption?"

"No one," Ashton said quickly, hating for anyone to know of her disease or weakness.

Mrs. Gurney set the tray on a nearby table and pointed her finger at Ashton, wagging it unmercifully. "You need to get married, young lady. That's a sure-fire way to prevent getting consumption."

Ashton bit back her laughter. "Marriage?"

"That's right. I read it myself in a book called *The People's Medical Lighthouse*. That's one of the reasons I married my daughters off when they was fourteen. You need to get rid of all the worry in your life. And corsets. Those gotta go, too." The woman spread out her arms and inhaled deeply. "A woman's gotta be able to take air deep into her lungs."

David cleared his throat.

Ashton brought a hand to her mouth to hide her smile at David's obvious discomfort.

"Ain't been sick a day in my life," Mrs. Gurney said with a quick nod of her head. "Corsets. That's the secret. Gettin' rid of the durn corsets. That contraption had to be invented by a man who didn't like women. That's all I got to say on that matter. Now you folks eat up my cookies and drink my tea. It helps to go to bed with something on your stomach." She bustled out of the room.

Ashton reached for a cookie. "In all my reading, I somehow overlooked that book."

"It was interesting," David said quietly.

Ashton snapped her gaze to his. "You read it?"

He blushed and she thought she'd never loved her brother more. "You did read it."

He shrugged. "I was looking for a miracle."

"That's not the reason you asked Kit to marry me, is it?"

"No, unfortunately, marriage supposedly only prevents consumption, it doesn't cure it."

Ashton nibbled on the cookie. "Thank you, David."

"Don't thank me, Ashton. I've yet to find a cure for your disease nor a way to grant your wish to be a bride."

"At least you tried, and that means the world to me."

Bloody damned hell!

Kit paced the small confines of his office unable to erase Ashton's jubilant smile from his memory. In sleep, in joy, she was a fragile beauty, an earthbound angel soon to touch the heavens.

She took delight in the simplest things, putting his cynical side to shame. Dear God, in truth, it had been years since he'd known happiness. Long before the night he learned that Christopher was to marry Clarisse.

"Mind if I join you?" Christopher asked.

Staring into the fire, Kit simply waved his hand magnanimously over the decanters on the table beside his chair. "By all means, if you can find one that still has anything left in it." With an unsteady hand, he brought the glass to his lips, wondering how much more he'd have to drink before he drowned the pain.

Christopher came to stand before the fire.

"You're blocking my view of hell," Kit muttered.

"I just had the most unbelievable conversation with Father."

Kit lifted his glass in a salute. "As unbelievable as the one I had with him earlier? Interesting, how he broke the news to me before he told you."

"I swear to you, Kit, I did not know he was going to arrange a marriage between me and Clarisse."

Kit scoffed. "For the good of Ravenleigh . . . or some such. I am having some success at forgetting his exact wording." He sipped the brandy.

"Her father would not allow her to marry a man who is not titled."

Kit grinned crookedly. "Don't suppose you'd do me the great service of dying?"

Christopher sat in the chair beside him, planted his elbows on his thighs, and leaned forward, his face incredibly serious. "If she does not marry me, she will go to someone else. She can never be yours."

"You make her sound like a mare on a bloody bidding block."

"She has been raised expecting to marry a man with a title. She deserves one."

"She deserves love."

"As my wife, she will have that . . . in abundance."

Dumbfounded Kit stared at his brother. "You love her?"

"You attend so few balls, Kit. In the beginning, even though I believed your hopes unrealistic, knowing how you felt about her, I was merely trying to ensure that no one else captured her fancy—"

"Does she love you?"

"I believe she has a fondness for me. I was not actively pursuing her—or anyone else, for that matter—which is the reason Father took the action that he did. He grew impatient waiting on me to choose a wife."

"Bloody hell, Christopher." He squeezed his eyes shut and shook his head. "I knew I could never have her. What has a second son to offer any woman of distinction?" He opened his eyes and met and held his brother's gaze. "Give me your solemn vow that if she is not in favor of the match, you'll find a way to get out of the marriage that will not cause gossip."

"I swear it."

A promise his brother had never had to fulfill, and that knowledge had hurt even more.

Kit could not pinpoint the exact moment when he'd become aware of his unhappiness, but it seemed as though it had always hovered nearby. Never having the ability to meet his father's expectations had not helped, nor had loving his brother but coveting his acquisitions. He wondered if he'd ever been truly happy. He certainly was unhappy now. If he did not marry Ashton, nothing would change. If he did, still nothing would change. He would continue to wallow in a past he could not alter, but she might know another moment of joy.

David was right. Her dream was an incredibly small request. It would not change Kit's life, but it might ease Ashton's dying.

He strode from his office into the night, leaving his common sense locked behind iron bars.

He neared the boardinghouse. Light shone from one lone window, and within its glow he saw the silhouette of a woman gazing at the stars. He wondered if she was making a wish.

She sought no pity for her condition but seemed intent on appreciating each moment that remained. Perhaps through her he could again learn to appreciate what life had given him, instead of longing for what it had denied him.

He leapt onto the porch, grabbed the beam, and hoisted his way up to the top of the eves. Bracing her hands on the sill, she leaned out the window.

"Mr. Montgomery, what are you doing?" she asked, concern clearly etched in her voice.

"Coming to see you, Miss Robertson."

"Are you insane? You could break your neck."

"It would be no loss, I assure you." Balancing precariously, he cautiously made his way across the slanted roof over the porch until he reached the area that was even with her window. He held out his hand. "Come and join me."

Her eyes became as round as the moon. "And risk breaking *my* neck?"

"I swear to you that I will not let you fall."

She seemed to hesitate as she clutched the front of her nightgown. "I'm in my nightgown."

Her unnecessary revelation amused him. "I assure you that I have seen women in much less. Besides, with the slant of this roof, there is not a great deal I could do to compromise you, but if I were to slip in through your window—"

"I'll come out," she said quickly.

He smiled and reached for her. "I thought you might."

She gathered up her hem and slipped a shapely leg out of the window. He grabbed her elbow, wrapped his arm around her waist, and guided her safely onto the roof.

"This is madness," she whispered as she settled beside him.

"Yes, but you can see the stars much more clearly. Were you making a wish?"

"No, I was just thinking about today. I shall remember it for as long as I . . . forever." She peered at him. "Thank you."

"It was my pleasure."

She ran her finger just beneath his chin. "I noticed this scar earlier today. How did you get it?"

"A gift from my father."

She furrowed her brow, her eyes mired with confusion. "But it looks like a burn. Why would he hurt you like that?"

"I have a twin brother. Christopher. He was born first, and as such, he is the heir apparent. My father wanted to ensure that no one ever mistook me for him so he applied a hot poker just below my chin shortly after I was born."

"How incredibly cruel!"

He shrugged as though his father's action was of no consequence when in fact he'd often held the same sentiment. "I have no memory of the pain."

"I find it odd that his name is Christopher and people call you Kit. I always thought Kit was a nickname for Christopher. Do they call him Kit as well?"

"Good God, no. As the future Earl of Ravenleigh, he carries my father's second title, Viscount Wyndhaven, and is always addressed formally. When we were lads, Christopher said Christian was an inappropriate name for me when I was constantly getting into trouble, so he bestowed his nickname upon me, since he would never have a need for it."

"It sounds as though the two of you were close."

"Very." He smiled warmly at the memories of his youth. "In some ways, our closeness is frightening. One day, I was at school, writing an essay, and suddenly pain shot up my arm, my pencil went flying, and I could not write. Even when the teacher threatened to smack me, I could not make my hand obey, and the pain would not abate."

Her delicate brow creased. "What caused it?"

"No one knew. They called in a physician. He examined me. He had no answers. They sent word to my father. He arrived quite pale. It seemed Christopher had fallen from a tree and broken his arm." He held her gaze. "During the same hour that I was to write an essay."

Her eyes widened. "Incredible."

"Sometimes we weren't certain if our thoughts were our own or each other's."

"Do you look alike?"

"Exactly." He rubbed his scar. "Except for this."

"I still think that was exceptionally cruel of your father. It must have been hard growing up knowing your brother would gain all."

"There was only one moment when I regretted that

I was not born first, and it has lasted forever."

"When was that?" she asked quietly.

He looked toward the stars, his throat still tightening after all these years. "The moment Christopher took as his wife the woman I loved."

Her small hand covered his larger one with a gentleness that he had not known for a good many years. "I am so sorry," she said softly.

He watched a star arc through the sky. "My father arranged the marriage so I never felt that Christopher had betrayed me. He was given no choice, just as I had no say in the matter. But, happily for them, he loved Clarisse, and she him."

"What an incredibly lucky woman to have possessed the love of two men."

He threaded his fingers through hers, brought her hand to his lips, and held her gaze. "She fell ill and died shortly before I left England."

Regret swept over her features. "I remember the grief in your eyes when you told us at dinner. David's request was incredibly cruel."

"He did not know that I loved her or that I held her as she died with my brother's name upon her lips."

"Why did your brother not hold her?"

"He could not bear to see her die, so I stood in his stead, allowing her to think I was him."

Tears welled within Ashton's eyes as she cradled his cheek. "You have known too much sorrow, Mr. Montgomery. I'm incredibly sorry for all you have suffered."

He laid his hand over hers, turned his head slightly,

and pressed a kiss to the heart of her palm. "Will you honor me by becoming my bride?"

Gasping, she jerked free of his hold. "Did your activities this afternoon knock your common sense loose?"

No, it had been her triumphant smile after she'd captured five rings on the end of her lance. How could he explain so she would accept his offer? Suddenly it seemed imperative that she agree. "Before Clarisse died, she spoke of wishes. I could grant her but one. I would have sold my soul to the devil to have possessed the power to grant them all. David said you also have a wish—to be a bride."

"But the ceremony would be real. You would be bound to me by a document and vows."

"Ashton, I have no one in my life—no one. I loved once, deeply. I do not expect to love again. Taking you as my bride will deny me nothing, but perhaps it will give you everything you have dreamed of."

Tears rolled along her cheeks and glistened in the moonlight. "Everything, Mr. Montgomery. And more."

Chapter 5

Sitting on the edge of the mattress, Ashton gingerly touched the lovely dress spread across the foot of the bed. David was so sure of his plan's success that he had brought her mother's wedding dress with him.

Had he never found her in the dress, she might not be waiting for the arrival of evening and her wedding to Kit. Dear Kit, who had been a permanent fixture in her dreams since she'd first met him.

Why wasn't she filled with joy? Because David, with his good intentions, had misinterpreted the words she'd spoken in the attic. She wanted to be more than a bride. She wanted to be deeply loved.

She knew that in a few minutes she would have to remove the plain dress she now wore and slip into the dress decorated with lace and tiny pearls. David would be incredibly disappointed if she didn't don her mother's gown after he'd gone to the trouble to ensure it was here, yet how could she wear it? Her mother had worn it to please the man who loved her. Although Ashton desperately wanted to please Kit this evening, she knew he didn't love her.

Sighing deeply, she closed her eyes. It was such a simple thing that David expected of her, yet somehow wearing her mother's dress felt incredibly wrong, as if by doing so she would taint its purpose.

"Having second thoughts?" a deep voice rumbled into the room.

Ashton's eyes flew open as she pressed her hand to her throat and jerked her head around. Kit sat on the window ledge studying her. She jumped to her feet and stepped to the end of the bed, trying to hide the dress. "What are you doing here? Don't you know it's bad luck for the bridegroom to see the bride before the wedding?" she asked.

He angled his head slightly. "I thought it was bad luck to see her in her gown before the wedding." Shifting slightly, he brought his legs inside and slowly came to his feet. "Besides, you don't truly expect an attentive groom to go the entire day without visiting his bride."

She wrung her hands together. "I'm not sure what I expect. I can't believe this is actually happening, that I'm going to get married."

With a pantherlike grace, he crossed the short expanse separating them. As light as a shadow, he grazed his knuckles across her cheek, his gaze holding hers. "Believe it, sweetling."

The endearment thrilled her as she pressed it close to her heart like a flower flattened between the pages of a book so it would forever be remembered. She had so often thought of him whispering romantic things in her ear. In her journal, she'd childishly written a list of the names he would call her, and she realized that she could no longer envision any endearment passing between his lips except for the one he'd just spoken, one she hadn't written but now knew was right for him. "I wanted to have this day so badly," she confessed.

Understanding softened his eyes and lifted a corner of his mouth. "I know, and now you shall."

"I wish Madeline were here. I don't know what to do."

"I have control of all the details," he assured her with a confident grin. "All you have to do is get dressed."

He touched the ribbon holding her hair in place. She felt two slight tugs, and then he was wrapping the lavender silk around his finger. It seemed such an intimate gesture, as unsettling as if he'd loosened her buttons and removed her dress. "Don't bind your hair," he ordered gently.

Unable to locate her voice, she could do little more than nod. He looked past her to the bed. "Is that the dress you plan to wear?"

She cleared her throat. "Yes, it was my mother's. I'm not sure I should wear it, though."

His gaze warmed with appreciation. "You should. It's perfect." He reached inside his jacket and removed an oblong box, wrapped in white paper and secured with a white ribbon and bow. He extended it toward her. "For you."

Her gaze darted between the gift and the blue of his eyes. "What is it?"

"A wedding gift." He moved it closer to her. "Take it."

With trembling fingers, she took the package and

sat on the bed, turning the gift over. "I don't have anything for you."

"Your presence at my side this evening will be gift enough."

His words, spoken with such sincerity, were more precious than the present he'd given her. She peered up at him. "Can I open it now?"

She saw infectious delight dancing in his eyes. "Of course."

Slowly she untied the ribbon, then removed it and the wrap. Carefully she opened the box, her breath catching as she gazed at a strand of pearls. At their center hung a miniature cameo. "It's beautiful," she said on a sigh. She glanced up at him. "I can't accept this."

He knelt before her and took the jewelry from the box. "Certainly you can." He slipped each end of the necklace around her neck, holding her gaze as he fastened it behind her. "It's a gift from the man who is to become your husband in less than two hours."

Her eyes stung as she brought her fingers to her lips and rasped, "It's too much."

With his thumb, he captured the solitary tear that rolled along her cheek. "It's only the beginning. I have so much more planned. Enjoy each moment, smile as you did yesterday, and I shall be the happiest man in all of Fortune." He cradled her cheek and slowly leaned toward her. His eyes darkened, his lips parted—

A harsh knock on the door had them both jumping back, Kit shooting to his feet, Ashton pressing her hand above her pounding heart.

"Ashton? It's Jessye. Thought you might need some help getting ready."

"Yes, thank you, just a minute," Ashton called out.

Suddenly at her side, Kit bussed a quick kiss across her cheek and whispered, "Until this evening. Remember, hair loose."

He unfolded his body, walked rapidly across the room, and climbed out the window. He looked over his shoulder and blew her a kiss before disappearing. All her doubts dissipated like fog warmed by the sun.

She touched the cameo. For tonight, she would be a cherished bride.

Ashton studied her reflection in the cheval glass. Her mother's dress fit her perfectly. The straight tall collar fit snugly around her neck. The string of pearls circled it and the cameo lay nestled against the lace just below her throat. Something old. Something new.

"Kit's gonna be right pleased when he sees you," Jessye said.

Ashton felt her stomach quiver at the mention of her soon-to-be husband. She met Jessye's gaze in the mirror. "Do you really think so?"

"Wouldn't have said it if I didn't think so."

Ashton smiled at the no-nonsense tone of Jessye's voice. She'd forgotten how forthright Jessye was, so unlike most of the women she'd ever met. "I *do* want to please him."

"Course you do," Jessye said as she straightened the veil held in place with a circle of flowers. "Getting to the church on time would be a good way to begin. Come on, let's go."

Ashton took a deep breath to calm her jitters and again looked at herself in the mirror. If her smile remained that large, her jaws would ache by the end of the evening. But she couldn't stop smiling. She was going to get married, be a bride . . . and only she and David knew she was marrying the one man she'd ever dreamed of having as a husband.

Jessye opened the door. "I'll see you at the church."

"Jessye?"

Jessye stopped and turned toward her.

Ashton took another shuddering breath, grateful she was wearing gloves to absorb the moisture coating her hands. "Jessye, I know it's the last minute, but would you stand at the front of the church with me?"

Smiling brightly, Jessye walked back into the room and gave Ashton a hug. "Be happy to. You just hurry along, now. These Englishmen don't like to be kept waiting."

After Jessye left the room, Ashton took one last glance in the mirror and smiled at her reflection, knowing that for this night, at least, her happiness would overshadow her illness.

She stepped into the hallway, her face warming as David gazed at her with appreciation reflected in the brown depths of his eyes.

"You look beautiful, Ashton," he said as he took her hand, lifted her arm, and slowly twirled her around.

Anticipation shimmied through her, and amazingly she wasn't the least bit tired. She was beginning to understand why Mrs. Gurney had recommended marriage. David extended a bouquet of delicate white roses and late-blooming bluebonnets bound together by what she recognized as her silk lavender hair ribbon. Kit had taken it with him earlier. "Are these from Kit?" she asked, almost certain she knew the answer.

"Yes," David admitted. "He seems to have thought of almost everything."

Something borrowed, something blue.

She was almost giddy with delight at Kit's thoughtfulness. David crooked his elbow. "Shall we go?"

She entwined her arm around his. She brought the flowers to her nose and inhaled their sweet fragrance. "Is he here?"

David escorted her down the stairs. "No, he's waiting at the church."

They walked outside, where a buggy and two dappled gray horses waited.

"The church isn't that far away, but Kit didn't want you to get dusty walking along the street," David explained as he helped her clamber into the buggy.

The vehicle rocked as he climbed in beside her. He lifted the reins, and she placed her hand over his. He stilled and looked at her.

"Thank you, David."

Love filled his eyes as he touched her cheek. "I wish it could be more, Ashton."

She knew that he wanted her to be well, but no one could grant her that wish. "It's enough, David, that I have tonight."

He nodded before slapping the reins over the horses' rumps and setting the carriage into motion. Ashton settled back against the seat as twilight eased around her. She saw the first star appear in the sky and smiled softly, knowing any wish she could have made would pale in comparison to the dream unfolding this evening.

"I cannot believe that you agreed to this idiotic scheme," Harry whispered harshly as he stood beside Kit at the front of the church.

"I don't recall asking for your opinion on the matter," Kit snapped, waiting for his bride to arrive and begin her walk down the aisle. He did not need to hear his own misgivings echoed aloud.

Word of his impending marriage had seeped into every ear within hearing distance and the strength of the pews was being tested as a crowd of people gathered to gain sight of the woman who had supposedly captured their marshal's heart with a solitary smile.

"Have you given any thought to the fact that you might meet someone you wish to marry before you become a widower?" Harry asked. "What then? Do you ask the woman to wait, when physicians have predicted death's arrival in error before? Do you honor vows that demand you forsake all others—"

Kit sliced his gaze to his friend. "What I *do* demand is that you shut up!"

"—Forsake all others until death do you part," Harry continued. "You cannot be celibate for six weeks, much less six months. Will you make a mockery of these vows?"

"I will make a mockery of no vows I take this day. I am giving one woman a chance to live her dream. Would you do no less for Jessye?"

"But I love Jessye. You do not love Ashton. Therein lies the difference, my friend. You are simply sending yourself more deeply into the bowels of hell."

"Or perhaps I am seeking absolution. All I know is that no harm shall come of this day or this arrangement because no woman in this world gives a bloody damn what I do. There shall never be a woman other than Clarisse whom I shall love."

The preacher cleared his throat.

Kit gave Harry a level glare. "Now, either walk away from my side, or cease your condemnation and remain the stalwart friend that I need at this moment."

Harry gave a brusque nod. "I pray to God that you never come to rue this day."

The organist began to play, sending music to the far corners of the rafters. Kit took a deep breath before turning his attention to the doorway that led into the church.

Bloody damned hell! His mouth went dry, and his breath backed up into his lungs until he thought he might never again draw air into his body.

His bride strolled down the aisle toward him, her arm intertwined with her brother's, and God help him, Kit thought he'd never seen a more beautiful sight. Her white gown whispered across the wooden floor. A gossamer veil was draped over her head and covered her face, but it could not hide the luminescent glow of happiness in her eyes.

Perhaps he was stepping more deeply into hell, but for the first time, he did not object to the journey. She had worn her hair loose as he'd requested. It flowed past her shoulders to her tiny waist, and he experienced a moment of misgiving. The man waiting for her before the altar should be one willing to brush her hair each night before she slept.

Her dream was to be a bride, but at what point did a bride become a wife?

At the moment of consummation, he supposed. For them, that moment would never arrive. Why was he always so quick to make a pact with the devil? How many times could he bargain away his soul?

At least this time, he would not give his heart.

Ashton stopped before him, and he saw a flicker of doubt in her eyes. He smiled as though he was a besotted fool who thought himself the luckiest man on earth. Her eyes warmed with gratitude, and all the doubts plaguing him melted away.

"Who gives this woman to this man?" the reverend asked.

"I do," David said.

With a fluid movement, Kit took Ashton from her brother and nestled her against his side. He lowered his head and whispered, "Speak the vows as though you mean them."

Ashton watched her future husband straighten and wanted to take him away to a corner and explain why David had chosen him. She wanted to tell him what her journal revealed of her feelings for this man standing beside her now on the verge of making false vows to grant her one solitary day of happiness.

She adored him. It was as simple and as complex as that. From the moment she had first heard tales of the Englishman David had met on his journey abroad, she had been fascinated with him. Then she had met him at her brother's party, listened as he spoke with a deep voice accentuated with grandeur, and watched his every courtly gesture, mesmerized. She had desperately wanted to dance with him, but the subject of Clarisse had come up during the conversation at dinner. After that, Kit had been interested only in her brother's expensive wine, not in his companions.

Ah, yes, she would speak the vows as though she meant them, because she did. She prayed that her heart would not shatter when he repeated vows that were of little consequence to him or his heart.

Kit's gaze did not stray from hers as the minister spoke on the merits of love and the responsibilities of marriage. She had yearned to hear words such as these directed her way, surrounding her and the man who would make a life with her. She had not expected the words to echo within the church, a hollow sound that reverberated within her empty heart.

She and Kit had no life except for this one evening. They would have no children, no home, and no shared dreams to whisper about during the night as they held each other within their arms. She stood before the altar experiencing the wedding of a child, not that of a woman.

The minister turned to Kit and bade him to repeat his vows. Until this moment, Ashton did not realize that she dreaded the vows that would bind them through *sickness* until *death*. Words she loathed would weave their way into her special evening, tainting it beyond measure. Why had she not thought to ask that their vows be changed?

As though sensing her doubts, understanding her

misgivings, Kit took her hand, brought it to his lips, and pressed his lips to her fingers, the warmth of his mouth seeping through her gloves.

"Repeat after me," the minister began.

Yet before the minister uttered another word, Kit spoke his vow in a voice that rang strong, clear, and true. "I, Christian Montgomery, take thee, my dearest Ashton Robertson, to love, honor, and cherish as my beloved wife."

Everyone seemed to fade away except this man who stood beside her, giving her in ways she'd never imagined an evening she would never forget. Gladness filled her heart and joy swirled within her as she tightened her fingers around his, her gratitude immeasurable. He had mentioned no illness, allowed no reference to the inevitability of death. Only the inevitability of life.

Ashton recited the vow that was now etched on her heart. "I, Ashton Robertson, take thee, my dearest Christian Montgomery, to love, honor, and cherish as my beloved husband."

As though he'd never been interrupted, the minister announced, "Whom God has joined together, let no man put asunder. You may kiss the bride."

Holding her breath, Ashton waited as Kit slowly lifted her veil. Like an intimate caress, his gaze moved over her face as though he wanted to etch this moment into his memory as much as she did. He cradled her face between his large, strong hands, angled her head slightly, and lowered his mouth to hers. He brushed his lips lightly over hers, sealing their vows and their fate with only the shadow of a kiss.

The absence of passion sent disappointment reeling through her. She latched onto the gift of his vows, knowing that somewhere between the boundaries of dreams and reality she had to find contentment.

"So sweet," he murmured against her temple. "This evening, I am indeed the most fortunate man in all of Fortune."

Tears stung her eyes as he returned his mouth to hers with a gentle pressure that weakened her knees and hinted at secrets that had yet to be shared. He lifted his head and held her gaze. She smiled for all the gifts he'd given her this day.

He captured the tear rolling along her cheek with his thumb. His mouth curved into a tender smile as he crooked his elbow. "Mrs. Montgomery, shall we see what other secrets this evening's moments reveal?"

Joy spiraled through her with the realization that she was truly Ashton Montgomery, Kit's wife. She slipped her arm through his, relishing the sturdiness.

As he escorted her along the aisle, she was vaguely aware that people rose from the pews as they passed, but her world had narrowed to the light blue eyes that held hers as though nothing was more important than this moment shared with her.

In all her dreams, she'd never dared imagine him looking at her as he did now: as though he loved her with all his heart.

Chapter 6

"Oh, I'm not at all surprised she won the marshal's heart," Mrs. Gurney announced to her enthralled audience, as she slapped a child's hand away from the cookie tray. "Why, that first morning at breakfast, he could hardly take his eyes off her and I thought then, 'He's taken a fancy to her.' I ain't never been one to read a man wrong."

Overhearing Mrs. Gurney's words, Ashton suppressed her smile. Holding onto Kit's arm as they greeted the guests who arrived at the boardinghouse to celebrate Kit's marriage to her, she cast her husband a furtive glance. "I didn't realize you were quite that taken with me."

He smiled rakishly. "Trust Mrs. Gurney to embellish the tale a bit."

"I think we've created a scandal. I've never done that before."

"Scandals are my stock in trade," he assured her.

"As I recall, that's the reason your father sent you here."

"Among other reasons," he admitted with apparently no shame.

"I suppose most people know much more about their spouses when they marry than we know of each other," she said quietly.

He brought her hand to his lips and brushed a light kiss across her knuckles. "I know all I need to know of you, and trust me on this, you know all that you *want* to know of me."

After this evening, she would know little else of him, because tomorrow she would leave with David in order to return to Dallas and the terrifying wait for death. "I was wondering if perhaps we might . . . correspond . . . now and again . . . just a bit of news."

"If you like, although I confess my penmanship is as disgraceful as my reputation."

She laughed lightly. "Thank you for this evening."

"Don't thank me until it's over." He gave a curt nod to some men sitting in a corner, and as one, they lifted their instruments and began to play a tune, sweet and slow. "I believe the first dance is yours."

She felt as though a thousand butterflies had suddenly taken up residence within her chest. She took a deep, calming breath. "I'm not very skilled."

"I am. Just follow my lead. I once danced with a woman three times my width and not once did we bump into anyone." As people moved back against the walls, Kit led her into the center of the room. He bowed slightly, bestowing upon her a warm smile, before taking her within his arms, the one place she desperately wanted to be. With movements born of experience, he guided her through the waltz, his eyes mirroring adoration as his gaze held hers.

"You are good at the pretense," she said wistfully, now that she owned the dream, wishing that she also possessed the reality.

"That is why David chose me, is it not?"

"I'm not complaining. I consider myself fortunate to be your bride."

His hand on her waist curled more closely around her as he brought her nearer until she could feel the warmth radiating from his body.

"Then know that this evening, I have given no pretense," he said quietly. "Our vows were true. You are my bride, and I adore your courage in the face of adversity."

"But our vows were to love, honor, and cherish."

"Honor and cherish are easily given to you, Ashton. As for love, it comes in many forms. I am certain in your heart of hearts you would have preferred a groom who would have vowed a deeper love than I did, but make no mistake, my vow of love was not false. Can the same be said of yours?"

Her heart bounced against her ribs as she thought of all the times her mind had drifted to memories of him. "I meant the words I said in the church even though they merely echoed yours."

"Then all is well, and this evening you have your dream."

She nodded, smiling with gratitude. "And more. When you were in Dallas before, I wanted to dance with you."

He furrowed his brow. "I don't recall dancing with anyone."

"You didn't, but that didn't stop me from wishing."

"Then tonight we shall dance as long as you desire."

He swept a path across the floor, and other couples joined them. One of his hands held her waist while the other cupped one of her hands. She felt the roughness and the calluses on his palm that she was certain had not arrived with him from England.

Since she had seen him last, the sun and wind had carved lines within his face, sculpting his aristocratic features into sharper edges. His manner held the same arrogance she'd noted when he visited in Dallas. Life could turn him into a beggar, yet he would always retain the heritage of a nobleman.

When the music fell into silence, Kit stopped moving but his hands didn't leave her, they only brought her closer. In his eyes, for a brief moment, she thought she saw desire, true desire . . . and her heart raced wildly. But just as quickly it passed, and she wondered if it had been there are at all, or was just wishful thinking.

The musicians began filling the room with gentle strains from their violins. David approached and bowed slightly. "I can't let the evening pass without dancing at least once with my sister."

Kit released his hold on her. "One dance." He touched her nose. "I shall return."

She watched him walk away before she moved toward David. She had seen him dance numerous times with Madeline, but never had he danced with her.

"You seem pleased," she said as he waltzed her around the room.

"I am. Kit plays the role of adoring groom very well."

Her heart lurched at the reminder that it was all a game. She tripped over her own feet, and David caught her, balancing her until they could resume the dance.

"I'm sorry," he said quietly. "That was unthinking of me to remind you—"

She shook her head quickly. "It doesn't matter, David. The thought is never far away." But it had been. For a time while she danced within Kit's arms, she'd almost forgotten that tonight was only pretense. She glanced over her shoulder, searching for Kit. She wanted him back. For however many dances remained in the evening, she wanted every one to be with him.

She and David finished the dance in silence. When the music ended, all she wanted to do was find Kit, but Grayson Rhodes approached, then asked permission to dance with her, and she could not deny Kit's friend so simple a request. She'd seen him dancing with Abbie, so she wasn't surprised to discover that he was almost as smooth with his steps as Kit was.

"Harry is not at all pleased that he can no longer dance," Grayson told her. "So this dance is for him and me."

She smiled demurely. "What a good friend you are."

"Only because he has been a good friend to me. As has Kit. I don't recall ever seeing Kit look as content as he does this evening."

She felt the heat suffuse her face as she averted her gaze from his.

"You don't have to look away, Ashton. I know the reason behind the marriage."

She snapped her head back around, her eyes holding his. She hoped Kit returned to her for the next dance. He was the only one who didn't constantly bring up reminders that tonight was but a dream.

Tears burned the back of her eyes. "Does the whole town know?"

He tilted his head slightly, never missing a step. "That he cares for you? I should think so. It's rather obvious in the way he looks at you."

Overwhelming relief swamped her. He didn't know the true reason behind the marriage, and she certainly wasn't going to tell him. If Kit had managed to fool one of his friends . . .

The final strains of the song drifted away. She smiled at Grayson. "Thank you so much."

"The pleasure was all mine."

She felt a hand come to rest on her waist and glanced up to see Kit standing possessively beside her. "Go dance with your wife, Gray," he ordered.

"Ah, jealousy. You wear it well, Kit." Laughing, Grayson strolled away.

"Another dance, sweetling?" Kit asked.

Smiling softly, she nodded. He took her in his arms as the music once again filled the room.

"He thinks you care for me," she told him.

He looked at her, bewilderment evident in her eyes. "I do . . . immensely. Never doubt that."

The confusion left his gaze, leaving behind what she'd seen all along and failed to recognize: a deep and abiding fondness for her.

She lost count of the number of dances that filled her evening as more of the townsmen approached her. But she enjoyed most her waltzes with Kit. With him, she felt as though she tripped lightly over billowing clouds. Was that how the trek to heaven would be?

"You're tired," he pointed out.

She jerked her gaze to Kit's, shaking her head in denial of the truth.

"People will begin to talk," he said quietly. "Most husbands are not this patient when it comes to ending the wedding celebration. I think it is time we retired for the night."

Before she could protest, he lifted her into his arms. She wound her arms around his neck.

"You are all free to enjoy the music and refreshments until dawn," Kit announced, a wicked gleam in his eyes and a knowing smile on his face, "but now if you will excuse us, my wife and I will continue the celebration in private."

Scandalous! The thought reverberated through her mind, but she was too weary to protest. She snuggled her head into the crook of his shoulder and smiled as he carried her up the stairs. A perfect ending to a perfect evening.

He strode down the hallway, opened the door to her bedroom, stepped through, kicked it shut with his foot, and carried her to the bed. Gently, he laid her down. She smiled up at him. "Thank you."

"I told you not to thank me until the evening was over," he reminded her.

"It's over now," she told him, knowing consummation was impossible. Or so David had led her to believe.

"Someone must prepare you for bed, and it's obvious that I kept you dancing too long. You look like a wilting rose."

"I can see to my needs."

He pressed a kiss to her forehead. "As your husband, so can I."

A loud knock sounded on the door before it burst open. David stood in the doorway, legs akimbo, his fists clenched at his side. "What do you think you are doing? I warned you that she is too delicate—"

"I am doing nothing more than putting her to bed."

David stepped into the room. "I can do that. You may leave now."

"Not bloody likely," Kit said. "Tongues will wag enough as it is when my bride leaves on the morrow after one night in my arms. I'll not have them wagging before the night has ended."

Ashton sat up in bed, her hand pressed to her throat. "I hadn't considered that. The gossip you will endure when we depart—"

Kit knelt beside the bed and took her hand. "Do not concern yourself with my reputation. It is of no worth."

"Then there is no reason for you not to leave now," David said.

Kit slowly unfolded his body. "This ruse may have been your idea, but I play by my rules. You will leave this room. I shall prepare *my* bride for bed, and then I'll slip out the window."

David's gaze darted between the two of them. "Kit, she is too frail—"

"I won't make love to her. You can have a bloody physician examine her in the morning if you want and call me out if she isn't still a virgin."

Ashton watched her brother swallow. "I simply had not envisioned the two of you alone tonight."

"Well, rethink your vision and consider the embarrassment that will fall upon her shoulders should her husband be seen leaving this room five moments after he entered."

David nodded. "I see your point."

"Do I have a say in this matter?" Ashton asked quietly.

Kit spun around. "Of course you do. Do you want me to leave with David?"

Holding his gaze, she shook her head. "No."

"Then the matter is settled." He turned to David. "Say goodnight to your sister and wish her pleasant dreams."

David crossed the room and kissed her brow as he had ever since she was a child. "He is a good friend, but should he attempt to seduce you—"

"He is my husband."

David straightened and met Kit's gaze. "Will you be at breakfast?"

"Of course. What attentive husband would leave his wife to dine alone after their first night in ecstasy?"

David held up a finger. "Bride and groom. You are not to advance to husband and wife."

"Don't challenge me, David. You won't like the stone wall I can become."

"Gentlemen, I grow weary of this arguing and you are ruining my perfect evening."

David gave a brusque nod. "I'll see you at breakfast. Holler if you need me." He cast a glance at Kit. "Take care climbing out the window."

David stalked across the room and closed the door in his wake.

"He means well," Ashton said softly.

Kit turned to her. "Protectiveness is not always a good thing. Imagine if a mother bird never shoved her babies out of the nest. The trees would lack song and the sky would never know the graceful fancy of flight."

"Nor would a lady's hat ever be decorated with feathers."

Laughing, he took her hands and pulled her to her feet. "Let's prepare you for bed, sweetling. You do look tired."

Placing his hands on her shoulders, he turned her slightly so her back was to him and began to unfasten the row of buttons that ran from the high collar of her dress to her waist. His movements were slow, but not awkward, as though he relished the task. "You've done this often," she mused.

"A man's past is best not discussed on his wedding night."

The cool air tingled along her flesh as the material parted. She felt the softness of his lips press against the nape of her neck. She closed her eyes and relished the warmth of his breath and the gentleness of his kiss. So reminiscent of the one he'd given her following the ceremony. A brief touching of lips . . . as shallow as the vows they had exchanged.

"Do you remember the kiss I gave you in the church?" he asked as he slipped the gown from her shoulders and trailed his mouth along her collarbone. He dipped his tongue into the hollow at the base of her throat.

A shiver shimmied along her spine, and she had an incredible urge to lean into him. She swallowed hard. "I remember."

The room grew hot. Had August arrived without her knowledge?

"It was not the kiss I wished to bestow upon you, but the one I promised David I would give you." He cupped her face between his palms as one would hold a precious crystal sculpture. A smile teased his lips. "I have not given a chaste kiss such as that since I was twelve."

Her breath caught while her heart pounded painfully within her chest. "Indeed. What sort of kiss had you wished to bestow upon me?"

"It lies beyond the description of words."

Her eyes fluttered closed as he lowered his mouth to hers. She had always imagined a man's lips to be hard, his mouth demanding—perhaps because she had spent her life listening to her father and brother issue orders. Kit's lips were incredibly soft, but not in the same manner as hers, because beyond the softness she detected the strength, the power to wield without force in order to gain victory. His lips parted, and his tongue traced the outline of her mouth as though to memorize each dip and curve. With a sigh, she pressed her hands to his chest and felt the hard, rhythmic pounding of his heart while his tongue deepened his exploration until she no longer knew where his mouth began and hers ended—until she no longer cared.

He bestowed upon her a gentle patience that put her own forbearance to the test. She wanted more.

Her hands crept up his chest, and she looped her arms around his neck. With a feral groan, he pressed her body flush against his and the kiss deepened, intensified until it drew the very breath from her chest, the strength from her legs. With one arm, he held her steady, while his mouth tortured her with ecstasy.

Slowly, tenderly, he pulled back, brushing his tongue across her tingling, swollen lips in a bittersweet farewell. His breathing was as shallow as hers was, and she saw sweat glistening along his throat.

"Perhaps you'd best finish dressing for bed," he rasped.

She nodded mutely and stepped away from him.

"Ashton?"

She glanced over her shoulder.

"I would appreciate the honor of brushing your hair before you braid it."

"Tell me, Mr. Montgomery, do you brush hair with the same exuberance that you kiss?"

He offered her a devilish smile that was matched by the wickedness reflected in his eyes. "I think we are beyond such formalities, Ashton. You may call me Kit."

It was not until she was hidden safely behind the screen and changing into her nightgown that she realized he had avoided answering her question.

Chapter 7

Kit loosened his cravat and wondered what in God's name he thought he was doing. He should have clambered out the window long before he ever bestowed a true kiss upon his false wife. Ashton was like a shadow that could only appear in the presence of light and was doomed to non-existence with the arrival of darkness. And for her, the darkness would arrive far too soon.

Thank God, he would not have to bear witness to it.

She stepped from behind the screen. In her nightgown, with a solitary lamp providing a pale glow, she appeared incredibly thin. Narrowing his eyes, he scrutinized her delicate frame. Blushing, she crossed her arms over her chest before scurrying to the mirrored dresser. She sat, grabbed her brush, parted her hair down the middle, and draped it over each shoulder.

"You pad your clothing," he stated, both dumbfounded and amused by the discovery. "It was too dark to notice the other night when we were on the roof."

"It's not an uncommon practice among women,"

she announced, tilting her chin with her gaze riveted on her reflection.

"But it gives a man a false impression."

"Then he deserves what he gets on his wedding night if he never looks beyond the physical aspects of his betrothed."

Kit laughed as he crossed the room. "You play a dangerous game, sweetling. Why pad yourself if you never had any hope of capturing a man's attention?"

She stilled and dropped her gaze to the brush in her hand. "Because I have some pride."

Kneeling, he placed his hand over hers, his fingers circling the brush. "You promised me the honor of brushing your hair."

"You should leave before you discover all my faults."

"What makes you think I consider small breasts a fault?"

"Mine are more than small," she said in a tiny voice. "They are practically non-existent."

"I ask again. Why is that a fault?"

Her cheeks flamed red. "I often overheard David and his friends talking. They seemed to notice women with large bosoms more often than others."

He took the brush from her and glided the soft bristles through her silken blonde strands. "Never make the mistake of judging my preferences by others' standards."

He slipped his hand beneath the cascade of her hair and followed the trail of the brush along her neck, past her collarbone, halting when he reached her chest. Slowly, ever so slowly, he grazed his knuckles over the soft cloth that separated his coarse flesh from her tender nipple. He heard her sharp intake of breath and felt the tiny bud harden. "My tastes have never been those of the majority," he said quietly.

She licked her lips. "Did Clarisse have small breasts?"

He silently cursed the memories that slammed into him, memories best left unremembered. "No."

He moved his hand away from her breast and continued to brush her hair as she studied her clasped hands.

"I'm sorry," she whispered. "I had no right to ask about her."

"It doesn't matter. She has been gone a long time."

"But she still lives within your heart." She lifted her gaze and met his reflected in the mirror. "I hurt you with my insensitive question."

"I would prefer that you not compare yourself to her."

"I would always find myself lacking." She took the brush from him. "You should make your escape through the window now. The night has ended, and I thank you for making me a bride out of friendship for David."

Damn his already condemned soul. He had hurt her, not she him. He would have preferred that she had not mentioned Clarisse, but he was astonished to discover that the memories no longer held any bitterness. What cut into his heart was the knowledge that he had not given Ashton the full extent of her dream.

He cradled her cheek. "You think I took you as my bride out of friendship for David?"

"Why else would you do it? He asked—"

"I told him no. He could have asked a thousand times, and I would have answered the same."

She furrowed her delicate brow. "Then why?"

He stroked his thumb along the curve of her cheek, just below her eye. "Because yesterday afternoon, your eyes reflected delight, and it has been a long time since I have given a woman joy. I married you for selfish reasons. Simply to see the rapture in your eyes again." He slipped the brush from her hand. "Now the joy has retreated. I shall not leave until it returns."

She smiled warmly. "You have a gift with words. You should consider writing."

"I do write. Occasionally I send articles about my adventures here to a publication in London. I have even considered penning a complete history of my experiences in this wretched state—"

"You don't like Texas?"

"I miss England."

"Then you should return."

"I have little waiting for me there as I have here."

"That is too shallow an answer, Mr. Montgomery."

"Mrs. Montgomery, you are to call me Kit."

Her eyes brightened. "Say that again."

"Mrs. Montgomery."

She laughed lightly. "I love the way that sounds." She trailed her fingers along the curve of his jaw, the brightness in her eyes dimming. "Until this moment, though, I hadn't considered that you'll become a widower."

"I have told you before not to concern yourself with that aspect of this arrangement. Give me your smiles and your laughter, but never your tears, and I shall have no regrets."

He slid the brush through her hair. "Now on to important matters. Do you brush a hundred strokes?"

A sly twinkle came into her eyes. "Two hundred."

He slowly moved the brush through her silken tresses, relishing the softness against his flesh. If she could stay awake long enough, he would gift her with three hundred. "So I have a greedy wife," he mused.

"Only where brushing my hair and chocolate are concerned."

"You have a fancy for chocolates?" he asked, wishing he'd known sooner. He would have given her chocolates before bed.

"They are my weakness, although my physician has ordered me not to eat chocolate."

"Why?"

"He feels they will speed my decline."

"Is this physician of yours well educated?"

She nodded, the sadness flickering in her eyes. "He is self taught, as many physicians are in the West. But still, David would only take me to the best."

"Of course. My question was unfounded."

"But you're bothered by my answer. I've accepted my destiny. Please don't pity me or I'll be forced to give you the tears that you don't desire."

He gave a brusque nod. It seemed the longer he stayed, the less grand her dream remained. He was to make her a bride. Nothing more. He'd done his part. Why was leaving such a torment? He should be glad to be rid of her.

He contented himself with one hundred and twenty-five strokes before turning away so she could plait her hair. Once Christopher had taken Clarisse for his wife, Kit had given no thought to marriage. His responsibilities did not include providing an heir to Ravenleigh.

He wondered if his brother had ever brushed Clarisse's hair. He squeezed his eyes shut, banishing the thought and all the other wild imaginings that intruded on his peace—all the things his brother had held that had been denied Kit. He refused to resent what was not his by right. A small hand came to rest on his arm.

"Are you all right?"

He opened his eyes and smiled warmly at his wife. "I was contemplating my exit through your window."

She tilted her head slightly. "It's a good thing ours isn't to be a true marriage, because no trust resides between us. You don't need to lie. Just tell me your thoughts are none of my business."

Dear Lord, he found it disturbing that she somehow managed to read his moods so well. He strode across the room and jerked back the blankets on the bed. "Come on. Let's get you into bed so I can keep my promise to David."

She padded over and slipped between the sheets. Kit reached for the lamp.

"Not complete darkness," she said quickly. He glanced at her. "I'll have that soon enough."

He turned down the flame until its muted glow allowed the shadows to creep into the room. He leaned over and kissed her forehead. "Sleep well, sweetling. I shall see you in the morning."

He walked to the window, moved the curtain aside, sat on the ledge, and swung one leg over onto the roof.

"Christian?"

He glanced over his shoulder. She lay in the bed alone, such a frail creature, the blankets drawn up to her chin. Alone. She would sleep in solitude for the remainder of her nights.

She offered him a hint of a smile. "Now you can't argue that the dream isn't over, so thank you for all that you've given me."

"It was my pleasure." He leaned out the window, into the darkness. He would return to his room at the jail where a narrow cot and a full bottle of whiskey awaited him.

Tomorrow, he would escort her to the stagecoach and, amidst wagging tongues, give her a final farewell. As the months passed, he'd wait for the letter from David that announced he was truly free of her.

Truly free of her and her blasted dream.

Ashton clutched the blankets as she studied the part of Kit that still remained in her room. What was keeping him there? If he didn't leave soon, she'd lose the control she fought so desperately to keep and call him back, ask him at least to hold her for a while as she had so often imagined her husband holding her.

Oh, she had wanted to be a bride, but it had all been false. Not a true dream, only pretense. It wasn't truly what she'd wanted, but she refused to hurt the two men who had tried to give her what they thought she desired.

Kit slipped back into her room. She bolted upright, her fingers tightening around the blankets as he shrugged off his jacket and tossed it onto a nearby chair. His previously loosened cravat joined it. "What are you doing?" she asked.

"A bride should not spend her wedding night sleeping alone," he said quietly as he unfastened the buttons on his shirt.

Her heart bounced against her ribs. "But I thought . . . I mean, David indicated—"

"Sleep, Ashton. We will do no more than sleep."

His words stilled her escalating hopes that perhaps she would know the full measure of a man's love. That longing was her true dream. One she knew would never be realized.

He pulled his shirt over his head and tossed it onto the chair. The muted light from the lamp revealed his broad chest and shoulders in glorious splendor. Had he arrived from England with such hardened muscles and firmness of physique? She thought not. She imagined he'd arrived thinner, but just as elegant. His ancestry more than nature had shaped him.

The bed dipped as he dropped onto its edge and began to remove his shoes. With one hand, she grabbed the edge of the mattress to prevent herself from rolling toward him. Whatever would he think if he found her thin frame next to his powerful one?

The room contained more shadow than light, but still she could make out each of his movements. He stood, and with a single fluid motion, shucked his trousers and slipped beneath the sheets, sheets that bunched at his hips, leaving his taut stomach and chest visible. She gripped the blankets more tightly because to do otherwise might give her fingers the freedom to touch him as she desperately wanted to do.

"Come here, Ashton," he said, in a low seductive voice.

She jerked her gaze to his face. Even in the shadows, she felt the intensity of his stare. "I'm not certain this is a wise idea."

"Nervous?" he asked.

"Aren't brides supposed to be?"

"Not necessarily. I doubt either Abbie or Jessye was nervous on her wedding night."

"Yes, well, perhaps they knew more of what to expect."

"I've told you what to expect. Sleep."

"Then why do I need to come to you?"

"So I can hold you."

She took a deep shuddering breath. "You're not wearing a shirt."

"That fact did not seem to bother you yesterday when you rode on the horse with your back pressed to my chest."

He spoke the truth. She had enjoyed it, but far more articles of clothing separated them yesterday. She swallowed hard. "I guess no harm could come from one moment."

He raised his arm, and she slowly eased to his side, his warm side, his bare side where his flesh met the thin material of her nightgown. He lowered his arm and drew her into the circle of his embrace. He took her hand and pressed it flat against his chest, just below his heart.

"I've never done this before," she whispered, "lain so close to a man, especially one partially dressed."

"If you find it unpleasant, I'll leave."

"No!" She squeezed her eyes shut. "I mean, there's no need now that we're here, and since you're my husband nothing is wrong with our sleeping in each other's arms."

"Then relax. You are as stiff as a poker used to bring the dying embers of a fire to life."

She turned her head slightly, released a long, slow breath, and relaxed against him. She remembered as a child playing for hours with wooden puzzle pieces, putting them together until they created pictures. At this moment, she felt as though she had just fitted one odd-shaped piece into its proper place.

She breathed in and caught the scent of bay rum and the faintest aroma of sweat. He hadn't looked it earlier, but she wondered if he'd been as nervous this evening as she had been. She averted her head again and released her breath.

"What are you doing?" he asked.

She lifted her gaze to his. "I thought my breath going across your chest might tickle."

His chest rumbled beneath her cheek as he laughed. "Dear God, Ashton, what am I going to do with you? I forget how innocent you are. Have you never had a man court you?"

"Never. Nor a boy."

His laughter dwindled, and he rolled slightly until she felt as though she was wrapped in a cocoon. He grazed the back of his hand along her cheek. "Life has treated you unfairly. Today hardly makes up for it."

She licked her lips. "Is it true that a union between a man and a woman is as difficult on a woman as David hints?"

He threaded his fingers through her hair. "It can be vigorous . . . or not, depending upon the couple, the mood, the couple's feelings toward each other."

"So you could be gentle."

"On this matter, I must admit David's warning is best heeded."

She dropped her gaze to his chest, preferring the sight of it to the pity in his eyes. She laughed mirthlessly. "I don't even know why I'm pursuing this path when I know so little about what passes between a man and a woman."

He took her chin between his thumb and forefinger and tilted her head up. He skimmed his lips across her brow, her cheek, until his mouth rested near her ear. "I would possess your body, our flesh joined in a heated passion that would forever mark you as mine and me as yours. Right now, the parting will go easier because only words bind us." His breath became harsh as he moved back so he could hold her gaze. "I can grant you the physical pleasure, Ashton, but could you truly accept it, knowing that our hearts watched from afar?"

"Either way, it sounds as though I shall have regrets."

He cradled her face within the crook of his shoulder. "It was not my intent to give you any regrets, only to remind you of our original bargain."

"Then you have loved all the women you've bedded."

"I've loved none of them."

Her heart constricted with the knowledge he had unwittingly given. He'd never made love to his beloved Clarisse.

"Then how can you know there is a difference?"

She released a tiny squeak as he rolled her over, wedging himself between her thighs, her nightgown pulled taut across her legs.

"Do you want my body joined with yours? Give me your permission and I will make it so."

The lamplight cast a halo around the anger burning brightly within his eyes.

"No," she whispered hoarsely. She wanted adoration in his eyes, and his willingness without seeking permission. "I think you're right. We're overstepping the boundaries of the original bargain."

He pressed his forehead to hers. "I should leave. I am ruining what was to be a gift."

She dared to comb her fingers through his thick hair. "Please stay. I won't badger you for things you can't give."

He rolled off her and drew her snuggly against his side. "In the next few months, while you are in Dallas, should you meet a man who takes possession of your heart, know that I will fully understand if you grant him possession of your body."

"Then our vows today would become false. Will you seek solace with other women when I leave?" she asked, wondering at the pain that ricocheted through her chest with the thought.

"No."

"So you will honor the vows, but you don't expect me to?"

"I expect you to take advantage of every opportunity for happiness that life places before you."

"And *your* happiness?"

"Can wait."

She pressed her palm to his chest and marveled at the hard, steady pounding of his heart. "They say a girl does not truly become a woman until she marries. I thought only of what today would give me, not what it would take from you."

"You've taken nothing from me today."

"Except a chance for happiness."

"No, I lost that eight years ago when I placed the one thing I valued most above the only thing I treasured."

Chapter 8

Kit found nothing as comforting as the feel of a woman's body pressed against his, her curves nestled within the hollows of his frame. Yet never had the placement seemed so incredibly perfect. Reason enough for a man to marry, he supposed.

But was it reason enough for a woman? A woman needed love, even if it was only a pretense. He had not anticipated that once he settled into bed with Ashton his lower body would begin to rule his head, nor that she might desire it.

Although sleep eluded him, she had succumbed quickly enough to it once their chatter had ceased. He had no memory of ever talking with a woman in bed except for the erotic things he'd whispered in her ear. He should have gone out the window as planned.

Dear God, he should have thrown himself out head first.

Because now, all he could do was watch her sleep and wish for things that could never be. How many other dreams did she hold that would not bear fruit?

She shivered against him, and he tucked the covers

more closely around her. How could she be cold in this Texas heat? Perhaps because she had so little meat on her bones. He would ensure that she ate a hearty breakfast before she began her trip back to Dallas.

She rolled away from him and the loneliness eased in. Strange, how he had not noticed its absence, but was only now aware of its presence.

He considered drawing her back into his embrace, but he did not wish to take a chance on disturbing her. He folded his hands beneath his head, stared at the shadows dancing across the ceiling, and realized with increasing awareness that he desperately wanted to make love to the woman lying in bed with him.

She was correct in her assumption that men preferred women with more rounded curves, but it was not Ashton's physical attributes that attracted him. It was the calmness of her soul that reached out to him. He longed for more than a physical union. He wanted emotional gratification.

A dangerous thing to crave in his love-deprived existence.

Kit felt hell's blaze rise around him, engulfing him as forked flames scorched his flesh. He heard the harsh rise and fall of the bellows that breathed life into the fire. The dampness surrounded him and the earth trembled as he was consumed—

He shot up in bed, his breathing labored while his eyes adjusted to the muted shadows. The dream hovered, refusing to be banished. He wasn't on his cot. He was in a room, a room that carried the lingering fragrance of a woman. A woman. A woman curled on her side, shivering as though she were packed in snow.

Reality crashed in on him and he leaned nearer to her. "Ashton?"

Her breathing came in short gasps, followed by a hacking cough. He touched her shoulder. Her nightgown was drenched, and beneath it he felt the heat of fever. "Ashton, tell me what to do."

"Leave. I . . . can . . . tend to my needs."

"The bloody hell you can." He tossed aside the covers, scrambled out of bed, and hurried to her side. He reached for the buttons on her nightgown. Her fingers closed over his.

"No, please leave."

"It's bloody stuffy in here. Who closed the window?"

"I did. I woke up and you were asleep, so I closed it. It's a rule. Mother's rule. Night air is unhealthy."

A thousand curses rumbled through his mind. "You need fresh air, but I can't allow it in until you are dry. I'm going to remove your nightgown."

"It's improper."

"I'm your husband," he reminded her as he lost all patience and tore the gown in two. She screeched, frantically trying to hide what he'd just revealed, but had no time to notice. He grabbed the top blanket and began to gather the sweat from her body.

"Please, I can dry myself," she pleaded, her voice small and frightened.

"I can do it more quickly and efficiently. As for your modesty, I shall return it to you once you are no longer shivering."

He grabbed another blanket and wrapped it around her. Leaving her in the bed, he stumbled through the darkness, cursing when his shin hit the object he was seeking. He shoved the rocking chair to the window, tore down the draperies and flung open the window.

He crossed the room, and as gently as he could, he lifted Ashton into his arms. "You need fresh air."

"But Mother warned me—"

"I don't give a bloody damn about your mother's warnings. If I'm on the verge of suffocating in this room, how can you not be?"

He carried her to the rocker, dropped into it, and cradled her against his body. "You're fevered."

"It'll pass."

"Has this happened before?" he asked, wishing that his voice didn't sound like that of a panicked schoolboy. He rubbed her back and arms briskly, trying to work up a measure of heat to stop her shivering. How could she shiver when she was fevered?

"Yes," she finally answered, her teeth clicking together.

"Does David know?"

"No, and please don't tell him." With a violent shudder, she collapsed against him, nestling her head within the crook of his shoulder. "It always passes."

Gingerly, he felt her forehead, grateful for the coolness that greeted his touch. She no longer shivered or coughed. All that remained were the shallow breaths that barely caused her chest to rise and fall.

He took a deep shuddering breath and relaxed against the chair, gently rocking while he held her more snuggly against him. The cool night air seeped into the room. It did not yet hold the heaviness of summer, but it was crisp and clean. Perhaps he was wrong and it would do more harm than good, but for right now, he was content with her stillness. He released a slight chuckle.

"What's so funny?" she asked quietly.

"I have done many things with many women, but I have never done this." Although his mind began to weave possibilities. If he were to turn her so she faced him, her legs straddling his thighs . . . he closed his eyes and fought back the images. The last thing his innocent bride needed was to feel against her thigh the direction of his thoughts. "Why have you not told David of these episodes?"

She sighed. "Because he would hire a nurse to sleep in the room with me, and the last of my independence would be forfeited. I've had so little in my life that I treasure the smallest liberties, and sleeping alone is the greatest of those at the moment."

He opened his eyes and met her gaze. "You should have told me the truth about why you wanted me to leave. I had no desire to relieve you of your independence."

"I'm glad you stayed. I didn't feel like a prisoner even though you held me in arms that seemed as strong as iron. When I first awoke, I watched you sleep. You do it with such ease, as though you have no demons to haunt you."

He smiled sardonically. "It is only in sleep that the demons do not torment me, so I always welcome it."

He watched as she studied his face and the furrow

between her brow deepened. "What if they are wrong about consumption?"

"In what way?"

"They say it is a disease of the family. Yet neither my parents nor David has ever showed signs of it."

"Surely the physicians know its cause."

"They don't know everything."

Pain sliced through his heart, for she could not have spoken truer words. They had not known how to stop the disease that took Clarisse. "What is your theory on its cause?"

She averted her gaze. "It lives inside my lungs. It seems to me that it could easily escape with each breath I release, and if someone were close enough to take my breath into their bodies—"

She shoved against him. "You shouldn't hold me so close."

Pulling her back, he banded his arms around her. "It's a bit late to worry about that now, don't you think? Especially after I kissed you."

She swiveled her head. "I didn't breathe when you kissed me."

"It was that good, was it?"

She smiled timidly. "You arrogant man. You know it was heavenly."

He combed his fingers through the strands of hair that had loosed from her braid. "Are you in pain?"

"No, I hear that frightening aspect comes later, near the end."

"Why did the physician predict you would die this winter?"

"Because winter months are the hardest on me. Summer comes and I feel better, but last winter he truly didn't expect me to survive, so he says this year will be my last." She cradled his cheek. "What if I *have* given you this disease?"

"I can think of better wedding gifts."

She hit his shoulder. "Do not make light of my fears."

Cradling her face, he studied the lines that had not been shaped by happiness. Her parents had obviously protected her to the extremes and now her brother was determined to carry on in their stead. "Ashton, I learned long ago that there is much in life I cannot control. Worry does not alter them."

"But you could die because of my stupid dream. It was a child's wish, not a woman's. I'll worry constantly—"

"You are not to worry about me at all. I do not fear death." He trailed his thumb across her cheek. "Do you?"

"I don't fear the dying or even what awaits me beyond. I think I simply regret all that death will deny me." She smiled softly. "Although it did give me you, didn't it?"

His stomach clenched at the warmth in her eyes. "Only temporarily, Ashton. Until the stagecoach arrives tomorrow."

He hated watching the light dim in her eyes, but by God, he had played his role of groom and more.

She curled her head into the nook of his shoulder until her face became lost in the shadows. "Thank you, Christian, for traveling with me into the night."

His throat tightening, he held her closer and continued to rock her until she fell asleep, a woman who would die with a child's innocence and his family's name carved on her headstone for eternity.

He could not decide if it would be a tribute to dreams or a mockery of them.

The blanket slipped from her bare shoulder and a moonbeam captured the perfection of her small breast. Her smooth pink nipple fascinated him. Usually by the time he had removed a woman's clothes, passion had hardened it into a little bud. The temptation to run his tongue over it and feel the bud form in his mouth was almost more than he could bear.

The breeze gently brushed over them, and he watched her nipple pucker. Yet the temptation remained. What had he given her this day? Nothing really.

An opportunity to dress up and play a part. A few dances. A kiss. A tuck into bed. The opportunity to sleep within his arms.

And now he rocked her as though she were a child.

Gingerly, he brought the blanket back over her shoulder and tucked it securely into place until her tempting flesh was hidden from his sight. Unfortunately, he could not erase the image of it from his memory.

The knock sounded at precisely eight o'clock. Kit chuckled as he slipped the last button of Ashton's dress through its loop. "Your brother is timely."

Ashton turned slightly and smiled at him. "He doesn't want to miss the stagecoach."

She bid David to enter. Kit leaned against the dresser and crossed his arms over his chest, taking pleasure in David's indignant expression.

"Good morning," Kit said cheerily.

"There was certainly no reason for you to slip back into the room this morning," David said.

"There certainly wasn't."

David glared at him. "You never left, did you?"

"That answer rests between my wife and myself."

"Your wife?" David snarled.

Kit held up his hands. "My bride. If she came to this bed a virgin last night, then she is still one."

"You doubt that she did?"

"Oh, David, calm down," Ashton scolded. "Can't you see he enjoys riling you?"

She reached for a ribbon. Kit took it from her and picked up the brush. "Allow me."

His body ached in every spot imaginable. A rocking chair did not make a fine bed. He never thought he would have preferred his cot to a woman in his arms.

He brought her hair back and tied it in place with the ribbon. Black. He would send her some colorful ribbons and perhaps a letter or two just to keep in touch.

He extended his elbow. "Shall we see about breakfast?"

She slipped her arm through his. "David, stop frowning. You can escort me downstairs as well."

Kit walked beside her to the door.

"How did you sleep last night, David?" Kit asked as she wound her arm around her brother's.

"Poorly."

"Glad to hear it."

"Kit," Ashton chastised.

"This marriage was his idea, and I rather enjoy the thought that he lost some sleep over it."

"He didn't hold a gun to your head," she scolded as they descended the stairs.

No, she had held something much more lethal—joy in her eyes.

He pulled out her chair and waited until she was settled before taking his chair beside her.

"Land o'goshen," Mrs. Gurney said as she came out of the kitchen. "I wasn't expecting to see the newlyweds down here. I had planned to take something up to you later. You gonna be living here now that you got a wife, Marshal?"

Kit cleared his throat and took his napkin. "No, Mrs. Gurney."

She placed her hands on her hips. "You can't expect Mrs. Montgomery to sleep on that old cot in the jail."

"You need not worry yourself, Mrs. Gurney," David said. "Ashton is going to return to Dallas with me. My wife is expecting a child and has need of her."

"Her leaving so quick don't make much sense to me. I reckon the marshal was just stakin' his claim then."

"Yes," David murmured.

Mrs. Gurney returned to the kitchen, and Kit watched as Ashton took her usual small portions of food.

"Actually, Ashton will not be returning to Dallas with you," Kit said as he scooped up some eggs.

David's fork clinked as it hit his plate, and Ashton turned to Kit, a deep furrow in her brow.

He smiled warmly even though his mind screamed that he was carelessly adding fuel to the fire of misbegotten favors. "Every bride should have a wedding journey. I've decided to take you to Galveston."

Joy flashed into her eyes, then diminished. "But you have responsibilities here."

"I have not taken a holiday in three years. The town can live without my presence for a few weeks."

"I'm not sure this is wise," David said in a low voice.

"Since you arrived, nothing we have done has been wise, but we have set our course and we must follow it," Kit said.

"How long would we stay?" Ashton asked.

"As long as you wish."

"Ashton—" David began.

She met her brother's gaze. "I want to see the ocean." She turned her attention back to Kit. "But are you sure? You've already done so much."

"So I shall do a little more. What harm can come of it?"

Chapter 9

"Oh, Kit, it's beautiful."

His arms crossed over his chest, Kit leaned against the wall near the open door that led onto the balcony where his wife stood in the distant corner, her hands wrapped around the railing as she stared out to sea. He wondered how many women had done the same, waiting for husbands to return from their ocean mistress.

He and Ashton had traveled by stagecoach to Galveston, a journey of several days. As each night approached, they had stayed in a different inn along the route. Ashton had not slept well, and he was determined that she would do so while they were here. Sharing accommodations with people seemed to make her uncomfortable.

Upon their arrival in Galveston this afternoon, he'd secured her a room at a hotel. While she'd napped, he'd gone in search of something more pleasing. Fortunately, he'd managed to locate and secure this small cottage on an isolated part of the island. Sand dunes hid it from sight on one side while the bay circled it on the other.

"It looks like the ocean goes on forever," Ashton said.

"In a way it does, although from time to time, it runs into land masses: islands, England, Europe, Africa."

She glanced over her shoulder, her eyes filled with delight. "I know the layout of the world." She looked back at the water. "I hadn't expected the ocean to roar so loudly, and the keening of the wind makes it seem as though it's in mourning."

"No doubt it weeps for all the sailors lost at sea."

She spun around. "Do you really think so?"

He shrugged. "In truth, I doubt the wind cares that in its anger it has sent many a man to his death."

"Were you frightened when you traveled here on the ship?"

"Only the day we encountered the sea monster."

She laughed. "There are no sea monsters." She lowered her lashes and peered at him. "Are there?"

Smiling, he crossed the expanse separating them. "No, none that I saw. What I did enjoy was watching the dolphins." He pointed toward the bay. "That fellow followed me all the way from England."

She turned back around, and he heard her gasp as a dolphin arched gracefully out of the water before diving below the surface. Kit studied the nape of her neck, incredibly tempted to place a kiss there.

"He's beautiful. How do you know it's the same one?" she asked.

"I don't."

She twisted around, her mouth close enough to his

that he could close the gap in less than a heartbeat. The joy in her eyes was incredible to behold. His body was reacting to her nearness with a ferocity that made him doubt his wisdom in giving his bride a wedding trip.

"Why are you making fun of me?" she asked.

Because if he didn't, he might take her in his arms and kiss her until they both lost their senses. There was something about the salt air, the freshness, the thundering of an ocean that renewed life. He stepped back until he could no longer smell her fragrance. "I'm not making fun of you, sweetling, but the rake within me cannot resist an opportunity to tease."

She narrowed her eyes. "How long did you say we'd stay here?"

"As long as you wish."

"What about the people of Fortune and your duty to them?"

He grinned. "You will grow tired of me long before they realize I've gone."

She shook her finger at him. "Don't be so sure, Christian Montgomery. I might grow used to your teasing, and then what?"

And then what, indeed? He dared not contemplate that inevitability or the fact that he might grow more accustomed to her presence. He was finding it difficult enough to remember a time when she wasn't beside him offering smiles and pleasant conversation. As an added bonus, she neither spit tobacco nor cursed.

She returned her gaze to the sea. "I can't believe you found this cottage."

"We had a bit of good fortune. I've hired a cook to come each day and prepare our meals, but she won't be here until tomorrow morning, so I'm afraid tonight you must suffer through my poor attempt at a meal."

She glanced at him. "I'd offer to cook if I knew how."

"You don't cook?"

She shook her head. "I've always had everything done for me."

"Then I suppose it's a good thing that I've hired the cook's daughter to come and clean the house."

He saw disappointment in her eyes. "It sounds like we'll have a house full of people. Who else have you hired?"

"Just those two women, and they'll only stay until we finish dinner. Then they'll return to their homes."

"And we'll be here alone?"

"Yes." Although he was beginning to fear that aspect of this wedding trip was not the wisest part of his little plan.

"You've thought of everything, haven't you?" she asked.

"I enjoy managing details and leaving nothing to chance." He tipped his head toward the sky. "The sun will set soon. Let me prepare our dinner, and we'll eat it here on the balcony so you may continue to enjoy the ocean."

Ashton sat at the cloth-covered table with the ugliest lantern she'd ever seen decorating its center. With the breeze blowing, she knew candles were not an option. She also knew in her head that Kit had not intended the dinner to be romantic, but her heart had hoped. A foolish desire that blossomed daily within her breast.

She moved the food around on her plate and glanced at Kit, who had already eaten all of his. "Now, what did you call this?" she asked.

"A cowboy's fare. Beans, sourdough biscuits, and whatever else happened to be handy."

She nodded thoughtfully. "It's the 'whatever else' that worries me."

He leaned over and touched the fish on her plate with his fork. "That's flounder. One of my favorites. If you eat it very carefully, the meat comes off the bone, leaving the skeletal structure intact so you end up with no bones in your mouth. I coated it with butter and lemon. It's delicious, I assure you."

She grimaced. "But you left its head on. I can't eat something that's staring at me."

"It's dead. It can't see you."

"But I can *see* it." She placed her napkin over the plate and tucked it underneath to hold it in place against the wind.

Kit sighed heavily. "Ashton, you don't eat enough to keep a bird alive."

"I'm sorry. I know you went to a great deal of trouble to prepare the creature, but I just can't eat him."

He held up a finger. "Don't touch your plate. I'll fetch dessert."

Watching him disappear through the doors that led from their bedroom onto the balcony, she drew her shawl more closely around her and wondered how long they truly could stay here. She'd fallen in love with the area the moment she'd set eyes on it.

Kit walked out carrying a large box. He had been sitting across from her before. He moved the chair until he was beside her and set the box on the floor. He withdrew another box and held it up.

Her eyes widened with delight. "Chocolate. You remembered."

"I remember everything." He removed the top from the box and took out a small confection. "There is a store in town that sells nothing but sweets."

"Is that entire box full of chocolate?"

"Indeed it is."

"I think I may fall in love with you."

An emotion similar to worry flitted across his face. She laughed lightly as she realized her words had made him uncomfortable. "Don't worry. I know I'm not supposed to love you, but I can adore you for bringing me chocolates even though you know my physician cautioned me against having them."

"No disrespect intended, but your physician was foolish. No harm can come from chocolate."

"I suppose you have that on good authority?"

"Quite. My brother is the healthiest man I know, and he has a ravenous appetite for chocolate that he appeases at all hours of the day or night. Now, open your mouth."

She did as he bade, not certain which she enjoyed more: the taste of the chocolate or his fingers. The decadent thought made her grow warm. His fingers didn't stay in her mouth long enough so she relished the chocolate, closing her eyes and moaning as she did so.

"Delicious," she murmured. "I'll take another." She popped open her eyes and stared at her fork that now sported some white meat on it. "What's that?"

"Your flounder."

She darted a glance to the table and discovered that while she'd been enjoying her chocolate, Kit had moved her plate so it was now in front of him.

"I have no difficulty staring at a fish that is staring at me," he said calmly as he moved the fork closer to her mouth. "Eat. Two bites of fish and I'll give you another chocolate."

She wanted to be angry at him, but for some unfathomable reason, she found him incredibly attractive sitting there holding her fork, tempting her with chocolate while trying to make her eat. "That's bribery."

"Indeed it is."

She narrowed her eyes. "One bite of fish in exchange for two pieces of chocolate."

"One fish, one chocolate."

She opened her mouth and unenthusiastically welcomed the fish. Much to her surprise, she enjoyed the flavor. She licked her lips. "It's not bad."

"Liar. It's delicious."

"Not as good as chocolate."

Grinning, he popped a confection into her mouth. "No, not as good as chocolate."

Sitting in the chair on the balcony, Ashton stared at the night. Kit had taken the dishes downstairs, leaving the chocolate behind. She ate another piece. It tasted different when his fingers hadn't touched it first. Not nearly as enticing.

If she were wise, she would suggest that they leave for Dallas tomorrow. Kit could easily steal her heart, if he hadn't already. Strange how she had always resented everyone waiting on her, but adored the way he saw to her every need.

She had to constantly remind herself that he was simply being kind and held no true affection for her. Still, the memories were sweet to hold, as sweet as the chocolate she chewed.

She heard footsteps and glanced over her shoulder. Carrying a blanket, Kit stepped onto the balcony, grabbed his chair, and dragged it across the wooden floor. He draped the blanket over her before sitting beside her.

"I can't believe there are so many ships out there," she said quietly. "I find that one particularly intriguing." She pointed toward a ship whose light shone brighter than any other.

"It's the only lightship on the Gulf Coast. Others have come before it, but according to the clerk at the hotel, the *Galveston Lightship Number 28* only just arrived in Galveston this past January."

"What's its purpose?" she asked.

"The same as a lighthouse. It's moored at the entrance to Galveston Bay to warn ships that land is near and to guide them when necessary."

Ashton drew the blanket more closely around her. "For some strange reason, I feel safer knowing it's there."

"Are you cold?" he asked quietly.

She glanced at him. "A little, but I'm not ready to go inside yet."

He reached for her. "Come here, then, and I'll warm you."

Instinct warned her to stay put, but her heart and shivering body obeyed his request, and she moved to his lap. He tucked the blanket snugly around her before wrapping her within his embrace.

"How can you be so warm?" she asked.

"I grew up in a colder climate. After five years here, the heat bothers me less, but still I don't much care for the summers."

"I love the summers. It's the only time I'm not cold. August is my favorite month."

She felt his exaggerated shudder, knowing the action was intentional and not brought on by the slight chill in the night air.

"I dislike August the most," he said, "And not only because it's the month that we first picked cotton."

"I can't imagine you working in a cotton field," she said.

"I find it difficult to imagine as well, but I stuck it out because Gray was so determined to see the stalks plucked clean. I loathed every moment of it."

"You're all fortunate to have such good friends in one another."

"I've always thought so."

She nestled her head within the crook of his shoulder. "You've told me about your brother and father. What of your mother?"

"She was a saint."

"Was?"

His arms tightened around her, and she glanced up to see him staring out to sea.

"She became ill the winter before Clarisse died. Whatever it was, the disease took her quickly and unexpectedly. I was holding her, reading to her, and when I glanced down, she was gone."

Ashton pressed her palm to his cheek. "And here you are holding another dying woman."

"Tragedy comes in threes, does it not?"

"How unfair for you." She covered her mouth, trying to stifle her yawn.

"The hour is late, sweetling. I should put you to bed."

She wrapped her arms around his neck as he stood. "I can walk, you know."

"I might as well carry you, since you're already within my embrace."

"You're going to spoil me."

"In ways you can't even imagine," he promised as he walked into the bedroom.

She glanced at the four-poster canopied bed and her mouth went dry as he released his hold and she slowly slid down his body. As casually as she could, she removed the blanket and draped it over the bed. "There's no changing screen."

"You won't need one," he assured her, and her heart sped up as she slowly turned to face him.

"I won't?"

"You'll have privacy here. I've taken the room across the hall."

Disappointment slammed into her. "You didn't need to do that."

He held out a hand as though to explain better. "We are the only two within a house on an isolated part of the island. Our sleeping habits will not be the fodder for local gossip as they would have been in Fortune."

She nodded briskly. "Of course."

"It's for the best, Ashton, if we are to hold to the original intent of our marriage."

"I understand," she said, wringing her hands. "Truly I do. I'll see you in the morning."

"The cook should arrive in time to prepare our breakfast."

"Wonderful."

He leaned over and kissed her forehead. "Sleep well, sweetling."

He walked out of the room, closing the door behind him.

She turned and kicked one of the bedposts. She'd wanted a kiss on the lips, not the forehead, as though she were his sister or worse, his child. She wanted to curl against him as she slept.

She plopped down on the bed. She had wanted to visit Galveston, and he had brought her, as a friend, not as a husband. He was right, of course. Their sleeping arrangement was for the best.

Still, for reasons she could not explain, that knowledge hurt.

Kit paced the confines of his room while some damned clock downstairs bonged twice. Two o'clock in the morning, and he had yet to sleep a wink.

After several nights of holding Ashton in his arms while he slept—first the night they were married; and then each night along their journey when the stagecoach stopped at an inn—he didn't know what to do with his bloody arms when they were empty. They thrashed about, searching for her, keeping him awake. How could he grow so accustomed to her small frame nestled against his while he slept? It was ludicrous that his body should torment him with the memories of her scent, her warmth, the sound of her breathing.

He was beyond exhaustion, having spent the entire afternoon making all the arrangements for their stay here. Sleep should have come quickly. Instead it eluded him as much as absolution.

What if she were having another attack as she had on their wedding night? Would she call out for him? He should have given her instructions to yell if she needed him. But her voice was so soft, would he hear her even if she screamed?

Tomorrow he would purchase a cowbell, and she could clang it if she had one of her spells. Yes indeed, that action would solve his little problem of knowing if he was needed. Now all he had to determine was how he could sleep without her in his arms. He glared at the bed as though it were his enemy. He should have searched for a house that had only one bedroom. Then only one option would have been available to them. The one he desired.

He stopped pacing and stared at his door. He could

check on her. He *should* check on her. Make certain she was comfortable and sleeping well. As her husband, he was ultimately responsible for her welfare. With that matter settled, he stalked across the room and flung open the door.

He came to an abrupt halt at the sight of Ashton standing within her doorway. Her screech echoed down the hallway as she pressed a hand just below her throat and stepped back.

"What's wrong?" he asked.

"You scared the living daylights out of me."

"I realize that. Why are you out of bed?"

"I couldn't sleep. I thought some warm milk might help," she explained.

"I have a better solution." He crossed the hallway and lifted her into his arms.

"What are you doing?" she asked as he walked toward her bed.

"Unfortunately, I have discovered that I have grown accustomed to sleeping with you." He laid her on the bed. "If you have no objection, I would like to sleep in your bed tonight."

"And you want me to go to your bed?"

"No! If I wanted that, I wouldn't have carried you in here. Didn't you listen to what I just said?"

"Yes, but it's confusing when you sound so angry."

He sighed deeply. "I'm not angry. I'm tired. It's two o'clock in the bloody morning."

She slipped beneath the sheets and scooted over. "Join me, then."

Grateful for her understanding, he turned down

the lamp, removed his trousers, and climbed into bed. He raised his arm, and she came into his embrace as though she belonged there. If he weren't so tired, the thought would have kept him from sleeping.

Just as he was drifting off, he heard her soft voice. "Kit?"

"Mmm?"

"I lied."

"About what?"

"I wasn't going to get some warm milk. I was going to sneak into your bed. Seems I've grown used to sleeping with you, too."

Chuckling low, he pressed a kiss to the top of her head. "Oh, Ashton, what am I going to do with you?"

Chapter 10

As a gray haze eased into the room, Kit felt his wife stir, moving from within his embrace. He tightened his hold on her and mumbled, "Where are you going?"

"I want to see the dawn."

Before he could prevent it, she slipped away from him.

After several days of travel and with less than four hours of sleep last night, he'd hoped they might stay in bed until the late afternoon. "Come back to bed, sweetling. The dawn will be there tomorrow."

"For you," she said softly.

He squeezed his eyes shut more tightly, listening to her bare feet pad across the floor as she scurried onto the balcony. Was her life nothing but waiting for death or was she so concerned with death that she avoided life?

He threw back the covers, snatched up his trousers, and jerked them on. He stepped onto the balcony and crossed to where she stood, staring at the sun lightly stroking away the evidence of night. He drew her back against his chest, wrapped his arms around her, and settled his chin on top of her head.

"You didn't have to get up," she said.

"I know."

She placed her arms over his. "It's so incredibly beautiful."

"The sun does seem to favor the skies of Texas, although I prefer the sunsets."

She twisted her head slightly to look up at him. "Why?"

Because it placed one more day of guilt behind him, while the sunrise signaled another day to endure. Perhaps they were more alike than he thought, avoiding life because death held them within its unmerciful grip. "I don't know," he lied. "Perhaps because I enjoy the night." He yawned. "And the sleep it brings."

She turned her gaze back to the sunrise. "Last night the bed felt incredibly empty before you joined me."

"It was empty. You take up no room at all." He gave into temptation and kissed the nape of her neck. She rolled her shoulder inward. "I shall have you looking like Jack Spratt's wife before we're done here," he promised.

She giggled and her hands tightened their hold. "Don't suppose I could have chocolate for breakfast."

"Sweetling, you may have anything your heart desires."

She pointed in the distance where a carriage became visible just beyond the dunes. "Someone is coming."

"Probably the cook and her daughter. I'll tell her to delay breakfast for an hour until we've finished our morning stroll."

She turned around. "Our morning stroll?"

"Yes, I enjoy a brisk walk before breakfast. Since I indulged you and shared the sunrise with you, now you must indulge me and join me while I take my walk." He patted her bottom. "Now, get dressed and meet me downstairs. No need to bother with stockings or shoes."

He strode out of her room and into his. He glared at his reflection in the mirror. "Inviting her to join you on your walk was a damned stupid move, you ass. You don't want to grow overly fond of her."

His reflection glared mockingly back because it already knew the truth. He was extremely fond of Ashton and her innocence.

He grabbed a shirt and yanked it over his head, securing the remaining buttons as he stepped into the hallway at the same moment that his wife did.

With a shy smile, she wiggled her toes. "I've never gone barefoot. It seems indecent."

His laughter echoed along the hallway as he took her hand. "Ah, sweetling, I could tell you of indecent things that would make your hair curl."

"Like what?"

He laughed harder as they went down the stairs. "You don't want to know."

She stopped abruptly. He turned slightly and looked at her.

Her face was solemn. "I do want to know."

He heaved a deep sigh. How in the world had he managed to get himself onto this path of conversation?

He retraced his steps until they were even, leaned

toward her, and whispered into her ear. With satisfaction, he drew back, expecting her mouth agape and her eyes wide.

Instead, she simply shrugged. "Oh, that." And started down the stairs.

"What do you mean 'oh that?' " He hurried after her as she walked into the kitchen. "Ashton—"

He came up short at the sight of the cook and her daughter. He'd given them keys to the house when he'd hired them so they could come and go as needed without disturbing him or Ashton. He tilted his head slightly. "Mrs. Edwards, Miss Edwards, I'd like you to meet my wife."

Both ladies curtsied. "It's a pleasure to serve you, Mrs. Montgomery," Mrs. Edwards said. "We're lookin' forward to seein' after you while you're here."

Gently Kit grabbed Ashton's arm and guided her toward the door. "We're going for a morning stroll. Have an enormous breakfast ready in an hour."

As soon as they were on the porch, Ashton wriggled free of his grasp and hopped to the ground. "What are those pink and white flowers on the shrubbery by the house?" she asked.

"Oleander. They're not native to the area but they grow in abundance here. Galveston is famous for them."

She neared one, plucked a blossom, and brought it to her nose. "It smells sweet."

"Ashton, on the stairs—"

"Do you think I could take a plant back to Dallas with me?"

He didn't care about the plants, but he did care

about her wishes. "Not one of these. They're too large, but perhaps I could locate a small shrub."

She smiled sweetly. "I'd like that. I wouldn't be able to enjoy it for long, but I think Madeline would like it. I wanted to take something back that was unusual."

"That would certainly be unusual. Ashton, when we were on the stairs, why did you say, 'Oh, that?' " he asked quickly, before she could start another thread of conversation.

Holding her arms out, she spun around. "The sand feels wonderful beneath my toes. I'm glad you said no shoes." She started walking toward the shoreline. "Should we go to the water?"

Dumbfounded that she was blatantly ignoring his inquiries, he hurried after her. "Ashton, you're avoiding my question. What did you mean by 'oh, that?' "

She glanced over at him, a twinkle in her eyes that made him suspect she was annoying him on purpose. "What should I have said?"

"I don't know. Perhaps, 'How scandalous!' "

She arrived at the water's edge and planted her feet so the shallow waves could creep forward, wrap around her toes, and retreat. She wrinkled her nose as though concentrating deeply. She shook her head. "I don't think it was scandalous."

"You don't find it scandalous that Harry's mistress had her portrait painted while she wore not a stitch of clothing—"

She spun around, her smile bright and a look of relief on her face. "So it was Harry's mistress? You didn't say whose mistress she was."

He groaned. He'd left out that little tidbit of information on purpose. "What difference does it make whose mistress it was?"

"I suppose he had the mistress before he got married?"

"Good God, yes, and don't you dare mention this conversation to Jessye. She'll have my hide and Harry's as well. She would not like it at all if she discovered I was gossiping about his past lady friends."

"Did you see the painting?"

"How could I not? His mistress hung it over the hearth in a gaudy gold frame."

Her eyes alight with interest, she stepped closer. "Was it scandalous?"

"Of course. She left nothing to the imagination and seemed quite at ease flaunting her attributes."

"So you didn't like the portrait?"

"Whether or not *I* liked it is not important." He rolled his eyes. "How did we manage to wander so far off the point of this topic?"

"You wanted to shock me until my hair curled and you're upset that you didn't. Now, had it been his wife, then I might have found it scandalous."

The woman baffled him, but her eyes held a special glint that hinted she was enjoying the direction of the conversation. So he decided to indulge her. "What possible difference could that make?"

"A mistress should be scandalous. She's supposed to be bold and daring, all the things a man's wife isn't supposed to be."

Kit scoffed. "She is supposed to be discreet."

Ashton turned away and took several steps into the

water, until it swirled around her ankles. "I've seen sketches of the human body. In its natural form, I think it can be quite . . . provocative." She lowered her lashes. "Of course, you're the closest I've come to seeing a man in the flesh, and you're very careful to keep some things to yourself."

Careful? His wife had a gift for understatement. With his heart and his head, he'd made a personal vow before he asked her to become his wife. The lower part of his body seemed intent on rebelling, and only because he was extremely careful that he maintained his modesty was he able to keep the heathen in control.

His wife also had a captivating manner of looking like an innocent standing on the precipice, wanting to jump into a pool of improper knowledge. He threaded his fingers through hers, enjoying the intimacy of the contact, palm to palm, so much better than her hand simply resting limply on his arm. "Come along. We were supposed to take a brisk walk."

Her fingers tightened around his as she strolled beside him. "Do you think I'm shameful for not being shocked?" she asked.

"No, even though it caught me unawares that you weren't shocked."

"I don't like being so innocent, Kit. Sometimes I feel like a child when I desperately want to be a woman."

He tucked a stray strand of hair behind her ear. "Hold on to your innocence, Ashton. Once lost, it can't be regained."

"Do you wish you were still innocent?" she asked with a rebellious tone in her voice.

He met her gaze steadily. "Sometimes, I wish it with all my heart."

Chapter 11

Kit couldn't recall taking an afternoon nap since he was eight years old. He'd only done it then because his mother had insisted, and he hadn't wanted to disappoint her.

Today, he'd been exhausted, more so than he was last night. After lunch, he'd laid down for a nap. The final thing he remembered was Ashton removing his boots.

He stretched his body and opened his eyes to see dust motes waltzing in front of the open balcony doors as the late afternoon eased its way into the room. The temptation to stay here until dawn was strong, but he had to tend to Lancelot's needs.

The horse had traveled tethered to the back of the stagecoach. Kit had brought the gelding so he could ride him after he returned Ashton to Dallas. He preferred the freedom a lone horse would give him to the predictable route and monotony of the trail a stagecoach followed.

He turned his head slightly and could see no indentation in the bed where his wife might have taken her rest. Perhaps she'd decided to use the bed in his room.

With a yawn, he got up and pulled on his boots. He glanced at the empty balcony and search beyond it to the shoreline. He saw no sign of Ashton. He checked the other bedroom. Empty.

He went down the stairs into the kitchen, welcoming the aroma of cinnamon. He heard Mrs. Edwards singing a song about the Red River Valley. He'd visited the area once. As far as he knew, he'd seen most of the state.

As though sensing his presence, she stopped singing and smiled at him. "Have a good nap?"

"I slept like a babe. Have you any notion where my wife is?"

"Yep. She went to the infirmary."

Kit felt as though his heart had stopped. "The infirmary?"

Wiping her flour-coated hands on her apron, Mrs. Edwards nodded. "St. Mary's in Galveston. Martha took her."

"Dear God in heaven, why didn't you let me know immediately?" Kit yelled as he stormed across the room.

"Because Mrs. Montgomery said we wasn't to disturb you," Mrs. Edwards shot back.

"Don't ever follow my wife's orders again," Kit called over his shoulder as he hurried out the door and down the steps. If there ever was an *again*.

Why hadn't Ashton told him that she wasn't feeling well? What was she thinking to let a woman she barely knew take her to a hospital while Kit slept?

He approached the lean-to where he kept Lancelot and hastily prepared him. He mounted the horse and urged him into a gallop toward town. He could only hope that he wasn't too late.

He could not bear the thought of Ashton dying with no one beside her.

"Then Sir Kit, the bravest of all the knights, thrust his powerful sword into the heart of the dragon. It roared out its anger and blew flames into the heavens, knowing that it had been defeated. It fell to its side, deader than a doornail. Sir Kit took the princess from the dragon's lair and they lived happily ever after."

As the children surrounding Ashton clapped, Kit decided he would strangle his wife. He'd rushed into the infirmary like a raving lunatic, demanding to know where his wife was, only to discover she was regaling children with tales of damsels in distress.

She wasn't ill at all. He knew he should be incredibly grateful, and once he stopped shaking, he would be. But right now, he could only envision his hands around her soft throat as he placed his thumbs below her chin . . . and tilted her face toward his to receive a deeply satisfying kiss.

The woman had scared the bloody hell out of him, and he didn't like it, not one bit. She was destined to die, but he didn't want it to happen while he was within reach of her.

She walked around the room, giving each child a hug, most with dark smudges at the corners of their mouths. Then Ashton spotted him and gave him the most beautiful smile he'd ever seen, and his heart melted like the damned chocolate she'd eaten last night.

"What are you doing here?" she asked as she approached him.

"The question, madam, is what are you doing here? I thought the worst when Mrs. Edwards said you'd asked to come to the infirmary."

Her smile withered, and he cursed his temper for making his words clipped and harsh.

"I thought I'd be back before you woke up." She turned briefly, smiled at the children, and waved as they scampered back to their beds.

She followed him into the hallway. "I'm so sorry. I didn't think that you'd mind if we brought the leftover food from lunch—"

"Ashton." He spun around and faced her. "I don't give a bloody damn about the food. I thought you were having another spell like the one you had the night we wed, and that you'd come here"—he swallowed—"instead of coming to me."

A softness touched her eyes as she laid her hand reassuringly on his arm. "I didn't mean to worry you." She nibbled on her lower lip. "Although I'm glad you were worried. I'm an awful person for being glad."

He touched her cheek. "You're not awful. How did this adventure come about, anyway?"

"Martha asked if she could bring the food that we didn't eat at lunch, and I asked to come along. Actually, we were very quick about delivering it, but then I saw the children . . ." Tears surfaced in her eyes. "I just wanted to make them smile. It's horrid to lie there in bed with nothing to do but wait to get better."

He took her arm and led her outside. "As frail as you are, a hospital is probably not the best place to spend your time."

"I know." She looked up guiltily. "I brought them all my chocolate."

"We can purchase more. We can even make arrangements to have some sent here daily if you like."

She smiled warmly. "I'd like that."

"Just please give me your word that you will not go on another adventure without telling me."

"I promise."

He nodded thoughtfully. "Sir Kit, heh? I didn't catch the princess's name."

"Why, she was Princess Ashton, of course." She clutched her hand more firmly around his arm.

"And he killed the dragon deader than a doornail? What exactly does that mean?"

"It's just an expression."

He dared not ask the name of the dragon, for he feared he already knew it. Consumption. Unfortunately, Sir Kit had no powerful sword with which to defeat it.

Standing alone on the balcony with the remnants of a hellish nightmare rippling through him, Kit watched the mist roll in from the sea, thick and heavy, silent but menacing. He heard the deep timbre of a horn blasting from the lightship, its light a muted glow hovering in the dense fog.

Wrapping his hands around the railing until he felt the wood bite into his palms, Kit tried to decipher his dream. The gossamer images were unclear, and he was certain of only one thing: he'd been lost, confused, stumbling in the dark, struggling to find his way.

He'd awakened bathed in sweat that he could attribute to the warmth of the night coupled with Ashton's heat as she lay within the circle of his arms, but the chills, the trembling, the inability to form concrete thoughts had forced him to gasp for air like a drowning man.

Was that how the end would be for Ashton? Desperately trying to draw in air when there was none to be found?

He took a deep shuddering breath. Perhaps his concerns for Ashton had prompted the dream. Within the past week, since their arrival at Galveston's shores, his fondness for her had deepened, and the thought of her facing death was becoming increasingly unbearable, but he didn't think his emotions had prompted the dream. He'd been frightened, disoriented, like a ship tossed on a turbulent sea, unable to find mooring.

He'd felt ill upon awakening—as he had aboard the ship when he'd traveled from Liverpool to Galveston. Two weeks of heaving his meals over the side before he'd managed to adjust to the constant roiling of the boat. Poor Grayson had never adjusted. Harry had never gotten ill. Luck always rode his shoulder. Well, almost always.

"Kit?" Ashton whispered.

He glanced over his shoulder. She stood near him, a

blanket draped around her, the hair he'd loosened from the braid while she slept hanging in wild disarray around her face and shoulders. It had become a game between them. She braided her hair each night before bed, and once she drifted off to sleep, he unwound the strands, careful not to disturb her. He found her unbound hair incredibly enticing. He'd considered a dozen times convincing her that they should sleep without clothing, but he didn't think he could withstand the assault on his senses. To have the full length of her flesh pressed against his—the thought alone was dangerous. His restraint was being sorely tested. Perhaps the demons he fought had brought on the dream.

"What's wrong?" she asked quietly, studying him warily. "I woke up and you weren't there."

"Nothing more than a disturbing dream. Go back to sleep. I'll be there shortly," he said.

With the fog swirling around her, she seemed to glide toward him, ethereal, and he wondered for a moment if he still dreamt.

"It's scary out here," she said in a low voice. The horn sounded, and she jumped.

Smiling gently, Kit reached out, took her arm, and pulled her into his embrace, nestling his chin on top of her head. "It's only a bit of fog."

"Isn't this dangerous for ships?" she asked.

"It could be, but since there's no wind, the ships are probably just bobbing on the water."

"The fog distorts everything. Maybe that's what disturbed you."

"No, it was the dream."

She turned in his arms, bent her head back, and studied his face. "What happened in the dream?"

"The images were foggy." He grinned. "No pun intended. The thoughts, however, were clear." He gazed past her and stared at the lone light struggling to serve as a beacon. "The thoughts were crystal clear," he repeated. "Perhaps they weren't mine. Maybe they were Christopher's."

"You can read his mind even though he's an ocean away?" she asked incredulously.

How to explain what he didn't begin to understand? "It's not reading minds so much as sensing his feelings." He shook his head in exasperation. "It's impossible to describe what I experience."

"Try," she said with the determination in her voice that never failed to amuse him. "You've explained it a little, but I still find it odd."

He dropped onto a nearby chair and drew her onto his lap. "Odd, you say? A fitting word for my relationship with my brother. Had my father not always been so quick to point out that Christopher were the older, and therefore the favored, I would have thought us equal."

"It's not as if years separate you," she pointed out.

Kit settled more comfortably into the chair and pressed her head into the crook of his shoulder where it felt that the shallow curve had been created expressly for her face. He liked having her there, feeling her breath skim across his bare chest. "Actually, only a few moments separated our births, and yet, they were deciding moments, elevating Christopher to the exalted position of heir apparent and marking me as the lesser second son."

"You're as important as he is," she said indignantly.

He wrapped his arms more tightly around her, deeply touched by her defense of him. Christopher had been equally protective, never one to lord his position over Kit, but at times seemingly uncomfortable with the hierarchy of their family. "Not within the realm of English inheritance laws."

"I don't like your laws."

"I have no quarrel with the laws. They serve a purpose."

"Tell me how you and Christopher share thoughts," she prompted.

He grimaced. "Not thoughts, exactly. Impressions. At first, I always think it's what I'm feeling, but when I analyze the sensations, I begin to realize that they aren't mine. Tonight I awoke feeling unanchored, betrayed, angry. Something is troubling Christopher, but I don't have a strong enough sense of what it is. By the time I write him and he sends a missive, the crisis will have passed."

"Crisis? You think something horrible happened?"

He gazed into the fog. "Not horrible. Baffling. Not to worry. He'll sort it out." He brought the blanket up to shield her face from the dampness in the air. The foghorn blew.

"That's such a lonely sound," she murmured.

The moments passed until he eventually felt her grow limp against him, her breathing becoming shallow and even. He needed to carry her to bed and remove the dew from her hair. Instead, he gathered her more closely against him. He'd been adrift for too many years, and now one frail woman was beginning to serve as his mooring. The thought troubled him more than his dream.

Chapter 12

What harm can come of it?

As Kit sat on the blanket spread over the sand not far from the cottage, he feared the answer to the question he had tossed out with such nonchalance in Fortune more than a month earlier.

Wearing a white dress, Ashton lay beside him on the blanket, raised on her elbows, her small breasts jutting up as proudly as the largest ones he'd ever seen, her face tilted toward the sun, her eyes closed. She was lost in her surroundings and damn his already condemned soul, but he was becoming lost in her.

Each day she was like a small child allowed to take her first outing. She took joy in every sight, every sound, every aspect of life that touched the senses and yet, she would be denied the greatest sensation of all.

The warm ocean breeze billowed her skirts and lost itself somewhere between her ankles and her thighs. He knew the extent to which a delicate breath skimming over flesh could delight and arouse, a coolness that had the power to ignite a fire.

"Can you hear the roar of the ocean?" she asked

quietly as though she feared silencing it. "I never thought it would sound so powerful."

All he heard was the thundering of his blood between his temples. She had stopped padding her clothing, and now in her supine position, her bodice stretched taut across her chest to reveal the tiniest of alluring buds. Three loosened buttons, four at the most, and he could close his mouth around one of those hardened nipples and run his tongue across it in a variety of ways: up and down, side to side, a figure eight, a complete circle—

"Are you listening?" she asked.

He snapped his gaze to hers, trying to control not only his breathing but his errant body. Each morning and evening, they took long walks along the shore. He was beginning to realize he had made a grave error in judgment. He should have left his walks as a solitary endeavor, a private time for himself, but he enjoyed her presence so damned much. He cleared his throat. "I beg your pardon?"

She smiled at him as though he were a child to be indulged for daydreaming during lessons. "I asked if you had any idea what created the waves?"

"The waves?"

She nodded. "You see way beyond them, the water is incredibly calm. The waves seem to begin with no rhyme or reason, huge and majestic and then they fade away against the shore. What starts their journey?"

"How the bloody hell should I know?" He surged to his feet and stalked to the water's edge. He closed his eyes and inhaled deeply. Ah, God, he was not a man prone to losing his temper. Even when Christopher had taken Clarisse as his wife, Kit had maintained his dignity as he stood at his brother's side, repeating vows within his head that were not his to keep. Breaking them had come much harder than he'd expected, but easier over time. He could never have carnal knowledge of the woman he loved, and now he could not make love to the woman who was his wife.

The irony of life made him want to laugh like that lunatic in the saloon shooting at the floor.

"I've made you angry with my incessant babbling," she said softly behind him.

"No." Surprised him was more like it. He had not expected to be undeniably attracted to her. He had thought they could travel here as friends, and by God, that was what they would be. Friends. Husband and wife in name only. He could hold his body and his thoughts in check for a few more days. Then he would cart her back to Dallas and she'd have memories of the ocean. He faced her.

She was standing, the infuriating wind blowing her skirt against her legs and creating a hollow that stopped at the juncture of her thighs. Was the woman not wearing a petticoat? Her feet were bare. That he could understand. What was the point in shoes when you wanted to feel each grain of sand beneath your soles—but undergarments? It suddenly occurred to him why her bodice gave him such a clear image of her breasts.

Was she an innocent or a seductress? It made no difference. He would not make love to her, and his decision had nothing to do with her health, her frailty, or her brother's warnings. Responsibility was the sole thread that kept him tethered to a personal vow he'd made the night he asked her to marry him, but the thread was wearing thin and if it were to break, he feared his sanity would snap.

Ashton sat at the table while Mrs. Edwards heaped food onto Ashton's plate. Kit had charged back to the house like a man with a dog nipping at his heels.

They had both changed into proper clothes for the evening meal. He wore a jacket and cravat, and she wore all her undergarments beneath a light blue dress.

He had spoken hardly a word since her question about the waves, and he seldom looked at her. Was this what marriage evolved into over time? Silence in place of understanding?

Although he denied it, she knew she had done something to upset him. Perhaps he regretted bringing her here. They had stayed far longer than she had expected them to, but not nearly as long as she wanted.

As soon as Mrs. Edwards left the room, Kit glanced at Ashton over his wineglass. "You need to eat."

She shoved her plate aside. "I'm not hungry."

Anger flared in his eyes as he set down his glass but continued to hold it. "If you do not eat, tomorrow when we take our walk along the shore, the wind will no doubt carry you out to the sea."

"I'll eat when you've told me why you're angry."

"I am not angry," he said in a tightly controlled voice.

"Liar."

He snapped the stem of his glass, and Ashton watched in horror as red wine spewed across Kit and the table, along with his blood. Grabbing her napkin, she jumped up, rushed to him, and took his hand. She recoiled at the sight of the turned-back flesh and the river of blood that flowed from the wound. She pressed her napkin against his palm. "Why are you upset with me? What did I do?"

He cradled her cheek and tilted her face, his gaze capturing hers. "You've done nothing, sweetling, but be who you are."

"Perhaps I should go back to Dallas tomorrow."

"No." Gently, he took her free hand. "I am not angry, Ashton. I am attempting to control a body that has no desire to be controlled and am having damned little luck at it."

Warmth suffused her face as joy rippled through her because he was attracted to her; guilt followed in its wake because to give in to temptation would make the parting that much harder. She wanted to change his mood back to what it had been all the days before this one. "You're attracted to Mrs. Edwards, then."

His eyes widened. "Good God, no! She's at least eighty if she's a day."

"The maid—"

"The cook's daughter?" He smiled and brought her hand to his lips. " 'Tis you and you alone that makes me feel as though I have made a pact with the devil."

"Then I should leave."

With his uninjured hand, he cradled her cheek, sorrow and something she couldn't quite understand woven within his eyes. Regret, perhaps. Would she ever understand this man she'd married?

"My father sent me here because he feared I would bed my brother's wife. It is ironic that I have vowed not to bed my own."

Ironic and incredibly disappointing. Lying with him night after night, she was discovering an intimacy growing between them that seemed to know no bounds. She loved the way her head fit within the crook of his shoulder, the constant beating of his heart, the rumble of his chest as he breathed. How often had she woken up before dawn simply so she could watch him without his knowing. She loved the beard that shadowed his face when he awoke and the smile that eased across his face when his gaze first fell on her as though he were glad that he'd discovered her in his bed.

She looked at his hand, grateful to see that the bleeding had stopped. "I would rather you break a vow than have memories of your anger."

He kissed the top of her bowed head. "If you do not wish to incur my wrath, then eat your dinner."

She rose to her feet. "Someday, Christian Montgomery, I'll find a way to stop you from always changing the subject just when it gets interesting."

He smiled at her. "Someday, sweetling, I shall make you glad that I honored my vow."

Within the darkness of midnight, Kit awoke, his head warning him that he'd drunk too much wine. The breeze from the bay whispered over his flesh.

What he found comforting his wife would no doubt find chilling.

He sat up to draw the blankets over her and discovered that he had no one to cover. He was alone, not only in the bed, but also in the room. She had been extremely quiet as she'd prepared for bed. He had held her until he'd fallen asleep.

In the dimness of the room, he couldn't see her. The lamp was gone. Perhaps his earlier mood, which he deeply regretted, had prevented her from sleeping.

He got out of bed and walked through the open doors onto the balcony. He saw the inlet and an ethereal white shadow sitting where the land, buttressed with rocks, jutted into the bay. On the other side lay the Gulf of Mexico, but it was the small crescent moon that seemed to hold her attention.

He quickly donned his clothes before grabbing two blankets from the bed. Daft woman. She was probably shivering like a leaf in the wind, sitting out there. The ocean breeze coming off the water was always cooler than that which came from the land.

He rushed through the house and into the night, wondering at his own reaction. The way his heart was pounding, he would have thought that she'd been attacked by villains. They were isolated, but still, anyone could happen by. He stalked across the small strip of land until she was clearly visible. "What in God's name do you think you're doing out here?"

Without turning her gaze from the ocean, she said, "I needed solitude. Will you please leave me?"

"Leave—" His bare foot hit the lamp, its flame extinguished recently judging by the heat that scorched his toes. He uttered a curse as he stumbled and nearly fell over the edge into the thrashing waves below. He regained his balance and clutched the blankets. "Have you no sense?"

His gaze fell upon her face, limned in the moonlight, her tears a beacon to his cynical heart. He knelt beside her and draped a blanket around her shoulders. "Why are you crying?"

She released a harsh, almost hysterical laugh. "Because I can't always pretend to be brave. I can't always pretend that I am not bothered by the fact that Death holds out his hand to me and that his touch will be cold and dark and eternal." She swiped the tears from her cheeks. "Thank you for the blanket, but you can leave. I prefer to spend these moments of weakness in solitude."

"Then you should have never taken me for a husband," he said quietly as he eased behind her and nestled her between his thighs, bringing her back against his chest as he closed his arms around her.

"Kit, please—"

"Shh," he whispered near her ear. "The advantage to marriage is not that we have someone beside us when we are strong, but that we have someone to lean against when we are weak."

She shook her head. "But I am so often weak, and I yearn for things that I can never have."

Knowing even as he did it that he courted danger, he pressed his mouth against the nape of her neck. "What do you yearn for most?"

He heard the sudden hitch in her breath . . . then

nothing but the washing of the waves upon the shore. The moon cast so little light as to be nearly useless. He closed his arms more securely around her. "Weren't you the one claiming we needed to trust each other with our thoughts?"

She dropped her head back until it rested against his throat, and he could place his chin on the top of her head.

"Tell me what you want, Ashton, and if it is within my grasp, I *will* give it to you."

"*That* is the problem. Everyone has always *given* me everything." She released brittle laughter. "I wanted a husband, and now I have one without earning his love. I wished to come to Galveston and here I am because you brought me when I should have just purchased a ticket and brought myself. I want normalcy and independence, and I don't want to die with so many regrets."

He felt the shudder course through her body. "Ashton—"

"Can you please leave so I can wallow in my self-pity without anyone bearing witness to it?"

"Why do you object to my seeing that you are only human?"

"I object to your discovering that I am selfish and weak."

He slipped his thumb beneath her chin and turned her head slightly until he held her gaze. "Have you no friends?"

She shook her head. "David's wife is the closest thing I have to a friend." She lifted a shoulder. "And you."

His stomach clenched. Who would be with her at the end? He shoved the thought back into a darkened corner where he could hide it from his conscience. It did not matter who would be with her. It only mattered that it would not be him. She would have David and Madeline.

"I am not your friend, Ashton," he said kindly.

She started to turn her head away, but he held her in place. "If I were, you would not be bothered by my seeing you here, revealing your weaknesses. Although I consider both Grayson and Harry friends, Harry is the truer of the two. He knows my every weakness, my every sin. When I needed a confessor for the worst of all sins, the one that has condemned me to hell, he accepted the task without judgment."

He watched her as she scrutinized him, knew curiosity gnawed at her. He didn't know why he'd spoken as he had. He'd wanted to comfort her, and instead, he'd allowed his personal demons to surface.

"I cannot believe that you committed so grave a sin that you'll burn in hell after you die."

"Trust me, sweetling, when the situation warrants, hell arrives long before death."

She twisted within his arms until she could face him squarely. "What did you do?"

"What I did has no bearing on the purpose of this story, which is that a true friend knows your faults and yet his regard for you does not lessen. If you consider me a friend, then you must be willing to bare your weaknesses to me."

"All my weaknesses would repulse you."

"If that is the case, then I am not a friend and you would do well to be rid of me."

With a small laugh, she snuggled against his shoulder. "If I got rid of you, who would keep me warm at night?"

He slammed his eyes closed. Keeping her warm at night was only temporary. When he returned her to David . . . dear God, but he did not wish to travel that path. Not now, not tonight.

"Do you think the waves ever cease?" she asked quietly.

He opened his eyes and gazed past her to the blackness of the ocean, the white crests that seemed to have the power to hold the moonlight when nothing else did.

"No," he said in a low voice.

"I find that a comforting thought," she whispered, "to know there is something in this world that does not die."

He felt a tear fall onto his forearm as he held her and drew her more closely against him. He damned Harry for the wisdom of his words.

As he fought back the tears burning his own eyes, he realized that he'd just dropped more deeply into hell.

Chapter 13

With the late afternoon sun easing into the house, Kit quietly ascended the stairs and walked into the room he shared with his wife. The balcony doors were open as were all the windows. The salty breeze toyed with the loose tendrils of Ashton's hair as she slept on the bed, the pen in her hand creating a blackened stain of ink on the journal resting there.

He had no idea she kept a journal. He knew she took a nap every afternoon. He supposed that this afternoon she'd succumbed before finishing her entry. She had not slept well last night, not even after they had spent considerable time staring at the blackened sea.

He desperately regretted his behavior yesterday. He wanted her to find happiness during the time they were together. Yesterday, he'd brought her nothing but misery.

He was not accustomed to simply holding women while they lay in his bed. Yet he found a certain unexpected comfort in knowing she was there, demanding nothing of him except his presence. But holding her brought its own hell because he knew he could never move beyond it.

Thank God her innocence allowed her to find contentment with nothing more than his arms around her.

He shook his head as the blot of ink grew larger. Ashton's journal would be ruined by the time she awoke.

Careful not to disturb her, he removed the pen from her limp fingers and set it on the table beside the bed. Leaning down, he placed a soft kiss on her forehead. His gaze drifted to the journal and he read his name. He turned away. He would not impose upon her privacy.

He stopped and glanced back. He should move the journal from the bed. If she were to roll onto it she might smudge the pages or wrinkle them. He would simply place it on the table as well. He could do that easily enough without reading her words.

He picked up the journal. She had lovely script, each letter a schoolmaster's idea of perfection. Perhaps because she could not control her health, she had been determined to control her penmanship.

He closed the book. He would not read what she'd just written about him in spite of the fact that a cursory glance had revealed his name at least three times.

Curiosity gnawed at him. What harm could come of reading what she'd written before they were married, events and thoughts that did not deal with him? With a measure of guilt, he turned to the first page.

April 12, 1866

It seems significant that I should begin my latest journal following a night of awakening. I feel that until now I have slept my whole life.

This evening, I met Christian Montgomery at a party that David hosted. When David returned from England where he first met Mr. Montgomery, he had painted a portrait of a man larger than life. Imagine my surprise to discover his words were true. Never have I known a man to hold himself with such regal grace or to command such attention by simply speaking or moving about the room.

I could hardly take my gaze off him. Of course, he did not notice me. I was not witty, charming, or attractive.

I believe he was sent to Texas because of some scandal. I would love to know the details although they would not lessen my regard for him.

He strikes me as dangerous. A man who would break hearts. I would willingly offer mine up as a sacrifice to have his attention for a single moment.

Kit glanced at his wife. He wondered if David had read her journal and if it had influenced his decision to ask Kit to marry her.

He remembered Ashton's words spoken on Mrs. Gurney's front porch. "There is little about me to capture the attention of a man such as yourself."

Had he been so inattentive and uncaring of her feelings then? Probably. At that time, he had still been unable to look beyond his guilt.

He set the book aside and knelt beside the bed,

studying the way her blond lashes rested lightly on her cheeks. So four years ago she was willing to sacrifice her heart to him. And now, did she wish to take the memory of a broken heart to her deathbed?

He doubted it. Her words had been written before she knew death hovered, when she thought she would have time for her heart to heal and find someone else to cherish her.

Until this moment, he had not comprehended that whatever memories *he* gave her would shine the brightest as she lay waiting for death because they would be the most recent.

And what had he given her yesterday? Anger. Regardless of the fact that he was angry with himself, the fury had manifested itself to a degree that had upset her.

He had been correct in the beginning. Marriage to a dying woman was lunacy.

Why did he continue to prolong the farce when it would mean nothing except more regrets? Quietly, he unfolded his body and walked from the room, wishing he had no reason to return.

Guilt gnawed at Kit unmercifully as he rode through Galveston on Lancelot. He had desperately needed to escape death.

If he could but find a way to help Ashton elude its clutches . . .

He guided the horse along the waterfront. The waves that so intrigued his wife roared against the shore. He heard the boisterous guffaws of men, followed by the gentle laughter of women, the grunts of fishermen working to bring in their day's haul, ladies gossiping about the latest fashion.

He looked toward the blue sky. All around him, people acted as though nothing were amiss, while at the end of the island, a delicate woman fought not to touch Death's hand.

He was beginning to understand why Christopher had sent for him, why his brother had been unable to be with Clarisse at the end. Christopher had watched his wife wage the same battle that Ashton now valiantly fought.

It was not Clarisse's demise that he'd been unable to face, but her futile attempt to be victorious over death. He had not wanted to witness her defeat.

As one who did not belong, Kit merely watched the people mingling on the docks, yelling from the boats as the sun cast them in an orange haze. He looked toward the western horizon. Twilight would be upon the land soon. He had not meant to be gone so long, and yet a part of him wished to stay away forever.

He was to have made Ashton a bride only, not become her friend, not come to care for her, to resent that death would deny her so much of life.

He jerked on the reins and began the trek back toward the cottage that seemed more a prison than a home. Tomorrow, he would purchase the tickets for their journey back to her brother's. The decision came that simply and with unequaled difficulty.

He knew she would accept his decision, understand his reasoning, and bear him no ill will. But could he say the same of himself when his gut already clenched and he felt like a man headed for the dungeon of despair?

The house came into view, and he could not help but smile. She would no doubt be watching the sunset. In future years, when he saw the sun ease over the horizon, he would remember her. He would honor her as he continued to honor Clarisse. Tonight, he would tell her so. Perhaps the knowledge would bring her a measure of peace.

He drew his horse to a halt near the small stable and knew that referring to it as such was granting it a title it did not deserve. It had a roof, one solid wall, a trough for oats, and one for water. But the gelding could live without luxury for a while. It was a small request he asked of the beast, and he would make it up to him once they returned to Fortune.

Kit knew he'd want solitude during the journey back from Dallas. He might even take a few detours. Anything to rid himself of the guilt that was already flaying his conscience.

He heard the screech ring from inside the house, and raw fear speared his soul. Ashton had been sleeping when he'd left, but the cook and her daughter had been at the house. Only now did he realize that their carriage was not in sight as he heard his wife screech again.

Like a madman, he tore across the lawn toward the back of the house where the door that led into the kitchen was open. Not an uncommon habit in order to allow the breeze the freedom to keep the house cool. But he heard another tiny scream.

By God, if anyone so much as laid a finger on his wife, he'd rip off the man's arm.

He leapt onto the porch and staggered to a stop in the doorway, stunned by the sight of his wife shaking a broom over a pot of boiling water.

"Get in there, you wretched beast," his wife growled, but the crab clinging to the bristles of the broom didn't seem inclined to follow her orders. With a pair of scissors, she snipped off the straw and the crab plopped into the water. Ashton visibly shuddered before spinning around. Other crabs skittered across the floor.

Amused at her temerity, Kit crossed his arms over his chest and leaned against the doorframe. "Madam, what *are* you doing?"

With a squeal, she spun around. Breathing heavily, she stared at him. Her bun was askew as strands of hair that had gained their freedom flew wildly around her face with the breeze easing in through the doorway. Her face was covered in a mixture of white flour and black ashes. Her bodice was soaked and water had splattered over her skirt.

Damnation! The woman was without undergarments again. Lust slammed into him with a vengeance. Dear Lord, but no woman dressed in her finest for a ball had ever appealed to him more.

Tiny legs clicked as her prey moved across the floor. She jerked around, holding her broom as a weapon like some fierce warrior goddess. "Get away, you miserable creature," she said as she swiped at a crab, knocking him onto his back.

Avoiding the bucket that lay on its side, the other

crabs scampered across the floor, their claws poised high in the air.

Ashton twisted her head around and glared at him. "Don't just stand there. Help me!"

He unfolded his arms. "They are as afraid of you as you are of them, sweetling."

"I'm not afraid, but I don't like getting pinched."

"Did one pinch you?" he asked, not certain if he should be concerned or amused.

"Pinched my shoe. He's at the bottom of the pot now."

He fought back his laughter. "I should do well to remember not to pinch you."

She lifted her broom. "Don't you dare laugh at me, Christian Montgomery. I had everything under control until I knocked over the pail."

Along with the grin he could not hold back, he averted his face as he grabbed the bucket. Judging by the condition of the kitchen that he estimated would take a week to straighten, he and his wife had a different understanding of control. "Yes, I can well see that you did."

He glanced at her, wondering why he found her mutinous expression so intoxicating. Dear God, the mouse had a temper, and he loved it. "See if you can sweep them back into the bucket."

He held it on the floor while she trooped across the kitchen like a determined soldier. With quick, brief strokes and only a few jumps back, she urged the crabs toward the bucket. As soon as one or two made their entry, he righted the pail, walked to the stove, and dropped them into the pot of boiling water.

He heard Ashton's squeak and glanced over to see a crab dangling from the broom.

"They grab on and won't let go," Ashton explained as she stomped to the stove. "Move aside."

He obeyed quickly while she held the crab over the pot and snipped off more of the broom. At this rate, they'd have nothing left with which to clean the floor.

Twenty minutes later he dropped the last crab into the boiling water with a sense of accomplishment. But he noticed something now that he hadn't before. He turned to Ashton. "What's that stench?"

"Oh, no!"

She grabbed a towel, shoved him aside, and opened the oven. She jerked out a pan of blackened something. Biscuits, he supposed, or possibly rolls. She tossed the pan onto the table, dropped into a chair, and slumped forward.

He knelt beside her, his heart tightening at the solitary tear rolling along her cheek. Had it been more, he might have laughed, but one hurt him for reasons he could not fathom.

He brushed back the hair from her face. "Sweetling, don't cry. This debacle isn't your fault. Where the bloody hell is Mrs. Edwards? I hired her to prepare the meals, and when I've given her a piece of my mind—"

"I sent her home," she said in a voice that sounded as though she'd pushed the words past a lump in her throat.

"Why in God's name did you do that?"

She cast him a furtive glance. "Because I wanted to cook dinner for you. And now look, everything is a disaster. The rolls are burned, the crabs are obstinate, the flour sack burst. The recipe called for half a cup and I couldn't find one so I had to break a whole one which seemed such a waste, but how else was I to know if I had the right measurement? The kitchen is a mess." She lifted a frail shoulder. "I just wanted to do something for you because you do everything for me."

He cradled her cheek. "You have given me something."

"What?" she asked, hope sparking within her eyes.

An evening he'd never forget. Twilight shadows eased in through the doorway and windows, and he couldn't bring himself to tell her what she'd truly given him.

"English rolls," he said seriously.

She furrowed her brow. "They're burned."

"Which is the way the English cook them. I haven't had rolls such as these since I left England, and I've missed them terribly." He grabbed a knife and worked one out of the pan. He tossed it into the air until it cooled down so he could hold it. Then he began to scrape off the charred crust. "You see, cooking them as you have adds a special flavor. Then you open them, slather on lots of butter—" He tried to pry the obstinate thing open. "Of course, a true English roll needs to soak in milk for at least a week—"

She laughed. "The English don't eat rolls like that."

He crouched before her and smiled warmly. "No, they don't. I know you mentioned that you'd never cooked, but I thought surely you'd watched someone else do it."

She shook her head. "I haven't done anything in my life but lie around and be ill."

Taking a handkerchief from his pocket, he gently wiped the flour and soot from her face. "Ashton, I hired servants because we have servants at home. In England, I had a valet, a man who dressed me. He buttoned every button on my shirt and saw to it that I always looked sharp."

"You don't have a valet now," she pointed out.

"No."

"Do you prefer having someone do everything for you?"

This conversation hadn't gone where he'd planned, but somehow he wasn't surprised. Ashton had a way of turning his world around. "I did at the time because I knew no different."

With his thumb, he scrubbed the soot from her chin. "But you're quite right. I discovered that I preferred to do for myself."

She smiled. "I suppose I should have started with a smaller task."

"Well, for what it's worth, I think the crabs will turn out now that they're in the pot." An odor hit him. "Bloody hell. I think the water's boiled away."

He grabbed the towel, jumped up, and rushed to the stove. He moved the pot off the fire and carried it to the table.

Ashton stood, frowning. "Are they ruined as well?"

"Only the fellow on the bottom. I think the rest are salvageable."

Relief washed over her face. "Thank goodness. My dinner isn't a total failure."

With his handkerchief, he wiped away the soot on her neck. "I'm not sure we want to risk dining in, however. Why don't you grab a quilt, and I'll build us a fire near the shore? We'll watch the last of the sunset and the moon rise."

With a contented sigh, Ashton lay back on her elbows and looked at the grandeur of the sky. The moon was only a smile tonight, but the stars glittered in abundance.

"I've never seen you eat so much," Kit said as he stretched out beside her on his side. Behind him a driftwood fire burned low.

"Revenge," she said with satisfaction. "And guilt. I didn't like tossing the crabs into the water alive, but Mrs. Edwards said I had to. I didn't want any of them to have died in vain."

He laughed loudly, the sound such sweet music to her ears. Reaching out, he trailed his finger along her chin. Her heart pounded.

"Dear God, Ashton, but you are a delight. Whatever am I going to do with you?"

She shifted her gaze to him. "We're leaving tomorrow, aren't we? That's the reason you went away this afternoon. To make the arrangements."

"I made no arrangements for our departure."

"But you considered it."

He held her gaze. "Yes."

She looked back at the stars and inhaled deeply. "I like the air here. You can almost smell the life in the sea."

"Why do you not wear undergarments?"

She snapped her gaze to his. "How can you tell?"

"Because I'm not a novice when it comes to women or their clothing."

She shrugged. "I find them confining, and I think a woman in my position should be allowed certain luxuries."

"It drives me beyond madness, you know."

She studied him. "What do you mean?"

He eased closer, cradled her cheek, and pressed his lips against the side of her throat, working his way toward her ear. "I mean," he whispered hoarsely, "that it makes me want to rip away your dress and luxuriate in the glorious sight of your body."

Her heart fluttered, and the warmth of his mouth seared her flesh. Her breathing became shallow. "You've seen my body."

He trailed his mouth across her chin and brought it to rest at the corner of her mouth. "You mean the night you were shivering?"

She mumbled a yes, wondering how he could utter complete sentences when she could barely think.

"I paid no attention then and have regretted it ever since." He eased his mouth over hers.

She jerked back. "No."

"Don't deny me a simple kiss, Ashton."

"But what if my theory is right, and you get sick."

"It is a risk I am willing to take. What is the point in life if passion is forever held at bay?"

He pressed his mouth to her throat, and she felt his tongue taste her flesh. She wanted to do the same with him. To know passion and the full grandeur of life.

"Why seek to please me with a meal if you don't care for me?" he asked, nuzzling her neck.

"I do care for you, but we vowed—"

"Not to consummate the marriage. A kiss is not consummation."

His mouth came down hard on hers, silencing all protests, relieving her of any rational thoughts, save one: she wanted to spend the remainder of her life within his arms.

His tongue touched hers as he shifted his body, easing his leg between her thighs. Warmth swirled within her, cascaded through her. Instinctively, she raised her hips, pressing against his hardened thigh. If this was passion, she thought she would gladly die of it.

Moaning, she slipped her hands inside his shirt so she could clutch his bare shoulders. He moved his mouth from hers and blazed a path to her ear.

"I'm on fire," he rasped. "Let's go for a swim."

Opening her eyes, she gazed past him to the blanket of stars overheard. "Swim? In the ocean?"

He lifted his head, his eyes shadowed by the night, but his smile warm. "Do you know of some water elsewhere?"

"I'll catch my death." She slapped her hand over her mouth and laughed. "My mother always warned me against going in the water. I don't know how to swim."

"Then we won't go far," he said as he freed a button on her bodice, "and I'll hold you all the while."

He undid another button.

"What are you doing?" she asked.

"Helping you remove your dress."

"And your clothes?"

"Shall come off as well." He pressed a kiss to the shallow valley between her breasts, now exposed courtesy of his deft fingers. "You may remove them if you like."

He eased off her and drew her into a sitting position on the quilt she'd spread out earlier. She felt the breeze riffling with her loosened bodice as he pulled the pins from her hair.

She swallowed hard. "This seems a bit indecent."

He chuckled low. "There's no one about to see, and even if there were, you're my wife."

He tossed the last pin aside and her hair cascaded around her shoulders. Slowly, he eased his hands between the parted material of her bodice, his palms skimming along her flesh as he drew the material over her shoulders. Heat shot through her as the flames from his low fire cast dancing shadows around them.

He worked her arms free of her sleeves until her bodice was pooled around her waist. He trailed his finger along her collarbone. "Incredibly lovely," he said in a voice so quiet as to be almost wiped out by the roar of the ocean waves.

With trembling hands, she began to unfasten the buttons on his shirt. She had expected his hands to be as still as hers had been while he unbuttoned her bodice, but it seemed as though he were unable not to touch her. His hands ran up and down her arms, circled her waist, and traveled along her ribs, halting only when they rested just below her breasts.

Her mouth went dry. "I've finished with your buttons."

He made a low growl of approval before removing his hands from her and pulling his shirt over his head. She took the opportunity to cross her arms over her chest. "Kit, I don't know if this is such a good idea."

"My wife is timid," he said quietly. "Very well, remove the remainder of your clothes and meet me at the water's edge."

She watched him stand with grace and confidence. He walked beyond the light cast by the fire to the water's edge where he became merely a silhouette. He removed his trousers and cast them aside, but she could see little more than his form.

She undid the buttons on her skirt and wiggled out of it. She studied her husband, waiting patiently for her. She supposed most women came to know their husband's bodies intimately on their wedding night.

What did she fear?

Certainly not him. Perhaps like Eve, she felt she would gain knowledge this night that she was better off not possessing.

With a deep breath, she pushed to her feet and strolled across the sand, feeling remarkably vulnerable and incredibly free.

Kit watched his wife walk hesitantly toward him. What in God's name had possessed him to suggest this swim? He'd blame it on the wine if he'd had any to drink.

But the truth resided somewhere between insanity and obsession. Dear God, but he wanted her truly as his wife and that he could not have—ever. He had considered a dozen times taking her into the realm of pleasure and not traveling there himself.

Would she see his action as betrayal or a gift? He wanted nothing to cause her harm or regret.

He had not felt this possessive stirring for any woman except Clarisse. Yet now when he closed his eyes, he could no longer envision Clarisse's face. He could see only his wife. Too pale, too thin. Although she was eating more. Perhaps it was the salt air. It certainly increased his appetite and not only for food.

He held out his hand toward Ashton. She slipped her trembling hand into his.

"Cold?" he asked.

"No. I just can't see much out here."

Which he realized was no doubt for the best. "The water's warm," he assured her as he led her toward it.

"I guess you can swim," she said, but he heard the doubts laced within her voice.

"You assume correctly."

The waves swirled around his calves while the sand shifted beneath his feet.

"How far out will we go?" she asked.

"Until you tell me to stop."

"Do you think crabs are vengeful creatures?"

Laughing, he glanced at her. "Afraid they might come after you for eating their cousins?"

"Just being silly, I guess." Her hand tightened on his. "I like the way the water feels, and the wet sand. It's different."

"I want you to enjoy it."

"Do you ever think of sailing from here and returning to England?"

"Unfortunately, every day."

She stopped and he turned to face her.

"Do you really?" she asked, amazement in her voice.

"Unlike Harry and Grayson, who now have families, I have nothing to hold me here." As soon as the words were spoken, he knew she would hold him here. Four months, six months, a year. As long as she breathed, he would remain.

"Then why haven't you gone home?" she asked.

"Because there, I have nothing to call me back." He tugged on her hand. "Come along, let's go farther out."

The water lapped at his waist, the waves gentle but persistent. She released a tiny squeal and leapt at him. He grabbed her, holding her against his side, her feet finding purchase on his calf.

"Something touched my leg, something cold and slimy," she said, breathing heavily.

"No doubt a harmless fish." He slipped his arms beneath her and raised her well above his hips. "Lift your legs and wrap them around my waist."

Trembling, she did as he bade, her breasts pressed against his chest.

"We should leave the water now," she said.

"Why?" he asked, the warmth from her body seeping into his.

She leaned back slightly. "It could be a dangerous creature."

"It would have attacked by now." The only dangerous creature in the water was he. Supporting her with one arm beneath her hips, he wrapped his other arm around her back. Swallowing hard, he pressed a kiss just above her breast.

"Kit," she said on a sigh.

He'd expected her to push him away. Instead, she threaded her fingers through his hair and held him close. He turned his head slightly, took her budding nipple into his mouth, and suckled gently.

She dropped her head back. "Oh, my dear God."

He ran his tongue in a circle over her distended flesh before kissing her breast. "I want to know the feel of your flesh, all of you. I want to pleasure you, Ashton," he said in a roughened voice that he barely recognized as his own.

"I think you just did," she whispered.

"No, that was only the beginning." He tilted his head up. "There are ways to bring you pleasure without consummation, but you must want it and you must trust me."

She lowered her face and brushed her lips over his. "I do trust you, Christian, with all my heart, and I'll accept everything that you're willing to give."

He kissed the valley between her breasts and began walking out of the water, knowing even as he did so that he was wandering more deeply into hell.

Ashton stared at the flames of the fire, brought to life by the driftwood Kit had added to keep her warm. She lay within the path of their light, while he was stretched out on the other side of her, hidden in the shadows, trailing his hand slowly, provocatively over her thigh, between her knee and hip.

She closed her eyes. She should have told him that she didn't need the fire. The warmth he created deep within her was enough to ward off any chill that the night air might bring.

He nuzzled her neck, close to her ear. "Don't be afraid, Ashton."

"I'm not."

He slid his hand beneath her knee and raised her leg until he could skim his fingers along the back of her thigh. She purred low in her throat. His hands were unlike hers. His palms were rougher, yet his touch was gentler, so different from when she gave herself a bath. His movements were unhurried as though they had all night, as though the dawn would wait.

He moved his mouth along her neck and below her chin. "Like that?" he asked.

"Mmm," she replied, enjoying each liberty he took. Lethargically, she tangled her fingers through his thick hair and glided one hand over his shoulder, relishing the solid muscles residing beneath his flesh.

Most of her life, she had been tired, but this sensation made her feel alive even as it caused her bones to melt. She might never move from this spot. Perhaps she would die here.

He trailed his fingers along her hip, into the curve of her side, and brought them to rest against her ribs, his thumb sweeping along the lower swell of her breast. An intense shiver rippled through her, causing her fingers to spasm before pressing into his hot flesh.

He adjusted the positioning of his hand slightly and his palm swallowed her breast. "A perfect fit," he murmured, and she thought she'd never loved him more, for accepting her as she was.

"Kit—" Whatever she might have said on a dreamy sigh was lost as he covered her mouth with his own. The hunger she sensed coming from him surprised her. His tongue traced the outline of her lips as his hand glided down her body. She felt the heat intensify, her body quivering with needs she didn't understand. With skill and determination, he parted her lips as his hand cupped her intimately.

She tensed and he stilled, only his tongue teasing her mouth, daring her to follow where he led. When his tongue retreated, she whimpered and pursued, for the first time learning the secrets of his mouth, skimming her tongue across his lips, over his teeth until it met his tongue.

He groaned as he shifted his body until the hardened planes of his chest met the soft curves of hers. With his free hand, he cradled her head and tilted it slightly, kissing her more deeply, his tongue waltzing with hers until she swore she could hear the echo of violins, a ghostly reminder of their wedding night when they had danced.

At the juncture of her thighs, his fingers began a slow, gentle caress in direct contrast to the rapacious hunger of his mouth. Her hands tightened their hold on his shoulders, anchoring her to the earth when she wanted to reach for the heavens.

With his mouth and hands, he was an artist creating a tapestry of sensations she'd never dared to imagine. She grew hotter, her body quivering from her toes to the top of her head. Even though he wasn't touching all of her, he may as well have been. She'd never known the journey to pleasure encompassed every aspect of a person: her heart, her body, and her soul. Intertwined, inseparable. He made them all tremble with wonder.

Sweet pleasure spiraled from her core, shimmied up her spine, and spread through every limb, and when she thought she could stand it no longer, it erupted into a maelstrom of passions that knew no boundaries. She cried out, her back arching, her hold on him tightening.

His hand stilled. His breathing as strained as hers, he rained kisses over her face, her jaw, her neck, and her shoulders. He moved his hands to either side of her ribs and buried his face between her breasts.

With her breathing growing even, she wished they could stay here forever. She might have died without ever knowing the pleasures of the flesh. She wanted to thank him but could think of no words adequate enough to express the awe with which he'd satisfied her.

She combed her fingers through his hair. With his tongue, he drew a circle over her flesh. She lifted her gaze to the stars.

Not one shone as brightly as the gift Kit had just bestowed upon her.

Chapter 14

Kit awoke, the unmerciful predawn light threatening him with another day.

He could not believe how something as innocent as a swim had resulted in him ultimately bringing pleasure to his wife. But while he cursed himself, a small part of him, male vanity no doubt, was glad, glad that he'd given her a taste of pleasure.

No one should leave this earth without experiencing it.

He'd carried Ashton into the house while they both wore only that with which they'd been born. Unless the tide had washed away all evidence, he supposed he needed to return to the shore and gather up the blanket and their clothing. Should the items be spotted by Mrs. Edwards or her daughter, Kit was certain they would guess what had transpired on the shore last night. Only their imaginations would take it a step farther.

Dear Lord, but he had wanted to. Giving physical pleasure while receiving none was not his usual style. But then normalcy had walked out the door with his common sense the night he had asked Ashton to become his wife.

Yet he had no regrets. Moments of anger, yes, unrequited frustration, undoubtedly—but no regrets. Only a deepening desire to give her more.

She was content with so little when he'd known women discontent with far more. Why could greed or avarice not be a requirement for disease? Why did it choose as its victims those least deserving of its wrath?

He felt the sheet shift and opened his eyes into narrow slits. Then he opened them fully, unable to believe the sight he beheld.

Raised up on an elbow, his wife had tucked her head beneath the sheet she'd lifted slightly. They were both nude, and he could well guess at what she was staring.

Although he was not by nature a modest man, still he felt the heat suffuse his face. "Madam, what are you doing?"

With a start, she jerked the sheet down, clutching it against her breasts, her mouth as open and wide as her eyes. She blinked. "It changes. I couldn't see in the dark, but I thought last night that I could feel that it seemed . . . to be different . . . at times."

Ah God, he was torn between laughter and despair. He raised a brow. "It?"

She nodded vigorously and wiggled her finger toward the center of his side of the bed where the sheet was rapidly peaking. "Your anatomy."

"My anatomy?"

"Stop repeating everything I say and making it into

a question so I sound like a dunce. I read all the medical books I could find hoping to discover a cure for my illness. Therefore, I am familiar with anatomy, and I know *it* has a name. It simply escapes me at the moment."

"I don't know how it was referred to in your anatomy books, but I could give you a whole list of names to use, although I don't think any should pass between a woman's lips."

She furrowed her brow. "Why does it change?"

Inwardly he groaned, biting back several curses. He cleared his throat. "Because when a man makes love to a woman fully . . . in order to join his body with hers, he requires a certain . . . sturdiness."

Disappointment filled her eyes. "I see. So last night you didn't make love to me *fully*."

"I brought pleasure to you, did I not?"

Blushing, she lowered her lashes. He cradled her face. "Making love comes in many forms." He brushed his thumb beside the corner of her eye until she opened both and met his gaze. "We agreed upon no consummation, but as far as I am concerned, I did make love to you last night."

She nodded slightly. "I felt as though you did. It was the most glorious moment of my life."

"Then that's all that matters, isn't it?"

She touched his bristly cheek and unexpected desire surged through him.

"Does it hurt when it's sturdy?"

Yes, by God, it was bloody well killing him right now. If he didn't get out of bed this instant, he was going to roll his sweet, delicate, innocent wife onto her back and consummate this marriage with a fierceness that terrified him. His needs were those of a barbarian.

He jerked the sheet aside and clambered out of bed. "Put on a dress," he ordered. "No undergarments."

"Why?"

With his back to her, trying to shield his uncontrollable body from her, he glanced over his shoulder. "We're going for a ride."

A ride. Why had she thought of a romantic excursion in a carriage at dawn?

Ashton wondered if there ever came a time when a wife knew exactly what her husband meant without his having to go into a detailed explanation.

She certainly hadn't envisioned herself sitting astride a great black horse with no saddle beneath her, her skirt whipping against her legs while she felt the power of the beast as he galloped along the shallow edge of the surf, spraying water in his wake.

She clung to his mane while her husband wrapped one arm around her like an iron band and held the reins with his other hand. She sat nestled between his firm thighs while they journeyed toward the rising sun, with the surf thundering through her ears.

She felt the heat from Kit's body burn its way through the thin material of her bodice. She loved the freedoms he showered on her. More, she loved his touch, his nearness, his honesty, and his blush.

Lying in bed this morning, asking questions, and watching the red stain of embarrassment creep into his face, she'd felt her heart burst forth like a flower unfurling its petals. She thought she'd fallen in love with him when she'd met him in Dallas.

But now she knew it had been nothing more than an infatuation. Four years ago, he had intrigued and fascinated her.

He still did, but her feelings had blossomed, were as radiant as the dawn. She loved him.

A blessing and a curse, for she would leave this world happier than she had ever been, yet grieving the loss of time with him as she'd never thought possible.

He brought the horse to a halt at the edge of the inlet. Kit drew in breaths much deeper than hers.

She tried to breathe and instead was hit with a coughing spell. With resentment at her body's reminder of her frail health, she took the handkerchief he offered and covered her mouth. He massaged her back until the seizure passed.

Expecting the worse, she glanced at the white linen. No blood. She released a shuddering sigh of relief as she stuffed the cloth into the pocket of her skirt.

"Are you all right?" he asked, genuine concern reflected in his voice.

She leaned back against his chest and nodded. "I was actually getting hopeful. I can't remember coughing since we've been here."

"It's good air as long as we're upwind of rotting fish," he said quietly.

"Have you always been such an early riser?" she asked.

He pressed his lips to the nape of her neck. "Mmm-uh."

She smiled slightly. "That must have been a disappointment to your mistresses."

"I've never had a mistress. The word implies a relationship of sorts, a commitment. I sought neither."

She twisted her head around. "But you've been with women."

"Too many to count, and I seriously doubt you want to traverse this conversational path."

She studied the lines of his face shaped by hardships, not joy. "Is Clarisse the only woman you've ever loved?"

"No. I loved my mother." She watched him swallow as he trailed his fingers over her face. "And you."

Her heart leapt at the same moment it plummeted. The joy and grief caused an unbearable ache. She forced a smile that she knew wobbled. "You are too kind to say that."

He touched the corner of her eye with his thumb. "If I were kind, I would have ignored your question. From the first moment I met Clarisse until the day I took you as my wife, I awoke with thoughts of her."

He gently touched his lips to hers. "Now the only time I think of her is when you mention her. I always imagined that when I died alone and with no family that my last thought would be of her. Now, I know it will be of you."

Her eyes burned as she swung her head back around to stare at the sunrise. Through the tears, she could see nothing but a kaleidoscope of colors. "You weren't supposed to love me."

He sighed deeply. "Believe me, sweetling, it was not my intention to fall for you."

"You're not to die alone and with no family. Promise me that there will be someone after me."

She heard nothing but the breeze whispering loudly over the ocean waves. She squeezed her eyes shut, forcing the tears to roll down her cheeks. "Promise me, Christian."

"A promise tossed onto the wind is forgotten the moment that the wind ceases to blow." He released his hold on the reins and brought both arms around her. The horse snorted and sidestepped. She felt Kit's thighs tighten as he controlled the animal with only his legs.

"The sunrise is especially beautiful this morning," he said in a low voice.

Her heart constricted and a lump rose in her throat. Unable to speak, she opened her eyes to welcome the dawning of a new day. But deep within her heart, she felt as though a tiny part of her had already died, knowing the life he had carved for himself.

She felt his breath skim against her ear.

"Don't concern yourself, Ashton. Time spent with you has been a gift I did not deserve."

She shook her head. "I don't want you to be alone."

"Then don't die."

Her heart constricted with his command.

"You say that as though I have a choice."

"I do sometimes wonder if you've accepted your fate with too much grace, and with acceptance comes fulfillment."

"It's easy enough to spout philosophy when you are not facing death."

He chuckled low, cynically. "I can spout philosophy because I have *been* death."

She twisted around. "What does that mean?"

Averting his gaze, he reached for the reins. "Let's go into town today and purchase some trinkets that you can hold as memories."

He turned the horse about. Anger burst through her. "You'll give me no promises or explanations."

He met her gaze. "I promise you this: I shall give to you no less than I gave Clarisse. A marble statue of an angel to watch over you in your eternal sleep and fresh flowers on your grave every day."

She grabbed his forearm, digging her fingers into him, stilling him. "Why would I want a promise that consisted of cold marble and flowers that wilt? What purpose could either possibly serve?"

She saw the confusion and fury swirl within his eyes at her questioning his promise.

"They show that you are loved and remembered."

"They honor my death and not my life."

Recognizing within the depths of his eyes that she'd truly hurt him, she laid her palm against his cheek. It was not his vow to her that was causing his pain, but his gifts to the woman he'd loved before her, gifts he'd thought worthy of her. "I don't doubt the sincerity of your gifts or that Clarisse was worthy of your devotion." She smiled warmly. "Fresh flowers every day and an angel to guard over her. Any other woman would be honored to be remembered in such a manner. But I have grown up and lived within Death's shadow. If you wish to honor me, whatever money you would spend on flowers or statues give to a physician who seeks a cure for any disease that causes suffering or death. I won't feel neglected if weeds cover my grave."

"You deserve more than weeds, and I won't allow you to settle for less than you deserve."

She touched her lips to his. "One flower then. A white rose like the one you gave me the afternoon when we had our first outing. But no more than that. Did you know that in this city known for its oleanders and grandness that half the deaths recorded each year are those of children? Find a more worthwhile cause than decorating my grave."

He narrowed his eyes, and she worried that he wouldn't capitulate. Finally, he sighed deeply. "One rose every day and a small statuette."

"A tiny statuette."

He cupped her head and brought it into the nook of his shoulder. She heard him swallow hard.

"If that's what you prefer, sweetling, then that is what you shall have."

"I'm not faulting you for sending Clarisse flowers. I simply don't want any."

"You like sunsets," he said quietly.

She nodded. "But I prefer sunrises. We take for granted the luxury of time, living our lives as though tomorrow were a guarantee instead of a gift."

Standing at the water's edge, Kit watched sandpipers dart and race along the shoreline. Overhead the seagulls vied for his attention, but his mind drifted to thoughts of his wife.

They'd decided to delay their trip to the heart of Galveston until later in the day, after she'd taken her nap. They were going to have dinner at a restaurant.

He'd gone into town earlier and rented a buggy. He'd visited St. Mary's infirmary and spoken at length with a physician. Long walks, a good diet, and dry air were his offerings as a cure for consumption. Sometimes consumptive patients recovered—even those who coughed up blood on occasion—and he had no idea why.

The physician had given him a spark of hope, but Kit would have preferred an absolute cure. Perhaps a cure would exist if he'd given the hospital the money he'd earned that first summer picking cotton instead of sending it to his solicitor in England so he could ensure Clarisse always had fresh flowers on her grave. She had so loved flowers. He'd wanted to give her in death what he'd been unable to give her openly in life.

With a portion of the money from his first cattle venture, he'd had a statue sculpted for Clarisse. Christopher had written him that it had turned out handsomely.

Kit crouched and bowed his head, his chest tightening. He dug his elbows into his thighs and clasped his hands, an aching grasp that was doing little to stop the pain. He had not wept when Clarisse had died. At her funeral, he had remained stoic and strong, his feelings known only to himself and his brother.

Every wilted petal represented a tear he had not been allowed to shed in public and been unable to release in private.

He saw a drop of water hit the ground between his

feet. The sand greedily absorbed it. And then another drop. Five years of holding grief at bay, and just when he thought Clarisse no longer mattered, he was discovering quite the opposite.

He felt slender arms slip around him, a body nestle against his back as a woman placed her head against his shoulder. She held him so he couldn't wipe the disgrace of tears from his eyes.

"I thought you were taking a nap," he said brusquely.

"I thought you said the advantage to marriage was that it gave us someone to lean on."

Damn the woman for tossing his words at him. "If I lean against you, we'd both tumble over."

Her arms tightened around him. "I'm sturdier than you think, Christian Montgomery."

He shook his head, unable to stop the tears now that he'd given a few their freedom. "I didn't want Clarisse to be dead. That's why I send her flowers every day. Although if she's looking down from heaven, she probably thinks they're coming from Christopher. All the little surprises I left for her, she thought came from Christopher." He released a shuddering sigh. "Remember when I told you how connected Christopher and I were?"

"Yes."

"Sometimes I wonder if it was his love for Clarisse that I felt and not my own." Damn his chest for aching as though it was caving in on him and the tears that flowed more freely.

She sidled around him, met his gaze, and tenderly gathered his tears with her fingers. "You loved her. I saw it in your eyes the first night I heard you speak of her at David's. And I see it now."

He bowed his head. "You should return to the house."

She threaded her fingers through his hair and pressed her bosom against his face. "So you can wallow in grief alone."

"I prefer it."

"Then you shouldn't have married me." She kissed the top of his head, his forehead before leaning low to kiss the tears that dampened his cheeks. "I love you."

His spirits soared with such joy before they plummeted with unequalled despair. "I don't deserve your love."

She gave him an innocent smile and cradled his face between her hands. "You judge yourself too harshly. How can you doubt your feelings for Clarisse were real? They are the reason you have flowers laid on her place of rest every day and gave her a stone angel to watch over her." She touched her lips to his. He opened his eyes. "She had an angel in life, Christian. Just as I do."

"I am no angel!" He surged to his feet and stalked to the water's edge. He felt her presence more than he heard her approach.

"Didn't you marry me to ease my dying, give me memories, and lessen my regrets?"

He released a strangled laugh. "I don't know anymore, Ashton. My misguided reasons have turned against me because the one thing I do not doubt is what I feel for you." He turned to face her. "I love you."

He circled one arm around her, bringing her closer. He touched his knuckles to her cheek. "I don't want to see you suffer."

She gave him a tremulous smile. "I'll be back in Dallas long before I reach that stage, and you'll be in Fortune doing your best to stop men from murdering floors."

The ache in his chest was almost unbearable. Love was hell. Why in God's name couldn't he ever love a woman who would live long enough for her hair to turn silver?

Chapter 15

Clutching Kit's arm, Ashton strolled along the shell-paved path known as The Strand. As twilight eased in, the gaslights that lined the streets of Galveston were already casting their faint glow to ward off the approaching darkness. Sighing contentedly, Ashton refrained from pressing her hand to her full stomach. She couldn't recall ever having eaten so much. It seemed with each meal that she ate more than she ever had before.

"I cannot believe the grandeur of this city," she said quietly. The ornate buildings and the three-story homes with turrets, spires, and columns fascinated her. "Next to Galveston, Dallas seems like an unwanted stepchild."

Kit smile warmly. "Don't underestimate Dallas. It has an aura about it, and I have no doubt that it will someday take its place among the notable cities of this state." He placed his free hand over hers and squeezed slightly. "But you are perceptive. Galveston is special. In some ways, it reminds me of London." His smile deepened. "I should take you on a walk along The Strand there."

"I'd like to see London."

He shook his head. "I spoke out of turn. It's a long journey, and I fear the weather would not be agreeable to you. You shiver in the night here. It is much cooler there."

"Then I'll be content with Galveston. Thank you for bringing me. I would have never imagined a city such as this or that oceans never ceased to move."

He brought her hand to his lips and pressed a kiss to her fingers, sending warmth cascading through her. His gaze held hers. "It's been my pleasure."

She felt the heat brighten her cheeks as she remembered the physical pleasure he'd brought to her the night before. The pleasure had been *all* hers.

She looked away, trying to concentrate on the intriguing architecture, lingering oleander fragrance, and bustle of people surrounding her. Instead, her mind wandered and she wondered if Kit would gift her tonight with another journey into the realm of incredible sensations.

Distracted, she released a small gasp as she stumbled over a shell. Kit caught her, drawing her close. She caught a whiff of the bay rum he wore, mingled with a scent that captured the essence of his masculinity. She loved his scent, the impeccable manner in which he dressed, and the mien of nobility that was such a part of him.

He was not a Texan. He never would be. She thought it a shame that he didn't return to the home that he loved and missed.

"Are you growing tired?" he asked, concern clearly reflected in his voice. "We could take a mule-drawn street car back to the spot where I left the carriage, if you'd like."

"I want to walk. I don't think I've ever walked as much in my entire life as I have since we arrived here."

"I'm afraid I may have forced my passion for walking on you. As a lad, I enjoyed walking great distances just to prove I could do it."

She studied him, trying to make sense of his words. "Why would you need to prove anything?"

He cocked his head and leaned near as though to impart a secret. "When I was a boy, I was quite sickly."

Her eyes widened. "You're teasing me."

He gave her a grim smile. "I wish. I spent much of my time abed with a cough or a fever or simply not feeling quite right. I always seemed tired, and I could see in my father's eyes that he detested my weakness. I'm certain he thanked God every night that I was the second son born and not the first."

"But you look perfectly healthy now."

He shrugged. "I forced myself to get out of bed, to walk when my legs trembled, and to eat when I had no appetite. My mother coddled me, my father loathed me, and Christopher promised that if I became strong enough, we would fool everyone and switch places."

"And did you?"

"Only once," he murmured quietly, and she knew without asking that it was the night Clarisse had died.

"You see," he continued, "in my desire to become stronger, I also became obstinate and contrary. While Christopher remained the perfect gentleman,

I became a rapscallion. As I grew stronger, I took pleasure in embarrassing my father. I imagine over time, he came to wish that I had remained weak and died."

"No father would wish that."

"Perhaps not. He had Christopher, the perfect son, and me, whom he constantly sent hither and yon, out of sight and out of mind. I enjoyed earning his wrath. It was much easier to accept than his pity."

She narrowed her eyes. "You constantly shove food into my mouth."

He nodded brusquely. "Because you do not place it between your lips yourself."

"Each day our morning and evening walks grow longer."

"I saw no harm in it, and I keep a close watch to ensure you don't wear yourself out."

"You manipulated me," she accused.

"With the best of intentions, I promise you. I discovered I have no desire to become a widower."

She pressed her head against his arm, needing more contact with him. "I don't want to make you a widower, but I fear I have no choice. Last January, the doctor was certain that I would not survive another winter. Yet I feel less tired than I've ever felt. Maybe it's the salt air and the excitement of seeing everything. I don't want to miss a single sight. What if everything changes when we leave?"

"Then we'll come back." He began walking, and she was conscious of the fact that he took smaller steps when he was with her. She'd watched him walk along the shore when she wasn't beside him, his strides long and purposeful.

"This city actually has culture that you can't find elsewhere in the state," Kit told her. "There are theaters and an opera house. Would you like to see a performance while we're here?"

She squeezed his arm. "I'd love to. I've never been to a theater."

"I'll make arrangements tomorrow."

"I suppose you've seen many plays and operas," she said.

"In London, yes. I miss the finer aspects of British life, which is one of the reasons Galveston appeals to me. The people here are more educated and wealthier than most in the state. Regrettably, though, I think all cities must have a balance. You'll also find the poorest and filthiest of wretches here."

"Have you seen much of the state?" she asked.

"I traveled its length and width shortly after we finished our trail drive. The state is so diverse that it fascinates me."

"But you prefer England."

He furrowed his brow. "I don't know that I prefer England. I only know that I miss Ravenleigh."

She heard the wistfulness in his voice. "Then you should return to your home."

He laughed. "I've told you before that I have nothing awaiting me there."

"Is your home there similar to any of these?" she asked, grandly sweeping her arm around to encompass the Georgian- and Victorian-styled homes.

"I could not even begin to describe the manor house. It is three, nay, five times the size of the largest home you would fine here. Too many servants to count scurry about dusting and polishing all the furnishings and decorative pieces that have been in our family for generations. It's rather like living in a museum."

"I don't understand its appeal then. It sounds cold and uncaring."

"I can't explain it, but it's in my blood, I suppose."

She stopped abruptly, and he turned to look at her. "While we're here, you should talk with one of the architects or builders and have something similar built for you in Fortune," she suggested.

"So I could hear my footsteps echo along the empty hallways for the remainder of my life? No, thank you."

He began to walk away. She grabbed his arm and spun him around. He raised a brow. Although they'd spoken as though she would not die, she knew it was a false hope and reality would one day intrude, bringing death with it.

"You're a young man. You'll find someone else to marry."

"I'm not going to search, sweetling."

The obstinate man! She wanted to bop him with the broom only she'd snipped off all the straw while catching the escaped crabs. "Then you'll stumble into her."

"No."

She placed her hands on her hips. "Christian Montgomery, if you don't find someone else, marry, and raise a family, I swear I shall haunt you from the grave."

Sadness touched his eyes. "I fear, Ashton, that inevitability shall come about regardless of what I do with the remainder of my life."

Lying in bed, with the lamp turned down until its light was almost useless, Ashton watched her husband prowl through their bedroom, slowly removing his clothes. She'd never in her life been so nervous, wondering if he would remove everything, if she should remove her gown.

One night of intimacy left her longing for more. She considered suggesting a late-night swim, but she feared he'd say no, although he had yet to deny her anything she asked. No moon outlined his form, yet her eyes had adjusted to the darkness and she could see his silhouette.

The doors to the balcony were open and the warm salt breeze whispered into the room. He'd discarded his jacket. She watched as he stepped onto the balcony and unbuttoned his shirt. What were his thoughts as he stood out there alone? Should she join him?

Pulling his shirt over his head, he walked back into the room and tossed it onto a nearby chair. He sat on the edge of the bed. "Why are you nervous?" he asked.

"I'm not," she answered, surprised that she sounded as though she had no breath in her body.

Even in the shadows, she could tell that he'd twisted his head to look at her. "You haven't moved since you finished drinking the milk I brought you."

She swallowed. "I . . . um . . . I was thinking is all."

"About what?" he asked in a low seductive voice that sent shivers rippling through her.

"Last night," she confessed. "I was wondering if married people make love every night."

"Depends on the couple, I should suppose," he said, before standing and removing what remained of his clothing.

Her breath caught as he lay beside her, raised up on an elbow, and trailed his finger along her arm.

"Every night, every morning, every afternoon," he said quietly, "if the mood should strike."

"During the day?" she asked, shocked to think of making love without the benefit of shadows, more dismayed to realize the thought appealed to her, to have the ability to clearly see Kit's hands moving over her flesh, to gaze into his light blue eyes.

He brought his mouth near her ear and whispered, "No rules govern passion, sweetling." He nibbled on her lobe. "Did you want me to bring you pleasure tonight?"

She closed her eyes and the heat swamped her. "Yes."

"Then why did you wear clothing to bed?"

"Because I didn't know there weren't any rules."

"Mmm. You smell like oleanders," he murmured.

"I took a sponge bath while you were seeing to the horses." She was grateful the night hid the blush that she knew was creeping up her face.

"So you liked my gift of scented soap," he said as he deftly unbuttoned her nightgown. "I should bring you back to Galveston when the flowers are again in bloom."

Next spring. To see them, she'd have to survive the winter. She held his words close to her heart, not daring to rebuff them. For tonight, for as long as he was with her, she would pretend that death would not come.

He slipped his hands between the parted material, cradling her ribs, and forcing her to sit. "Remove your clothes," he ordered quietly.

She slipped her arms out of the sleeves and squirmed until she worked her nightgown past her hips, along her legs, and over her feet.

"So much better," he said as he eased her back down to the mattress. He loosened her hair and fanned it over the pillow. "Gossamer wings," he murmured. "All angels have such delicate wings."

With a gentle nudge of his knee, he parted her thighs and placed himself between them. Her breathing became almost nonexistent. She had expected exactly what he'd given her last night, knowing only the feel of his chest against her breasts, his hands caressing her flesh, his lips teasing hers. She had not anticipated this position, of having the ability to press her thighs against his hips and feel his sturdiness at the juncture of her womanhood. She felt fear mingle with exhilaration.

With clothes to separate them, he had taken the same position on their wedding night, only anger had spurred his actions. She threaded her fingers through his hair, scraping her nails along his scalp. Tonight anger found no purchase within their bed.

Lightly, he kissed her temple, her cheek, the corner of her mouth. "Trust me, Ashton," he whispered hoarsely, "and I shall take you farther into the realm of pleasure than I did last night."

A shiver cascaded through her. "I don't know if I could survive such a journey."

"You will," he promised before possessively covering her mouth with his.

He tasted of brandy and fire, his lips hungry, his tongue insistent as he explored the confines of her mouth. His hands cradled her face as though he feared she might resist. Instead, she dug her fingers into his shoulders and returned his kiss with equal fervor.

She felt the dampness between her legs and realized that tonight she would know the full extent of love, the joining of bodies. He would give to her all that he had to give, and she would gladly receive it.

He withdrew from the kiss and trailed his mouth along her throat. "Trust me," he rasped.

An inane command when she already did, with all her heart.

He cupped her breasts, his hand gently kneading one while he paid homage to the other with his mouth, his tongue circling the budding tip. She raised her hips, pressing against his stomach, wishing he hadn't slid down, denying her contact with the hard evidence of his desire.

He licked at the valley between her breasts before taking his hot mouth on a slow sojourn over her ribs and along her stomach. The heat swept through her, flames licking at her core, creating needs stronger than anything she'd experienced before.

He dipped his tongue into her navel. She pressed her fingers against his head in an effort to urge him to bring his mouth back to hers. But he ignored her silent request and slid lower, kissing the sensitive flesh on the inside of each thigh.

Then with a gentle daring, he pressed his mouth to the intimate core of her being and circled his tongue over the budding flesh of her womanhood. She convulsed as intense sensations flooded her. He alternately stroked and suckled, the velvet smoothness of his tongue heightening the pleasure.

Her fingers tightened their hold on him as her body curled toward him. She began to spiral upward, beyond limits, beyond boundaries, until she thought she would die.

Brilliant colors exploded behind her closed lids, blood roared through her ears, she cried out his name, and her back arched as the sensations carried her into what she thought was surely heaven.

She fell back to earth, breathing heavily, not certain she would ever be able to move again.

Kit kissed the inside of her thighs, his mouth following the trail back to hers. He pressed his lips to hers, leaving behind the salty taste of her own flesh as he gently eased away from her and slid his finger inside her.

"You're still throbbing," he said in a quiet voice, but she heard the masculine pride emanating from him.

"Am I?" she asked breathlessly, turning her head slightly so she could gaze upon him.

His answer was a low growl of satisfaction. She

wanted to laugh, but she hadn't the strength. Of its own accord, her hand turned and circled him. Beside her, she felt his entire body stiffen.

"You're still sturdy," she murmured.

He kissed the sensitive spot below her ear, and she heard him swallow hard.

"Yes."

She thought she detected a note of sadness in his voice. Why would he be sad after giving so much to her?

She folded her fingers more snugly around him. He groaned.

"Am I hurting you?" she asked.

"God, no," he answered, his breathing harsh.

"Kit, I want to know what it feels like to have you inside me."

He buried his face within the crook of her neck. "There is little except pain for a woman the first time."

"I don't care. I want to experience the full extent of love, and if it includes pain, I'll welcome it if it means a joining of our bodies. I love you, and I want you to be my husband in the truest sense."

He lifted his head and skimmed his knuckles across her cheek. "You're crying."

Until that moment, she hadn't felt the tears. "From joy. What you give me fills me with gladness, and yet I feel empty. I think it's because as close as we've become, we're still separate."

"Our joining will make the parting so much harder, Ashton."

She cradled his jaw within her palm. "I don't want to die not having experienced the greatest of all gifts."

"Then I'll give to you what I can."

Tenderly, he kissed her as though it were the first time, as though no other moment had existed before this one, as though he'd never brought her pleasure or known her body as intimately as he had.

Love swelled like the roaring of the ocean that lay just beyond their balcony. When he shifted and nestled himself between her thighs, she knew that he was where he belonged, and this time he would gift her with what she had expected before.

Instinct made her lift her hips to welcome him. With one sure thrust, he joined his body to hers. The pain was slight, no doubt because he had already given her exquisite pleasure once.

She relished the full, hard length of him, filling her. She felt a shudder course through him, heard his harsh breathing. He kissed her passionately, hungrily, before raising above her. His movements were slight at first, like wading into the ocean, testing the current. The night covered his face in shadows, yet she could feel the heat of his gaze upon her as he rocked against her, increasing the tempo.

She had expected the pain. She hadn't expected to feel the pleasure rippling through her again. She gasped and he quickened his movements. She ran her hands along his sides, over his chest, until she could clutch his shoulders. Anything to keep her anchored, but she became like a ship tossed into a tempest.

All she'd experienced before paled in comparison

to what she felt now with each powerful thrust. His fingers had worked a miracle, his tongue magic, but these sensations went beyond earthly bounds. He was hers, completely, absolutely, making her his.

She writhed and moaned, tossing her head from side to side as the passion increased, undulating waves that never ceased, but only grew grander in intensity, broader in scope.

She shivered, felt him tremble, and then the storm washed over her, gloriously, taking her to the depths of passion and tossing her back to the height of sensual awareness. Her body curled, then arched, her fingers digging deeply into his shoulders.

Lost in oblivion, she felt his last thrust before he stilled, hovering above her, breathing harshly.

She trailed her hands along his quivering arms, his muscles tense and taut as any rope about to snap. Slowly, carefully, he withdrew and rolled off her, leaving her bereft for reasons she couldn't understand. She had wanted him to stay with her forever.

Lethargically, she eased onto her side and placed her hand on his chest. "You're so tense."

He twisted his head slightly and brushed a kiss across her brow. "Go to sleep now, sweetling."

She moved her hand lower. "You're still sturdy."

He grabbed her wrist and tucked her hand in close against her side. "Go to sleep."

He rolled out of bed and disappeared into the darkness of the balcony while confusion surrounded her. Why would pleasure leave a woman feeling completely relaxed and a man incredibly tense? Would they not, in some way, both experience the same sensations?

She clambered out of bed, jerked the sheet off the bed, wrapped it around herself, and padded to the balcony. She could see only a silhouette of Kit standing in the front corner, gripping the railing as he stared at the distant sea.

Quietly, she crossed the expanse separating them and pressed a hand against his back. He stiffened, but not before she felt the tightness that already existed within him.

"Go back to bed," he said in a controlled voice.

She pressed a kiss to his sweat-slickened flesh. "What did I do wrong?"

"Nothing."

She wrapped her hand around his arm. "I don't understand. Why is a man so tense after experiencing pleasure while a woman—"

"I did not—" She heard him swallow. "I did not experience the pleasure that you did."

Grief hit her with the knowledge that she'd disappointed him. Her experience was none while his was abundant. Why hadn't he shown her what he needed from her to experience the joys of love? "What did I do wrong?"

"I told you. Nothing."

"Then explain to me what I should have done so I'll know—"

"Nothing."

"Then why—"

"Ashton, for God's sake, if you read all those medical books you must know what happens when a man reaches the pinnacle of pleasure."

The brusqueness in his voice caught her unaware. After all his kindness, why now was he incredibly angry? She took a step back, knowing the answer but needing to hear it from him. "Tell me what happens."

He jerked his head around and glared at her. "I not only fill you with my cock, sweetling, I fill you with my seed."

His crudeness unsettled her, but not nearly as much as the implication of his final words. "Your seed," she repeated lamely.

A sudden chill swept through her, and she drew the sheet more closely around herself. "So you held back. You gave me pleasure, but denied yourself."

"The night I asked you to become my wife, I made a personal vow that I would not get you with babe. If your physician's prediction holds any accuracy, then my child would die with you. I will not be responsible for the death of another innocent."

She heard the wind blowing over the waves, like the howling of a child, a child she would never hold. During their time together, she'd never considered all the ramifications that this arrangement was costing him. She felt the tears well within her eyes and slide along her cheeks. Her mouth dry, she cleared her throat. "I think it's time that I returned to Dallas."

"I thought you wanted to see a performance," he said quietly.

"I fear, my dear Kit, that I have been living a performance for too long now while you have suffered through the reality. I want to go back to Dallas."

He turned his attention to the ocean. "Then we'll leave tomorrow."

Although he couldn't see her, she nodded. She had married a man of wise words. All that she'd experienced would make the parting unbearable.

Chapter 16

Kit had succeeded in giving Ashton what she had so long ago wished for—a broken heart.

He found no satisfaction in his accomplishment. Self-loathing pierced his soul. Frustration had caused him to blurt out his explanation in the crudest of manners. If the devil didn't already own his soul, he would trade it to have that moment returned so he could have explained kindly with words that would soften the truth.

Sitting across from his wife inside the jostling stagecoach, Kit felt the chasm between them widening. She'd chosen to wedge herself between the side of the coach and the obese man who had climbed aboard ahead of her.

When Clarisse had died, he'd felt a loneliness so deep that he thought the well of despair would forever hold him captive. Now, he was taking his very much alive wife back to her brother, and he feared he would have neither the courage nor the kindness to leave her.

God knew he didn't have the desire.

Loneliness already gnawed at his soul. Ashton was still with him in flesh, if not in heart, and he wondered how he would survive when he no longer had the ability at least to gaze upon her, to watch the wind whip stray strands of hair around her lovely face, to inhale her sweet scent of oleander, the flower of Galveston.

He had purchased her some more scented soaps and perfume before they'd left. Although she'd obliged him by dabbing a bit of the perfume against her throat, her eyes had held no joy, only resignation.

Death was her destiny.

Clarisse had belonged to Christopher. Although Kit had accepted that fact, only now did he truly understand the ramifications of that truth. He had loved Clarisse, but it was a love born of youth, a love deepened by denial.

His feelings for Ashton were those of a man staring down a long, desolate road that would never again know the touch of the sun or the light of the moon. He would live only because his heart continued to beat and his lungs to take in air, but his soul was already withering.

He would insist that David not notify him when the flame of her life had been snuffed out. He knew he would be unable to bear the sorrow. In his mind, she would live forever. When his hair turned gray, he would imagine hers silver. When his wrinkles deepened, he might add one or two to the memory of her face. Only when Death came for him would he accept that she'd gone before, and he could only hope that she would be standing at Heaven's Gate awaiting his arrival.

He closed his eyes. He'd doomed himself to hell when he'd poured the extra powder into the glass for Clarisse. Once he left Dallas, he would never again see Ashton. Not in this life, nor in any that lay beyond.

Opening his eyes, he again felt the stab of regret—for the personal vow he'd taken the night he proposed and for his lack in judgment that had allowed it to harm her. Still, the memories of her moans, sighs, and cries were a balm to the mental flaying he'd given himself. He would carry the song with him for the remainder of his life.

He hoped that in the passing months, she would forgive him and remember him with a measure of caring, perhaps a bit of love, although he feared it unlikely. He had wounded her greatly by not giving everything to her.

If only she knew how much he'd wounded himself. Never in his life had he become so lost in a woman when he joined his body to hers. Never had he reveled in the pleasure he could provide or felt such a belonging. Until Ashton, he'd never realized that he had been as a voyeur . . . involved but distant.

Strange for a man of thirty-three to discover that he'd never truly made love. Created passion, yes. Elicited pleasure, certainly, but his heart had watched from afar, a safe distance away.

Now, it was no longer safe. It hurt unbearably. God help him, he'd never known such pain, and he'd always thought he'd experienced the worst. He was beginning to realize he'd experienced nothing at all.

With longing, he watched Ashton, resisting the urge to reach across the expanse separating them and take her hand in his, cherish her touch, just one more memory to tuck away and carry with him into his dotage.

With her head bent, she stared at her clasped hands in her lap as though they were the only things that existed in her life. She had shut him out completely, absolutely. He might have thought the past month had never occurred if it weren't for his heart. It refused to forget a solitary moment that he'd spent with her since he'd first seen her on the porch at Mrs. Gurney's.

Memories of Clarisse were like ancient portraits, faded over time until they were little more than shadowy veils. He hadn't a clue how he could keep memories of Ashton vibrant. He only knew that she was all that mattered.

"You're missing the countryside," he said quietly, remembering how she'd enjoyed it on the trip to Galveston, how much she had wanted to see everything.

She lifted her gaze to his and the sadness within her eyes was like a dagger to his heart. "I've seen it before," she said softly.

"It's a bit different. We're taking another route. There are more trees, more greenery."

She lowered her gaze, and he could see her knuckles turning white. Reaching out, he wrapped his hand over hers, surprised to find her cold. "Come over here," he ordered.

She shook her head slightly.

"Ashton, I will make a scene if I must."

She nodded. One corner of her mouth lifted into a smile that quickly disappeared. He placed his hands on either side of her waist, helping her keep her balance as she crossed over to sit beside him. He slipped his arm around her and drew her against his side, cradled her face, and nestled it within the crook of his shoulder. He bent his head and whispered, "I never meant to harm you."

"I know, but I brought such misery to you."

"Not you, sweetling. Fate conspires against me. You have no control over fate or my heart."

He heard the obese man snort. He glanced up to see that the man was asleep. An amazing feat, considering the rumbling contraption. He looked down at Ashton. "Perhaps you should try to sleep as well."

"I'm not tired."

He nodded, grateful to have her near. How in God's name would he find the strength to leave her in Dallas? He could and he would, somehow. He had yet to turn his back on an obligation, and to keep her near would only add to her suffering at the end.

Guilt was an unforgiving and cruel master.

A gunshot rang out, and Kit heard the echo of pounding hooves. He cursed soundly, using profanity that he'd never spoken in front of a lady. His horse was tethered to the back of the stagecoach, and his rifle was housed in his saddle on the roof. The stagecoach increased its speed. He drew Ashton more tightly against him.

The obese man awoke with a start and fumbled with his clothing, removing a money pouch from around his waist and shoving it beneath the seat.

"What's going on?" Ashton asked.

"Robbers, no doubt," Kit said quietly, his voice calm, while his mind reeled with unfavorable scenarios.

"The whip don't seem to be stopping," their companion pointed out as the stagecoach swayed unmercifully.

"No, he doesn't," Kit replied as more gunshots sounded.

"The last stagecoach I rode in overturned three times, and it wasn't going this fast. Why the hell doesn't he stop?" The man reached up and pounded on the ceiling.

Kit heard scraping on the roof. No doubt the man who rode shotgun was trying to position himself better. The retort of a gun exploded overhead, followed shortly by a yell. An object passed quickly beside the window.

Ashton screeched and turned her face into Kit's shoulder. "That was a man," she whispered.

He felt her shivering uncontrollably. He stared at the man sitting across from him. "Have you a gun?"

The man nodded and withdrew a derringer from inside his coat. Kit swore beneath his breath. A lot of bloody good that tiny thing would do him. He needed his rifle.

Gently, he urged Ashton away from him. He heard the ping of a ricochet. The wood in the window of the door splintered. "I want you to lie on the floor."

Her wide eyes were filled with fear.

"It sounds as though they're gaining on us. You'll be safer in a lower position," he explained.

Their companion began to slide off his seat. Kit shoved him back into place. "There's not room for two."

"You can't expect me to remain a target."

"I expect you to keep an eye out and use that gun if any of the outlaws ride close enough to the coach for your weapon to be of any assistance."

He thrust the weapon toward Kit. "You can have it."

"I won't be here."

Ashton clutched Kit's shirt. "Where are you going?"

"The driver had only one man riding on top with him. I need to determine if it's best to stop or continue at this breakneck speed." He drew her close. "I need you on the floor so I won't have to worry."

"Kit—"

"We'll argue about it later," he said firmly as he urged her to the floor. She looked up at him with such incredibly blue eyes. He had so much he wanted to tell her. "Keep your head down."

Taking a deep breath, he put his hand on the latch. Dear God, he was inviting disaster, but he didn't see that he had a choice. He opened the door. The wind caught it and slammed it against the side of the coach. He glanced out. Eight riders. Bloody hell.

Reaching up, he grabbed the top of the opening to the door with one hand, the opening to the window closest to the front of the coach with the other. He swung his leg out and wedged his foot against the corner of the window. He heard a bullet whiz past his ear and drew up his shoulders as though that insignificant action could protect him. The wood near his hand split.

If he thought the men in pursuit would leave his wife in peace, he'd yell for the driver to stop the blasted vehicle, and he'd stay inside.

His muscles straining, he pulled himself up, clutching the roof as he moved his other foot to the window. The driver jerked his head around.

"What the hell do you think you're doing?"

"Coming to your assistance. I'm a marshal," Kit yelled over the din of stampeding hooves and rumbling wheels. He threw himself on top of the coach and, lying low, worked his way to his saddle that he'd tied down in a corner before they'd begun the journey. He slid his rifle out of its scabbard.

He knew his horse would be an enticing target. He was surprised the men hadn't already shot it. Dragging dead weight would slow the vehicle.

Lying low, he pulled himself forward on his elbows. Cursing his precarious position, he reached over the edge, aimed his rifle at the rope tethering Lancelot to the stagecoach and fired three bullets in rapid succession. The beast broke free and galloped clear of the coach, heading between the thick trees that lined the road.

Inching back, Kit leveled his rifle and fired at the riders who were in rapid pursuit of the coach. One man toppled from his mount. Kit quickly fired again, downing another man before ducking behind baggage to avoid the flying bullets. He heard the driver cry out. He looked back. The man clutched his shoulder briefly before urging the six tiring horses on.

Kit sighted his next target, the man he deemed to be the leader. The jostling vehicle made it difficult to keep his rifle steady. He slowly squeezed the trigger. His victim bellowed and grabbed his arm. Unfortunately, he also kicked his horse, spurring it to increase its speed.

"We got a damn fallen tree in the road!" the driver yelled.

Kit glanced over his shoulder to see the driver leaning back, pulling hard on the reins. Kit heard an explosion, felt a sharp pain slam against his temple, and was powerless to stop the darkness from consuming him.

Chapter 17

As he walked along Fortune's dusty street, Christopher Montgomery thought he'd known what to expect in Texas. After all, when Kit put his mind to it, he could paint a detailed portrait with words and his brother had often written to him about life in his new home. Kit had told him a great deal in his letters. He had also omitted quite a lot.

Christopher had stopped by the jail, surprised to find it locked. A peek through the windows had assured him that no one was inside. He hoped Kit wasn't in pursuit of some dastardly outlaw. Now was not the time for his brother to get himself killed.

He stepped onto the planked boardwalk. It echoed with other men's heavy treading, but Christopher had learned at an early age to walk quietly and with dignity. Aware of the wide-eyed stares, he resisted the urge to let anyone know that he noticed them. With his handkerchief, he dabbed the sweat from his brow. A man could expire from the heat alone in this state, a little fact Kit had failed to mention along with the dust, the mosquitoes, and the air that hung heavy with a suffocating dampness.

Christopher walked into the saloon. Despite it being the middle of the afternoon, the establishment was filled with men who sat at tables while drinking and playing cards.

"Wyndhaven?"

He turned, relief sweeping through him at the sight of a familiar face. "Bainbridge."

Leaning heavily on a cane, Harrison Bainbridge walked toward him. Christopher had hated hearing about Bainbridge's unfortunate incident with the jayhawkers.

Bainbridge firmly took his hand and shook it vigorously. "Good God, what brings Viscount Wyndhaven to my door?"

"I'm attempting to locate Kit. He wasn't at his office so I thought he might be here."

Surprise flitted across Bainbridge's face. "Actually, he's in Galveston."

"Galveston?" Christopher scoffed at life's ironies. "But our ship docked there."

"Our?" Bainbridge inquired.

Christopher cursed his stupid tongue. He must remember to take care so he could avoid lies in the future. "I brought my valet, of course."

Bainbridge nodded politely, but his eyes held skepticism. "Of course. Would you care for something to drink?"

"That invitation sounds marvelous. Port, if you have it."

Bainbridge laughed heartily. "I don't." He snapped his fingers, and a young woman stopped walking across the saloon. "Lorna, bring me a bottle of whiskey and two glasses." Bainbridge waved his hand toward a vacant table in a corner. "Let's sit over here."

Christopher took a chair and averted his gaze out of respect for his brother's friend. He had no desire to make Bainbridge uncomfortable with his presence, and he remembered him as a proud man. He did not wish to embarrass him by witnessing his clumsy attempt to sit.

Christopher watched the woman saunter over, her eyes brightening and her smile widening as she saw him. She set the whiskey and glasses on the table before sidling up next to him. Her perfume was overpowering, almost eliminating the odor of tobacco and liquor.

"I didn't think you'd come see me now that you was married," she said as she tiptoed her fingers across his shoulders.

"Lorna, this man is not the marshal. He's his brother," Bainbridge explained.

Her features crumpled into disappointment. "Oh. But he looks just like the marshal."

"Not if you look closely enough," Bainbridge assured her.

She narrowed her eyes, and Christopher resisted the urge to squirm under her scrutiny.

"Reckon you're right," the woman said. "He looks kinda dandified, don't he?"

Christopher cleared his throat. "I am not accustomed to being spoken about as though I were not present."

Bainbridge chuckled. "You'll have to show him a bit more respect, Lorna. He's a viscount, one day to become an earl."

"How come you keep changing your name?" she asked, her brow furrowing.

Shaking his head, Bainbridge said gently, "Never mind, Lorna. See to my other customers. I need to speak with him privately."

As soon as she was out of hearing, Christopher mumbled, "Kit got married." The words came out as a fact. He'd suspected as much, but he hadn't dared trust his instincts.

"You knew," Bainbridge said as he began filling the glasses. "Kit told me you two often know each other's thoughts."

"I sensed that he was in love."

Bainbridge jerked his gaze to Christopher's. "In love? Are you certain?"

"Relatively so." Christopher pointed to the glass, filled to the rim with whiskey that was now cascading over the sides, creating a waterfall. "You've overpoured."

"Damnation." Bainbridge slammed the bottle on the table. "When did you get this impression?"

"Some time back. I can't remember exactly, a few days, a couple of weeks. But I also know he's unhappy."

"Of course he's not happy. I warned him against treading into this marriage." Bainbridge picked up the glass and downed the amber liquid in one long swallow. "His wife is dying."

Christopher sighed deeply. "Then why did he marry her?" He held up a hand. "No need to answer that. My brother has a habit of playing Good Samaritan. A shame he never reveals that side of his nature to our father."

"It's more of a shame that he bound himself to vows that could cause such misery," Bainbridge said.

Christopher listened to the tale of his brother's marriage with a mixture of grief for all the suffering his brother would endure and relief because in the end, the outcome would be for the best.

"So he took Ashton to Galveston for a wedding trip as though accepting her as his bride wasn't sacrifice enough," Bainbridge finished.

"I didn't feel his presence when I was in Galveston, but that's not unusual. We seem unable to control what we pick up from each other."

"Still, I hate hearing that he may have fallen for Ashton. After Clarisse—" Bainbridge stopped abruptly, looking decidedly uncomfortable.

"I know how my brother felt about Clarisse. Dear Lord, he has fresh flowers placed upon her grave daily."

"So that's where his money goes," Bainbridge murmured speculatively. "He never would say."

"He also had a marble statue of a guardian angel made for her. It's exquisite, a true work of art. I'm certain he paid handsomely for it."

"Kit never cuckolded you, Wyndhaven."

Christopher had always envied his brother the friendships he'd developed that allowed those he cared about to defend him unconditionally as well as to call him by his first name. "I never thought he had or would. My brother is a man of honor, regardless of what Father perceived him to be."

Bainbridge narrowed his eyes. "What brings you here?"

"I have some news to impart, and I thought it best done in person."

"Not bad news, I hope."

"To be honest, I'm not sure how Kit will take it." Unease settled around him. "Have you any notion as to when Kit planned to return?"

"I only know he was going to take Ashton to Dallas before he came back to Fortune. I suspect that he could return at any time."

Christopher sighed. "Then I suppose my best plan of action is simply to wait here." He stood. "If you'll excuse me, I need to check on some other matters. It was good to see you, Bainbridge."

"You'll have to come to my home and meet my wife and daughters."

"If time permits, I'd like that." He gave a perfunctory nod and headed out of the saloon.

The interminable heat blasted into him. Kit had been sent to hell. As if the weather weren't bad enough, if he was not mistaken, there were no theaters, museums, or any semblance of civilization within miles. Kit had so enjoyed the arts.

Christopher strolled along the boardwalk toward the south end of town where he'd taken a room at a boardinghouse. Although a fine establishment, it was not the type of inn in which he was accustomed to staying when he traveled. But then little here was familiar. He would be glad to be gone.

He walked past the general store. Without warning,

a sharp pain bounced between his temples. Slamming his eyes closed against the agony, he staggered and found purchase against the building. Breathing heavily, he waited for the torment to pass.

"Just past noon and you're already drunk," a sharp feminine voice chastised.

Forcing his eyes open, he twisted his head slightly to see a woman standing beside him, her hand wrapped around a young girl's arm while the fingers on her other hand were holding a squirming young man by his ear.

"I saw you coming out of the saloon," the woman said, accusation reflected in her blue eyes. "I don't know why the people of this town saw fit to make you marshal, or why I'm turning to a womanizer with this problem. Reckon because I got no choice." Without releasing the young man's ear, she thrust him toward Christopher.

"Ow! Ow! Ow!" the lad cried, wincing.

"I want him locked up for the night," the woman commanded.

Christopher realized belatedly that she'd mistaken him for Kit. "My apologies, madam, but I can't—"

"You sure can, and you'd better. Take him!"

The woman's blond hair was askew, falling from her tightened bun, and her eyes blazed with fury and defiance. Deciding that the path of least resistance was the best course, Christopher wrapped his hand around the young man's arm and pulled him beyond harm's way. The shrew seemed in no mood to accept the truth. He straightened, grateful the pain at his temple had finally subsided. "What's his offense?"

"He was unbuttoning my Lauren's bodice, trying to . . ."—the woman blushed—"take advantage of her innocence. She's only fourteen."

He gave a brisk nod. "I shall handle the matter posthaste."

"See that you do, or I swear I'll have the town council throw you out of office." She trudged away, pulling her daughter behind her, a girl who glanced over her shoulder and gave the boy a forlorn look.

"Who was that termagant?" Christopher asked of no one in particular.

"The Widow Fairfield," the lad answered.

Christopher directed his attention to the young man. "How old are you, lad?"

The boy angled his chin defiantly. "Fifteen, and I ain't afraid of jail."

"I'm not going to put you in jail for being curious, but wait until you're sixteen before you unfasten any other bodices. Make certain the woman is older or a sporting sort who is willing to take money to satisfy your natural curiosity." Christopher released his hold. "Now, be off with you."

He watched the lad dart away. Amused at the situation, Christopher crossed the dusty street. In England, he'd never had the occasion to be mistaken for Kit. They had seldom ventured into the same social circles. It was a startling revelation to be spoken to as though he were little more than a gutter rat, but it was something he would no doubt grow accustomed to.

He walked into the boardinghouse and strolled to the room he'd acquired on the first floor in a corner that faced the street. Quietly, he opened the door and entered the bedroom that he was already beginning to loathe.

Gazing out, his father sat in a padded red velveteen covered chair by the window.

"Is he coming?" his father asked, his laborious words slurred, a result of the second stroke he'd suffered on the ship coming over. The first incident had happened at Ravenleigh. Christopher had debated the wisdom of bringing his father, but the man had exhibited a remarkable recovery. Christopher had been naïve enough to think it would continue, and when his father had stubbornly insisted on coming, he had not had the heart to deny his request.

He came to stand before his father. Out of habit, he planted his hands behind his back, just as his father had taught him. "It seems Kit has married. He's in Galveston on his wedding trip."

Slowly, torturously, his father looked up at him. "Don't . . . tell him."

Pity for his father swelled within Christopher. He'd agreed that he'd keep his father's presence here a secret so as not to cause him embarrassment by revealing his condition. His father was such an incredibly proud man. Had always been so.

"He has a right to know, Father."

"Damn you." His father turned away.

Christopher sighed wistfully. He was no doubt damning them all.

Chapter 18

Ashton had a shadowy memory of the stagecoach tumbling end over end, bouncing her unmercifully as she slid across the floor toward the open door . . .

But she couldn't remember how she'd been thrown clear, how she'd landed in a tangle of brush with only bruises and nothing broken, or how she'd managed to find Kit. He was unconscious, the blood flowing from a deep gash near his temple matting his hair. Thank goodness the foliage in this area was thick, and she'd had to shove him only a short distance to hide him beneath the brush.

She was stretched out beside him, trying to conceal them both from the men who were trampling near the stagecoach that now rested on its side. She'd pulled some branches in close behind her to shield them from the outlaws. Darkness would settle soon, providing additional coverage.

As quietly as she could, she'd torn off a section of her petticoat and now held it against Kit's head. She felt his warm blood seeping through the cloth. Would the wound never stop bleeding? Somewhere she'd read to apply pressure to stop blood from flowing and force it to clot. She knew a head injury usually bled a great deal but she couldn't remember the reasoning. Her thoughts were as scattered as the luggage that had been on top of the stagecoach.

She fought off the panic that threatened to consume her. She also knew she needed to wake him shortly because he'd certainly taken a blow to the head, but she couldn't risk him making any noise until the robbers left. Why wouldn't they just take what they wanted and leave?

"Hey, Jasper, there's one still inside here, but I think he done met his Maker."

"Damn it, Morton, I ain't interested in anyone inside the coach. I want the man who was up on top."

"The driver's over there but he's got a busted head," Morton said.

"Not the driver, you idiot," Jasper said. "I swear you got nuthin' under your hat but your hair. I want the man that was shootin' at us. I dadgum guarantee that he was that marshal we met up with in Fortune."

Dread rippled along Ashton's spine, and she slowed her breathing until it was almost nonexistent. A coughing seizure now would doom them both.

"But he said he don't use a gun," Morton pointed out.

"He said he don't wear one!" Jasper yelled, and Ashton heard a thud. He'd obviously thrown something against a tree in his anger and frustration. "A rifle ain't something you wear, and he sure as hell was shooting it like a man who knew how to use one. He killed two of my men and shot me, to boot. I want him found. Whether he's alive or dead, I'm stretching him out for buzzard bait."

Ashton's heart sank as she wondered if these men were the ones Kit had brushed off as merely trying to murder a floor. Now, their leader seemed intent on killing him slowly and torturously.

"He's gotta be dead, Jasper. I seen you shoot him," Morton said.

"I want his body!" Jasper cried. "Find his goddamn body so I know he's dead."

"We could have more fun with him 'iffen he was alive," someone said.

"We sure as hell could," Jasper said, "and we will, but you gotta find him first! So stop your jawin' and start lookin'."

Kit rolled his head and groaned. Ashton slipped her trembling hand over his mouth, pressed her lips to his ear, and cooed softly, "Shh. Shh."

"Hey!" another man yelled. "Look what I found hiding in the bushes."

Ashton's heart thudded against her ribs and her throat constricted. She squeezed her eyes shut as though not seeing the outlaws would stop them from seeing her. She heard branches snap and leaves rustle as someone cleared away some brush. She held her breath.

"What'd you find? Is it that marshal?"

"Nah, it's the strong box."

She jerked when a gunshot exploded nearby.

"And lookee here. Full of money, just like we heard it would be. That sure was a smart idea you had, Jasper, cutting down a tree so it blocked the road."

"That's on account of I'm a smart man, which is the reason I lead you bunch of no goods. I didn't want to take no chances on the driver not stopping so I give him a reason to have to stop. Now, you start splitting up that money even like," Jasper said. "Everybody else search for that marshal."

She heard the men thrashing through the brush and foliage. How long before she and Kit were discovered? She couldn't determine the extent of his injury while those dreadful men were prowling around.

"Well, well, what have we got here?" someone asked. "This bag's got women's clothes in it."

Ashton's stomach clenched. Although she was more worried about what they would do to Kit, she also realized they would not be very kind toward her. She could not bear the thought of one of those men touching her.

"You think there was a woman in the stagecoach that maybe helped that marshal get away?" Morton asked.

"Either that or someone had strange dressing habits. Dammit!" Jasper spat. "This ground ain't good for marking tracks, but they can't have gotten far. Mount up. They'll be traveling on foot and he's wounded. We ought to find 'em before the sun sets."

Ashton heard horses whinny followed by the pounding of hooves over hard ground. She pressed her cheek against Kit's. She wondered how diligently the outlaws would search and for how long. She had to find a safer place to hide Kit.

She didn't care about herself. Her time was already limited, but he had a lifetime ahead of him. She intended to ensure that he lived to enjoy every moment of it.

Kit awoke groggily, his head aching with an intensity that he thought would kill him. He was surprised it hadn't already. It had succeeded in blinding him. All he could see were blurry shadows, gray and black, shifting and swirling.

His mouth grew dry and tingled. He swallowed down the bile burning his throat. He was queasy, but he needed to find Ashton. She shouldn't walk along the shore by herself or wade out into the water when she couldn't swim.

"Lie still," a soft voice commanded.

"I'm blind," he croaked.

"I don't think so. We're in a cave. It's very dark in here because it's night. The men who chased down the stagecoach are looking for you."

Jarring pain thrummed between his temples as he laid his head back on the hard ground, trying to remember what had transpired. "They took exception to my killing them."

"The dead ones aren't after you. The live ones are."

"Live outlaws can be a bit more dangerous."

He heard a strangled laugh. "Are you teasing me?"

He didn't think so but the words slid from his mind as soon as he spoke them. What had he told her? "Water?"

"There's some in the canteen."

He heard her movements, felt her lift his head slightly as the canteen touched his lips. The water was cool and incredibly welcome, but he limited himself to a few sips, afraid he was going to be sick. With a weak hand, he pushed the canteen away. "Drink."

"I already did. I found some jerky. Do you want some?"

Nothing had ever sounded so unappealing, although at this moment the mere thought of the finest pastries in all of England made him nauseated. He just wanted to sleep. "No."

He felt sweet lips brush against his cheek and raindrops slide toward his jaw.

"Kit, I'm so afraid."

He fumbled in the dark until he found Ashton's hand. He brought it to his lips and skimmed his mouth over her slender fingers. "You're stronger than you think, sweetling."

Unfortunately, he was weak, too weak to ward off the oblivion of unconsciousness.

Ashton studied the silhouette of her husband. She didn't dare build a fire, and the stars and moonbeams provided so little light. His earlier words had made little sense. The blow to his head had no doubt addled his brain. She could only hope that he hadn't sustained a concussion or that the blow hadn't caused permanent damage to his reasoning powers. She'd have to wake him periodically so he wouldn't go into an everlasting sleep.

This afternoon, pride and fear had warred within her. Pride that he'd dared to face the outlaws against insurmountable odds. Overwhelming fear that they would kill him.

She thought of the three innocent men who had died today: the man who had been inside the coach with her, the driver, and the man who had ridden with him. She didn't even know their names and had been unable to take the time to give them a decent burial.

She shivered. The cave reminded her of a tomb, cold and damp. They were near the opening where the air was fresher. If she heard anyone approaching, she'd pull Kit farther back into the cave.

Her stomach rumbled. The jerky had been less than satisfying, but it was something to gnaw on through the night. Tomorrow she'd have to figure out how to use Kit's rifle. She'd located it and used it as a staff to support herself as he leaned on her while they walked away from the stagecoach.

She was fortunate he'd maintained consciousness for as long as he had. Once they'd entered the cave, he'd collapsed as though he'd only been waiting for them to reach their destination.

She heard him mumble and returned her attention to him. Part of her heart wished she'd never married him, yet she would not trade a single moment of their time together for a promise of immortality. She did not regret their last night together. She had never felt such completeness. Her love for him had transcended all boundaries, physical and emotional.

She only regretted that he'd paid such a high price for his generosity. Yet in the end, he'd been unable to give her everything because she could give him nothing, nothing but promises on the wind.

The pain ripped through her. If he clung to any memories of her, they would always be bittersweet. She wished she could return to him a portion of all that he'd given her.

She stroked her fingers along his cheek, wanting to offer him comfort. His wound had ceased its bleeding, and she'd wrapped a strip of her petticoat around his head. How lucky they were that the bullet had only creased his brow.

"Clarisse?" he rasped.

Her heart tightened unmercifully as he whispered his love's name. She leaned low and forced the painful words past the knot in her throat. "I'm here."

He scoffed. "You can't be here. I killed you."

She stilled, a frigid wind seeming to sweep through her body creating a numbing chill deep within her. With suddenly cold fingers, she cradled his face. This man was her husband, her Kit, her love. Surely, delirium made him utter such ugly words. "No, no, you didn't kill me. I was sick—"

"I think Christopher suspects what I did, but don't confirm it, don't tell him. He is a man of too much integrity. He'd never forgive himself for sending for me, for being generous and giving me a moment alone with you. One moment when I wished for a thousand."

She felt her mouth move, silent words searching for a voice that she no longer possessed. Her chin trembled, her throat constricted. She pushed the question out. "What exactly did you do during that moment, Kit?"

"I killed you." His answer echoed through the cave, resounded through her heart.

Sitting up slightly, he wrapped his hand around her arm. "Don't tell Ashton, either. Her innocence is a balm to my eternal regret. You'll meet her soon. I wish it were otherwise, but she is ill as well. She will be a lovely Christmas present. Another angel to fill the heavens."

He dropped his hand to his side, and Ashton realized he'd lost consciousness. She scooted away until her back hit the wall of the cave. She brought up her knees, wrapped her arms tightly around her legs, and began to rock. Delirious. He was simply delirious.

He hadn't truly killed Clarisse. He had loved her. Perhaps he only thought he had killed her. Maybe he somehow felt that he was responsible, blamed himself for the disease she'd contracted. But his conversation referred to an action he had taken. What had he done? If he thought he'd killed her, how had he done it?

She remembered the angel he'd had carved for Clarisse and the flowers laid on her grave daily. Love, not guilt, motivated his actions.

She had never dreaded death more than she did now. How would she survive eternity if through death she learned that the man she loved was a murderer?

Ashton watched the sunrise through the small opening to the cave. Her swollen eyes burned from lack of sleep. Her mind tumbled over Kit's words. Surely he hadn't meant to imply that he had killed Clarisse.

But she was also haunted by the words he'd spoken on the balcony their last night in Galveston, words that her grief had not fully absorbed until now.

I will not be responsible for the death of another innocent.

Another innocent.

Her heart had been breaking, and she hadn't questioned who the first innocent had been. Was it Clarisse? Or was there someone else? Someone killed in an accident?

Her body ached as she rose and approached the mouth of the cave. She heard thunder in the distance. She didn't welcome a storm, although the rain would provide water.

She knelt beside the small bundle of items she'd hastily gathered. She removed the canteen that she thought had belonged to the stagecoach driver. She and Kit had sipped what little water it had originally contained. Now she was incredibly parched and knew Kit would be thirstier. His voice carried a rough, scratchy edge to it. He'd spoken so often while unconscious. Fortunately, his low mumbling had not echoed within the cave and had not caught the attention of any wandering outlaws.

She glanced over her shoulder at him. His thoughts had seemed scrambled, darting between the past and the present. At one point, he'd told her he was craving the taste of bark from a tree. Another time when he'd awakened, he'd asked her how she enjoyed Ravenleigh, as though they were visiting his home.

Perhaps it was only the loss of his first love that had led him to state that he'd killed her.

During the night, she had not heard the outlaws nor seen any sign of a campfire. Hopefully, they'd gone elsewhere. She wasn't certain where she and Kit were, but she had the impression that water was nearby. Otherwise how would all the foliage and greenery flourish?

As the sun rose higher, light sparkled off the dew-drops on the nearby leaves. If it weren't for the manner of their arrival or the fact that Kit was hurt and outlaws were looking for him, she might think they'd arrived in paradise.

She slipped out of the cave. Thunder rumbled constantly but the sky was a brilliant blue that contained not a single cloud. The sky reminded her of Kit's eyes when he laughed or when he watched her with amusement. She loved the expression that would cross his face when something brought him joy, as though the emotion were unexpected, undeserved.

Carefully, she made her way through the brush, tying scraps of her petticoat to the limb of a bush here and a tree there so she could easily find her way back to the cave. The roaring of the thunder grew louder, incessantly rumbling through the heavens, echoing around her, surrounding her. Yet the brilliance of the day was remarkable.

She ducked beneath the low, thick branches of a tree and stilled. A brook flowed before her, the current rushing over rocks with a purpose. But it wasn't the brook that caught her attention or her imagination. It was the beauty of the waterfall that marked a new beginning as water from above cascaded down.

She released a sigh of wonder and walked toward what she'd originally thought was thunder. Incredible. It didn't contain the magnificence of the sea, but it was still breathtaking. She sat at the water's edge and wondered where the river above began and where the brook ended.

Closing her eyes, she listened to the songs of nature: the birds, the leaves rustling, and the wind whispering its secrets. Tranquility eased around her, through her. If she were to die here, she would die content.

"I'm not certain you were wise to leave a trail," a deep voice rumbled.

With a tiny screech, Ashton twisted around, pressing her hand above her pounding heart. Holding his rifle, Kit wove his way toward her, dropped to the ground, planted his elbows on his thighs, and buried his head in his hands with a groan.

"Are you in much pain?" she asked.

"My head feels as though a blacksmith is using it as an anvil."

"You should have stayed in the cave."

He lifted his head. "I was concerned when I awoke and you weren't there."

She held up the empty canteen. "I came to get some water."

She scooted to the brook's edge and leaned over carefully. She placed the canteen beneath the surface and concentrated on the gurgling of the water. Except for the bandage around his head, Kit looked the same to her today as he had yesterday. The words he'd mumbled about Clarisse had to be untrue.

Yet he despised talking about Clarisse. Was it memories of his unrequited love that haunted him, or guilt that he had played God?

She eased back and extended the canteen toward him. He gave a slight nod.

"You go first, but drink slowly. If you're as thirsty as I am, you'll make yourself ill if you swallow too much or drink too quickly."

She brought the canteen to her lips, savoring the cool water, studying the man who had married her. She considered all the things that he'd given her without ever asking for anything in return. Why would he murder the woman he loved?

She handed the canteen to him and watched his throat work as he took long, slow swallows. Sweat beaded along his neck. He stopped drinking and looked at her.

"This is a beautiful spot. All the greenery reminds me of Ravenleigh."

She gave him a tentative smile. "You spoke often last night. Most of it didn't make sense, but at one point you asked me how I enjoyed Ravenleigh as though you thought we were there."

"Obviously a bullet grazing a man's head can make him say nonsensical things," he said with a rueful smile.

"I suppose we should be grateful that it didn't stop you from talking completely. It could have killed you," she pointed out.

"Yes, I was most fortunate, although right now I feel as though I drank a case of whiskey with no help. Have you any idea where the stagecoach is located in relation to where we are?" he asked.

She shook her head. "I didn't leave a trail, but it took us a good hour to get to the cave."

He furrowed his brow. "How did we get there?"

"You were conscious for a while and able to walk as long as I held you upright."

"You held me upright?"

She nodded. "I used your rifle for support, so it wasn't too hard."

"Still, I'm impressed, Ashton. An hour's journey must have been difficult for you."

"I preferred it to the alternative of being discovered by those outlaws."

He glanced around. "I don't remember our journey. I don't remember anything that happened after I climbed to the roof. It's all a blur. What happened to the driver and the man inside the coach?"

She took a deep, shuddering breath and said in a low voice, "They were killed."

He released a heavy sigh. "I hope they had no family."

She swallowed, not certain if she should tell him what she knew, but she'd always believed knowledge was strength. That belief had made her read book after book. "Those outlaws seemed to recognize you."

He snapped his gaze to hers. "What?"

She nodded jerkily. "They knew you were the marshal of Fortune, and it was obvious that they don't like you."

He narrowed his eyes. "Were any names mentioned?"

"Jasper and Morton."

He clenched his jaw. "Bloody hell. Jasper was the man shooting up Harry's saloon. I'd planned to look over the wanted posters when I returned to my office, but I got distracted when I saw David."

"They didn't seem too happy that you'd killed two of their men."

"No, I don't imagine they were pleased. A pity I wasn't able to kill them all. They shall be even less pleased when I bring them to justice."

A tremor coursed through her. "You're not going after them?"

"Not at this moment, no. We'll spend a day here gathering our strength, and hopefully by tomorrow my wits will return and we can find a way to get back to Fortune."

"But I wanted to go to Dallas."

He touched her hand. Instinct made her jerk back. She saw the hurt flash briefly in his eyes before he retreated. She wished she hadn't rejected his offer of comfort, but she'd been unable to stop herself.

He wasn't a murderer. Her heart knew that, but the very thought of his killing Clarisse made her wary . . . and afraid. She treasured every moment of life and that he would deny someone the opportunity to do the same was incomprehensible to her.

"I'm sorry, Ashton, but there is a possibility that when these men don't find me here, they'll seek me out in Fortune. I can't risk their taking their revenge out on the innocent townspeople. I'm supposed to protect them."

"But we've been gone for a little over a month."

"The local merchants offered to enforce the law when needed, but they were not anticipating the arrival of a gang of outlaws."

She opened her mouth to speak and he held up a hand. "Perhaps they won't go to Fortune, but it is my responsibility to make sure that if they do, someone with experience is there to handle them."

She swallowed hard. "To kill them."

"If necessary, yes."

She held his gaze. "How many people have you killed?"

"I don't keep count," he answered briskly. "But if you have no desire to stay in Fortune until I'm reassured that all is well, then I shall find someone to escort you to Dallas."

Grabbing the rifle, he stood. He wavered and closed his eyes as though dizzy.

"Are you going back to the cave to rest?" she asked.

He opened his eyes, and she could see within them that he was still in a great deal of pain. "No, I'm going to find us something to eat. You should probably come with me."

She shook her head. "I'll follow my trail back to the cave."

She watched him disappear within the brush. If she stayed with him, as she'd so often considered, would a day come when her illness would force him to take her life?

Kit awoke to discover the cave once again empty. He silently cursed his wife. Did she not realize the danger that lurked in the area? True, they'd seen neither hide nor hair of Jasper and his men the previous day, but that did not mean they were not nearby.

He knew he had wounded Ashton during their last night in Galveston, and he missed the smiles she'd previously bestowed upon him. Last night, he'd held her while they'd slept, but she'd been as stiff as a poker. She spoke only if he asked a question.

He often caught her watching him as though he were a specimen beneath a glass. He could not expect her to act as though all was well when outlaws were searching for him, but her constant wandering off confounded him. Now was not the time for her to exert her desire for independence. She should have been hovering closer than his shadow. How could he protect her otherwise?

He removed the bandage from around his head and touched the tender place near his temple. He'd been incredibly lucky and well he knew it. His headache had abated and his vision had cleared. Now all he had to do was discover a way to get them back to Fortune.

He picked up the rifle and walked out of the cave. Ashton had again marked her trail. He had to give her credit for realizing she might get lost, but he would have preferred she not leave at all. When had the woman become so stubborn? Or perhaps, it was simply her melancholy. Maybe she didn't care that death could come to her in the form of a bullet. No doubt it was preferable to what she would endure at the end.

He followed the bits of her petticoat that she'd tied to branches. She'd gathered them up on her way back to the cave yesterday. He would have hidden them had he known she planned to use them again. He was not surprised by the direction of her path. She was headed toward the waterfall.

What did astonish him when he found her was that she was completely nude standing with her back to him.

His mouth went dry and the air backed up in his lungs as he watched the gently cascading water of the falls wash over her. She raised her arms, tilted her head back, and combed her fingers through her hair.

Never in his life had he wanted a woman more.

The temptation to remove his clothing and join her was almost impossible to resist. But resist he did because he didn't know if this time he would find the strength to hold back. He wanted desperately to fill her with all that he possessed, to experience the ultimate pleasure while his body was joined to hers. If only he knew she would stay with him beyond Christmas.

She must have felt his gaze boring into her, because she turned slowly. His gut clenched. She'd gained weight while they were in Galveston and soft curves graced her body. She stepped beyond the falls, grabbed her skirt, and began to use it to dry herself.

Kit set the rifle aside, unbuttoned his shirt, and shirked out of it. He set it on the ground. "Come sit here, and I'll dry you."

She hesitated before strolling over and gracefully lowering herself to the ground, her eyes watchful, never leaving his. He knelt beside her, took the skirt she was using to shield herself, and began using the hem to dry her foot.

She snatched the other end of the skirt and brought it up to her breast. Kit gave her a lazy smile as he tugged on the skirt. "Let me enjoy looking at you."

"I don't think it's wise."

"Nothing we've done has been wise, but I would not trade a single moment that I've had with you for a seat in heaven."

Ashton allowed the skirt to slip through her fingers. With her body carrying the drops of water from the falls, she should have been cold, but his touch, his presence, always made her feel incredibly warm. She wanted to run her fingers through his hair, wanted them to make love as a true husband and wife, without death's shadow spoiling what should be a glorious experience.

"I should think all you've done for the people of Fortune will guarantee you a place in heaven," she said.

He shook his head. "No, sweetling. My destination shall be hell." He moved closer and cupped her cheek with his palm. "I am already in hell. I desperately want to make love to you."

She felt the tears burn her eyes. "You make love *to* me, and I want you to make love *with* me. Teach me how to pleasure you, and I will, but I can't take what you offer any longer if I can't give something back."

"You've never taken, Ashton. I've given what I could because it pleased me to do so. Emotional pleasure is as gratifying as physical pleasure."

She looked at her hands "But it's not enough for me, and it's too much to ask of you. That's why I have to go back to Dallas."

He began drying her thigh. "I don't know if I can let you go."

She snapped up her head. "What?"

"You place too much value on the physical. I enjoy bringing you pleasure. I love your smiles and your laughter and the burned crabs you cook. I like waking up with you in my arms."

"When death hovers, will you like it then? Will you wait patiently for it or will you hasten its arrival, as you did with Clarisse?" She slapped her hand over her mouth, wishing she'd been able to stop the words before they were spoken, but they'd been running through her head all night and she'd awakened with them screaming in her mind.

She felt his fingers dig into her flesh as he narrowed his eyes into glittering slits of anger. "What are you talking about?"

She snatched her skirt from his hands and wrapped it around her body, shielding herself as much as she could. "Right after you were wounded, you woke up and thought I was Clarisse. You said you'd killed me and that I couldn't tell Christopher."

"Is that the reason you didn't want me to hold you last night, the reason you've been avoiding me?"

She licked her lips, tasting the lingering purity of the falls. She had so felt a need to be cleansed. "Did you kill her?" she dared to ask.

He sat back on his heels, his eyes hard, shuttering all emotion, hiding any thoughts. "What do you think?"

She felt a shiver slither along her spine. "I keep telling myself that you were delirious, that the bullet knocked something loose in your head, that you would never commit such a vile act as murdering an innocent woman, regardless of the circumstances. I keep telling myself those things."

"But you don't believe them."

Her entire body tensed at the lack of emotion in his voice. "I don't know what to believe."

"Yes, you do," he said with certainty.

She wanted to run but his gaze pinned her to the spot, and the words she uttered caused the bile to rise in her throat. "You did kill her."

"Yes, madam, I did. You married a murderer."

Chapter 19

Christopher walked out of Fortune's telegraph office not at all pleased with the latest bit of information he'd received. Could anything else go wrong?

"Marshal Montgomery!"

With a suppressed groan, Christopher recognized the termagant's voice. Calling upon every bit of gentlemanly resolve within his possession to hold his temper in check, he turned to face her.

Déjà vu slammed into him. She was again holding her daughter's arm and the young man's ear. Her daughter's face burned a bright red as she kept her gaze averted, but the young man didn't display any remorse.

"Madam—"

"He was doing it again. Unbuttoning my Lauren's bodice."

His patience wearing thin, he glared at the lad. "I told you—"

"I turned sixteen today, and you said I could have a look-see if she was willing to take money. I give her two bits."

Mrs. Fairfield's eyes narrowed with fury that was amazing to behold. "You told him he could unbutton my daughter's bodice if he paid her?"

"Not exactly. He misinterpreted my instructions," Christopher tried to explain.

"You worthless son-of-a-bitch!" she yelled as she thrust the lad toward him. "I want him in jail, and you along with him. I'm going to the town council."

He watched her march off, righteous indignation in every determined step. He shifted his gaze to the boy. "What's your name, lad?"

"Tommy."

"Where in God's name are your parents?"

"Dead."

Christopher sighed heavily. "Come with me."

"I ain't afraid of jail."

"I'm not taking you to jail." Christopher walked along the boardwalk, his steps not quite as soft as they had been a week ago. If he stayed here another week, he'd no doubt be sending his feet through the planks. He shoved open the door to the saloon.

"You gonna lie and tell 'em I'm old enough to drink?" Tommy asked, hope clearly reflected in his voice.

Christopher gave him a steely glare.

Tommy shrugged. "I reckon you ain't."

"Wyndhaven," Harrison said as he walked over. "What have you got here?"

"A lad with no parents and too much time on his hands. What can I do with him?"

Harrison looked the boy over. "Know anything about cattle, lad?"

"I know it all," Tommy said confidently.

"You don't know a bloody thing, you little liar," Harrison said, "but you will before the month is out."

"What are you going to do with him?" Christopher asked.

"Put him to work for the Texas Lady Cattle Venture. Let's go see Gray. We keep our cattle on his land."

Christopher looked at the two-story clapboard house and the land that surrounded it. It was a far cry from the magnificence of Ravenleigh, yet it held a charm he couldn't quite explain. "How much land do you have?" he asked Grayson Rhodes.

"As far as you can see."

He smiled with genuine gladness for Rhodes's success. "Your father is extremely proud, you know."

"Surprised is probably more like it."

Christopher turned to his brother's friend. "You'd think differently if you heard the way your father bandies your name about the gentlemen's clubs."

He was astonished to see Rhodes blush.

"Come around to the back of the house. I want you to meet Abbie," Grayson said.

With Harrison at his side, Christopher followed Grayson. A man named Magpie had taken Tommy off to introduce him to the cattle. Both Grayson and Harrison seemed to think Magpie would do right by the lad and teach him what he needed to know.

They rounded the corner and Christopher stumbled to a stop, shocked to see the termagant pacing back and forth in front of a woman with blond hair and violet eyes. Upon closer inspection, he realized they looked very much alike.

"That man is a disgrace to this town," Mrs. Fairfield said. "Telling that boy he could pay to look at a woman's body. I don't know what possessed the townspeople to make him marshal, but I dadgum guarantee that I'm going to see him run out on a rail—"

"Madam!" Christopher snapped sternly.

The woman spun around. "You lowdown skunk—"

"I take it you've met Elizabeth," Grayson said quietly, humor laced in his voice.

"Unfortunately."

She took a step toward him. "Unfortunately? I'm about to show you exactly how unfortunate you are. I told you to lock that boy away—"

"I might have if I'd had keys to the jail or if I *were* the marshal and had the authority to do so. As I've tried to tell you repeatedly whenever I could nudge a word in between your blathering, I am not Kit! I am his brother. Thank God. The very thought that he might chance running into you every time he stepped on the street is enough to make me wonder why he ever bothered to take up the position of marshal and risk his life for ungrateful wenches such as yourself. Now, if you'll excuse me, I must return to town." He turned to Grayson and gave a curt nod. "Thank you for your help with the lad."

As he walked away, he heard Harrison mumble behind him, "Since it's my carriage, I'd best go with you."

* * *

Christopher carried the spoon of soup to the thin line of his father's lips. He sighed. "Father, I know you can open your mouth because I hear you cursing me through the night when you think I'm asleep."

A knock sounded at the door.

"Not now, Mrs. Gurney!" he yelled. The woman was the only one to know that his father was here. She came in every day to straighten the room and change the sheets on the two beds.

The knock came again.

"Please come back later!"

Another knock.

"Bloody hell." He tossed the spoon into the bowl, sending soup splattering over the dresser. He resisted the incredibly strong urge to dump the bowl over his father's head.

He rose, stalked across the room, and flung open the door. "Mrs. Gurney—"

He stopped as he stared into Elizabeth Fairfield's blue eyes.

"Mr. Montgomery—"

He held up a hand. "Mrs. Fairfield, I apologize profusely for my earlier words. They were totally uncalled for and quite unlike me, actually. You disparaged my brother, and I took offense because I feel you've misjudged him. But those feelings aside, I did not act as a gentleman, and I beg your forgiveness. Now, if you'll excuse me, I'll bid you good day."

He started to close the door, and she placed her hand on it.

"I'm the one who should apologize," she said softly.

He forced himself to smile benignly. "I assure you, Mrs. Fairfield, no apology is necessary."

He closed the door another inch before she stopped him.

"Mr. Montgomery—"

"Mrs. Fairfield, now is not a good time. My patience is frayed. My father will not open his mouth to eat, even though he slings curses at me all night. My brother left Galveston several days ago to take his wife to Dallas. The stagecoach was apparently attacked by a band of outlaws. Three men were killed. There is no sign of my brother or his wife, so God only knows where they are. I've hired men to search for them, praying every moment that they are not dead. People continue to confuse me with Kit and ask me to handle matters over which I not only have no authority but I have no knowledge. The heat is unbearable. There are no theaters to offer an evening's respite from the worries—"

"Come have dinner at my house."

He knew his mouth was agape and that he must look like a bloody fool. "I beg your pardon?"

"When your brother and his friends first arrived, I scolded Abbie for not giving them a proper Texas welcome, and here, I've done the same thing with you that my sister did. I'd like to make amends. I've got no theater to offer you, but I have a piano and my girls can sing."

Sadly, he shook his head and spoke in a low voice. "My father has suffered a stroke. I promised him I would not let anyone know he was here save Mrs. Gurney, and here I've blurted out his presence to you.

I hope you will keep my lapse of judgment to yourself."

"I won't tell anyone he's here."

"Thank you. However, since you do know of his condition, you must realize I cannot accept your invitation. I dare not leave him."

She gave him a beautiful smile. "Mrs. Gurney can watch him. Besides, you'll probably both benefit from an evening apart." She handed him a slip of paper. "I took the liberty of drawing you up a map. I serve dinner at six. Be there."

She began to walk away.

"I can't promise."

She glanced over her shoulder. "Didn't ask for your promise, only your presence."

He closed the door and looked at the map. What a splendid calling card.

With a sigh of wonder and a stomach fuller than he'd ever known, Christopher sat in the rocking chair on Elizabeth Fairfield's front porch and watched the sun hover at the edge of the horizon, painting the sky in brilliant hues of orange and violet and pink. How could he have been here a week and failed to notice the sunset?

Beside him, Elizabeth sat in a rocker and her three daughters—mirror images of their mother—sat on the front steps. Elizabeth's house was not grand, but it filled him with peace. He thought of the contentment reflected on both Harrison's and Grayson's faces. Would he see the same on Kit's?

And if he did, what then? Should he reveal the truth he'd discovered?

"I love watching the sunset," Elizabeth said softly. "Daniel and I never had much money for fancy things. He used to say that was the reason God gave us sunsets so we could always have something pretty in our lives that didn't cost us anything."

"Was Daniel your husband?"

She nodded and slid her gaze toward him, sadness in her eyes. "He was killed during the War Between the States."

"I'm incredibly sorry," he said quietly.

"I might not have minded so much if we'd won the war." She released a small chuckle. "Nah, I still would have minded. Loved him something fierce." She returned her attention to the horizon. "Grayson said you're a widower."

"Yes, my wife took ill and died shortly before Kit and his friends ventured over here."

She glanced at him. "Do you still miss her?"

He gave her a sorrowful smile. "Every day."

She nodded as though with understanding. "I keep staring down that road expecting to see Daniel walking up it some evening. My head knows he won't, but my heart hopes."

"It must be hard on a woman who is alone," he said.

"Don't imagine it's any harder on a woman than it is on a man."

"But there are times when a woman would require a man's physical strength to get a job accomplished."

She peered at him with a glint in her eye. "And there are times when a man requires a woman's compassion to see him through the turmoil of life."

"You're quite right. I think I miss most having someone with whom I may share my troubles."

"Have you got a lot of troubles?"

He shook his head slightly. "Not really. Others are far worse off than I am."

A companionable silence surrounded them as the final rays of the sun disappeared over the horizon.

"Girls, you need to say goodnight to Mr. Montgomery before you get yourselves to bed," Elizabeth said as the darkness moved in.

He considered correcting her on exactly how he should be addressed, but decided it was of no importance here. The girls, ages fourteen, twelve, and ten, gave him a shy goodnight before hurrying into the house.

"I'm just going to tuck them in," Elizabeth said, "then I'll be back out."

He sat on the porch alone, knowing he should leave soon, but loathing the idea of returning to the room he shared with his father. When he wasn't cursing, the man snored. Christopher had always known that burdens came with being the heir apparent. He'd simply never realized how difficult they would be to carry.

A shadow crossing the threshold caught his eye. He glanced up and smiled at Elizabeth. "I should be leaving."

"Stay a little longer," she said quietly. "I haven't had a man sit on my front porch in a long time. I've missed it."

"Have you always lived here?" he asked.

"Not in this house, but in this area. I was born in a house just up the road. My brother lives there now with his family. This house, this land, belonged to Daniel's family."

"It's beautiful." Hot, but beautiful. He could sense her watching him as the night shadows crept closer. He turned his head slightly and raised a brow, although he doubted she could see the slight action.

"You sure do look like him, but you don't flirt like him," she said quietly.

"Ah," he said on a sigh. "I assume you're referring to my brother. As heir to my father's estate, I am expected to behave with a bit more decorum, which makes me a tad boring."

"I don't think you're boring."

He resisted the temptation to reach across and touch her hand. "Thank you."

She laughed lightly. "You don't thank someone for speaking the truth."

Averting his gaze, he shifted in his chair and looked at the stars. "I've missed Kit terribly."

"You're close then?"

Christopher was amused by the surprise in her voice. "Extremely. When we were lads, we made a pact that even though I was the rightful heir, we would manage Ravenleigh together."

"He's probably changed considerably from what you remember since he's been here."

He chuckled low. "Undoubtedly, yet I know that the moment I see him, it will be as though we visited yesterday."

The night unfolded before them, the conversation enlightening. She told him about her marriage, Texas, cotton farming. And he explained what he could of his life. But he relished most the moments of silence for he never had the feeling that they needed to be filled. They simply existed, to be enjoyed.

He watched the blackened sky turn a dark gray, pastel shades of blue weaving their way through to create an incredible tapestry. "What's happening there?" he asked.

She laughed lightly. "That's the dawn. Don't tell me you've never seen the dawn."

"The dawn?" He shot out of the rocker. "I've been here all night?"

"That's all right. I enjoyed the company."

"But your reputation!"

"I'm a widow. I've got no reputation to worry about."

"Still, a gentleman would have left long ago." He backed up and stumbled down the steps. "I apologize profusely—"

"If you apologize profusely to me one more time, I'm gonna knock you upside the head with my cast-iron skillet."

He stared at her, then began to laugh. "By God, you would, wouldn't you?"

She rose from the chair, walked to the edge of the porch, and wrapped her arms around the beam. "Yep. No two ways about it."

Briefly, he considered stepping back onto the porch and kissing her. "Elizabeth, thank you for inviting me over. It has been a very long time since I've enjoyed the sum of an evening so much."

She smiled softly. "I'll be cooking supper again tonight. You're welcome to join us."

He'd never before regretted with such magnitude the words he knew he needed to speak. "I think it would be best if I didn't. You see, I'm betrothed."

"Do you love her?"

Her frank question caught him off-guard. If he hadn't grown fond of her through the night, he would have told her the answer was none of her concern. "No, but our marriage will help strengthen both families."

"Doesn't sound like you'll be doing much sitting on the porch watching the sunset."

"Ravenleigh has no porch."

"Reckon that's for the best."

"Perhaps. Regardless, I thank you for a wonderful evening, night, and dawn. I shall remember them always."

"Just a little Texas hospitality."

He gave a curt nod before walking toward the buggy he'd hired. Duty called, and it was a harsh taskmaster.

Chapter 20

Kit scrounged through the wreckage of the overturned stagecoach. Finding it had not been as difficult as he'd feared. Although Ashton had taken care in covering their tracks as she'd managed their escape, she'd also noted landmarks along the way.

She was truly remarkable.

And obviously disgusted by his confession.

He'd considered denying the truth, blaming his words on a confused mind, but she deserved his honesty. He'd hoped for absolution, but he was not surprised by the revulsion reflected in her lovely eyes. His image in the mirror often carried the same expression.

In truth, the confession was a blessing because the temptation to break his personal vow had never been greater than it was yesterday morning. He'd wanted to lay her down on the sweet green earth and bury himself so deeply within her that they would never again be separate.

Now, his vow would never again be tested. Once they made their way back to Fortune, she would return to Dallas and the wait for death while he had already returned to hell.

"Where are the driver and the man who was inside the stagecoach with us? They were killed, but I didn't have time to bury them," she said in a dazed voice as she gazed around.

His first thought was that animals had probably carted the corpses away, but he had no heart to tell her that. "Many of our personal effects are missing. Someone has been here. They no doubt gave them a decent burial."

"What are we going to do?"

"Walk, I suppose. If we head back in the direction whence we came, we should come to that last small town where the driver stopped to change horses. If there's no stagecoach going to Fortune, we should be able to rent a carriage."

"I can get passage there for a stagecoach going to Dallas."

He narrowed his eyes. "You could, but I'll not have you traveling alone."

She angled her chin defiantly. "I'm a grown woman."

"You are also my wife, and I shall not leave you unprotected."

"I could send a telegram to David—"

"The passage of time has no doubt brought him a child by now. Besides, it defeats my purpose in not taking you to Dallas right away, if I have to wait for David's arrival."

She began to pace in agitation, her hands balled into fists at her side. "You don't have to wait—"

"Ashton, regardless of the low depths to which your opinion of me has plunged, I am not going to take your life. You are safe with me."

She spun around, tears welling within her eyes. "*Why* did you kill Clarisse?"

"Because I could not bear to watch her suffer."

"Who gave you the right?"

"*I* gave it to myself. I alone carry the burden of the decision."

She studied him as though she wanted to see into his sordid soul. "How did you kill her?"

He rolled his eyes toward the heavens. "What possible difference can that knowledge make toward what you now feel for me?"

"I just want to know." Her voice carried a slight quiver.

He sighed deeply, fisted his hands into tight balls, and glared at the leaves in the trees. "She was in pain. She asked for something to relieve it. A pinch of powder, the physician instructed me. I used an abundance." He returned his gaze to hers, afraid she'd recoil if he reached out to touch the deep furrows within her brow. "She wanted the pain to end. It was the one wish I could grant her."

"The one wish you could grant her," she rasped, horror reflected in her gaze. "The night you proposed you told me that you'd been able to grant her only one wish. That was *it*? Death?"

Anger surged through him at his own inadequacies. "Do you not think that I wish that I could have granted her something else? But of the many things she wanted, death was all that remained within my power to give her."

"I thought love made you send flowers to her grave every day. But it's guilt, isn't it?" she asked.

"It's impossible to separate one from the other when you murder the object of your affection."

She stared at him as though he'd grown horns and a tail. No doubt he would, once death held him within its grip and he truly plunged into hell.

"If you had it to do over," she asked hesitantly, "would you kill her?"

"Yes."

She simply nodded as though she'd expected his answer, but was still disappointed by it. "I suppose we need to begin our final journey together," she said.

He was about to agree when he heard a low neigh. He spun around as his horse plodded toward him. "Lancelot, you beautiful beast. I've never been more glad to see you!"

Reaching out, he rubbed the horse's neck, welcoming the contact, warmth, and absence of rejection. At least the beast could not understand the gravity of his master's actions. Kit wasn't certain he could accept any more condemnation. The sooner they began the journey, the more quickly he could see his wife safely returned to her brother.

Unfortunately whoever had visited the overturned stagecoach had taken his saddle. With reluctance, he turned to Ashton. "Come on."

She cautiously approached.

"It'll be just like when we rode him bareback along the shore," he assured her.

But as he placed his hands on her waist and felt her stiffen, he knew it would be nothing at all like it. Before, she had relished his touch. Now she loathed it.

Last night in the cave, they had slept closely together but never touched. Not once.

He swung her onto the horse's back. "Hold onto his mane," he ordered.

He grabbed what remained of the rope that had held the animal tethered to the stagecoach. He was grateful that he had shot the rope so it was short enough not to get tangled in the brush. He would have hated knowing Lancelot had perished because of his actions. He began to walk along the side of the road.

"Aren't you going to ride with me?" Ashton asked.

"No, I doubt the horse has had proper nourishment since our encounter with the outlaws. He's too weak to carry us both." He was certain some truth resided within the lie, but the absolute truth resided within his heart. He could not tolerate being near her knowing that she not only despised his touch but hated him for being the man he was.

"We'll stay here for the night," Kit said as he brought the horse to a halt.

Ashton glanced around the clearing. "Shouldn't we have reached that small town by now?"

Looking up at her, he held her gaze. "I've decided to avoid towns until we reach Fortune."

Irrational fear gripped her. "I'm not going to tell anyone you killed Clarisse."

Disappointment mingled with sadness filled his eyes. "That was not the reason behind my decision. I know it will make for a more arduous journey, but I have concerns regarding Jasper. Although he isn't a bright fellow, if he thinks I'm still alive, he may have his men stationed along the route. If he thinks I'm dead, then he may be off planning his next stagecoach robbery. Or he may at this very moment be riding into Fortune. But since I don't know exactly where he is, I prefer to ensure that if we do meet, it will be on my terms." He held up his arms. "Come along. Let me help you dismount."

When she voiced no objection, he slipped his hands onto her waist and lifted her from the horse, setting her on the ground with only a hair's breadth separating them. "You may announce my sin to the world and it will make no difference. I won't be held accountable here for a murder I committed in England."

"Your reputation would be ruined."

"My reputation has never been anything I valued, and I can walk away from Fortune without a backward glance."

She stepped out of his embrace and wrapped her arms around herself. She watched as he saw to his horse's needs. "Will you build a fire?" she asked.

"A small one, if you're cold."

She shrugged. "It's the middle of summer. I doubt I'll get cold."

"But now you fear things in the dark that you've never feared before," he said in a low voice.

"Are you deliberately trying to frighten me?"

"No need to try. I seem to have succeeded."

"I'm not afraid of you," she said firmly.

He stepped toward her, and she stepped back.

"Aren't you?" he asked quietly.

"Right now, I don't know what I feel or what I think," she snapped.

"At least you're honest. Do you want a fire?"

"Do you think it'll attract attention?"

"Probably."

She took a shuddering breath. "I can go without one, then."

"I have nothing for you to lie on but my shirt." He began unfastening the buttons.

"You don't have to give me your shirt."

"You are still my wife, and therefore your comfort is my responsibility." He pulled the shirt over his head and extended it toward her. "You can at least use it as a pillow."

They had stopped to eat late in the afternoon when a fire wouldn't be visible. For the first time in her life, she hated the night. She took his offering, dropped to the ground, rolled Kit's shirt into a tight ball, and tucked it beneath her head. His masculine scent surrounded her.

He sat nearby, the rifle across his lap.

"Aren't you going to sleep?" she asked.

"I'll stand watch for a while."

She studied the silhouette of the man she thought she'd loved. She remembered writing in her journal long ago that she would gladly allow him to break her heart. How was she to have known then the pain that action would cause?

"Did she know?" she asked quietly.

"Did who know what?" he asked.

"Did Clarisse know you were killing her?"

Silence, thick and heavy, filled the distance between them.

"No," he finally shot out. "She knew only that she was weary and drifting off to sleep."

"So you gave her no opportunity to say goodbye to everyone."

"Christopher said goodbye to her each time he left her room. She said goodbye to me thinking I was he so she had her final farewell."

"But she didn't give it to the man upon whom she wanted to bestow it."

"I am certain that Christopher and Clarisse had ample opportunity to share their feelings. I denied her nothing."

"Except life."

Suddenly, she was cold and wished she had asked for a fire. "What about your mother?"

"What of her?"

She heard the impatience in his voice. "Did you kill her as well?"

He barked out his laughter. "Dear God, Ashton, are you to suspect me now as the murderer of everyone who dies of an illness?"

She sat up, trying to sort out her feelings. "You told me that you held Clarisse as she died. You were reading to your mother when she passed away. It's a logical assumption that you might have taken her life as well."

He sighed heavily. "My mother was not in agony. I did not hasten her death."

She felt relief and a bit of the warmth returned.

"You should sleep. We'll leave before dawn. Tomorrow will be a long day," he said.

She settled back into place. "Kit?"

"For God's sakes, Ashton, I may as well have built a fire. Your incessant babbling will notify anyone within hearing distance that we're here."

"I just wanted to say that I'm not afraid of you."

"Perhaps 'disgusted' is a better word," he said caustically. "Or how about 'disappointed,' 'disillusioned,' repulsed?' "

She buried her face in his shirt, allowing the silent tears to fall, wishing she could understand not only him, but her own feelings as well.

"Marshal! Land's sakes alive, we thought you were dead," Mrs. Gurney said as Kit escorted Ashton into the boardinghouse.

Kit had never in his life felt so exhausted. Avoiding towns and traveling straight to Fortune had made for some uncomfortable nights, but he didn't want Jasper and his comrades to get word that he was still alive until he'd reached Fortune.

They'd arrived in Fortune just after nightfall. He'd taken his horse to the hostler so the man could see after the beast and stable him properly. Now all he wanted was to get Ashton settled. "Only weary, Mrs. Gurney. We'll need a room for the night."

" 'Course, you need a room. Can't have you and your bride sleeping on that old cot in the jail. Mrs. Montgomery, the room you had before is still available if you want it."

"That would be lovely, Mrs. Gurney. Thank you."

"You both look like you need a hot meal and a hot bath. I'll get both started as soon as I let your brother know you're here. He's been worried sick."

"David's here?" Ashton asked, and Kit heard the profound relief in her voice.

"No, ma'am, not your brother. The marshal's."

Kit felt as though a punch had been delivered to his midsection. "My brother? You mean Christopher?"

"Yep. He had half the state searching for you."

Kit watched her tromp across the front room.

"You weren't expecting a visit from your brother?" Ashton asked quietly.

Still stunned, he answered as though from far away. "No." Then a horrible thought struck him. He spun around and captured Ashton's gaze. "He knows nothing of what I did regarding Clarisse. I beg you, please, don't tell him."

"I didn't think you cared about your reputation," she said.

"I don't, but I do have a regard for his feelings. He allowed me to see her. I don't want guilt sitting on his shoulder because of my actions."

Ashton hesitated before nodding mutely. Relief swamped him at the same moment that the door to a corner room opened, and Christopher strode through it. Mrs. Gurney skittered out of his way and headed toward the kitchen.

"Good God, man, you look like you've been to hell and back," Christopher said as he took Kit's hand and pulled him into his embrace. "I feared the worst."

Kit heard the strangled emotions in his brother's

voice. "Only the good die young, Christopher. I shall long outlive you."

Laughing, Christopher stepped back. "Typical of you to make everything seem as though it were nothing. I received reports that you'd been attacked by outlaws."

"Yes, but fortunately for me, they did not count on my wife being incredibly resourceful or courageous." Kit turned slightly. "I'd like you to meet Ashton."

"Bainbridge told me you had married," Christopher said quietly. His gaze never leaving hers, Christopher took Ashton's hand, bowed slightly, and brought her fingers to his lips. "So you are the woman who captured my brother's heart?"

Grateful for her silence, Kit watched Ashton lower her lashes, her cheeks flaming red. Although he no longer held her heart, she still held his. She would until the day he died.

"We have much that we need to discuss," Kit said.

"Indeed, we do," Christopher said. "Why don't you take time to enjoy some of Mrs. Gurney's fine cooking and freshen up a bit before you see Father?"

Kit could not have been more shocked if Christopher had pounded a sledgehammer into him. "Father's here?"

"Yes, but unfortunately his health is poor, and I'd rather he not see you looking quite so unkempt. I've told him nothing beyond the fact that you had married and taken your bride on a wedding trip."

Kit's thoughts were as scattered as they'd been when the bullet had grazed his temple. He'd not planned for this turn of events, had never expected his father to venture to Fortune. "I'll have to see if I can get the mercantile owner to open the store. We have nothing but the clothes upon our backs."

"You can wear my clothes, of course, but I fear I have nothing suitable for your wife," Christopher remarked dryly.

"In case you haven't notice, Christopher, I've filled out a bit more than you have since I left England. I seriously doubt your clothes would fit or that anyone would confuse us with each other."

"You'd be surprised," Christopher said, smiling.

In an effort to save time, Kit had bathed at the jail while Ashton had readied herself at the boardinghouse. Now he stood outside her room, not certain what to expect from her, knowing that whatever it was, it was well deserved.

He tapped lightly on her door. She opened it and peered out.

"Are you ready?" he asked.

She opened the door farther. "I like Christopher, but I don't see the point in meeting your father."

"I feared as much. May I come in for a moment?"

She stepped back, and he walked into the room. The scent of oleander permeated the air. It pleased him to know she had used the soap he'd bought her. It was one of the few things she'd managed to salvage before their escape, before she knew her husband's sin.

He heard the door click closed and was grateful this conversation would be held in private. As much as he cared for Mrs. Gurney, she heard too much and repeated too loudly.

He turned to face his wife. "My father and brother have traveled a great distance to be here."

She crossed the room and sat in the rocker. "But they didn't come to see me. They didn't even know you were married when they began the journey. Christopher said he needed to speak with you. I don't see why I need to be present, especially since I plan to get on a stagecoach in the morning and go back to Dallas."

He clenched his fists at his sides and damned his English pride. "Ashton, I realize that you find me abhorrent—"

She stood and presented her back to him. "I'm not sure how I feel about you right now."

He fought against taking a step toward her. "I've never asked anything of you, but I'm asking now. Please, allow me to introduce you to my father. Pretend for a few days that all is well with our marriage so he may return to England free of any guilt he's harboring for having sent me here."

She spun around. "You think that's the reason he's here? To ease his guilt?"

"It's the only logical explanation I can envision."

"Guilt seems to run rampant in your family."

The truth of her words cut deeply. "As soon as my family leaves, I will make arrangements for someone to escort you to Dallas. After that, you'll not hear from me again." He gave her a sad smile. "Although I will keep my promise to place a white rose upon your grave."

"I no longer want the white rose."

Another slash to his heart. He tilted his head slightly. "As you wish. *Whatever* you wish I will grant, if you will but pretend for whatever time they are here that we are happily wedded."

She crossed her arms beneath her breasts. "I'm not much good at pretending."

"You don't have to be. Smile occasionally and stand by my side. That's all I'm asking."

"How long are they going to be here?"

"I haven't a clue, but I can't imagine that it will be long. They have responsibilities at Ravenleigh that require their presence."

He watched the doubts and wariness flicker over her face. She gave a brusque nod. "I'll give you tonight and tomorrow. After that I leave for Dallas. You can tell them that I have to help Madeline with the new baby."

Her answer was not all that he'd hoped for, but it was more than he'd expected. "Thank you. I shall see that you don't regret this kindness."

He opened the door. She took a deep breath before walking across the room and stopping beside him. "I'd rather you not touch me."

"Sweetling, I figured that much out a few days ago."

Her gaze swept over his face, and she furrowed her brow. "Is that the reason you walked while I rode the horse?"

"Yes. Believe it or not, Ashton, I only wished to give you your dream."

"Instead you gave me a nightmare."

"Apparently, I've managed to give us both one."

Chapter 21

Kit knocked briskly on the door to the room where Christopher and his father were staying. Christopher opened it, gave them a tenuous smile, and stepped back, allowing him to enter. Kit's gaze immediately went to his father, sitting in a chair by the window. He looked incredibly old. Even after Christopher had warned him that his health was not good, Kit had not expected his father to look so old.

It was obvious that his father could not rise and that his physical limitations infuriated him. His father had always expected as much of himself as he did of others. Kit walked across the room, knelt before his father, and smiled warmly. "Hello, Father. Missed me, did you?"

His father scoffed, but Kit was aware that his gaze never faltered as he searched his face. "Didn't expect it . . . to be . . . so boring . . . with no scandals brewing." He lifted a shaking hand. Kit took it and brought it to his face. A ghost of a smile played at his father's mouth. "You've done well . . . for yourself . . . here."

"I like to think so," Kit admitted.

"Your mother . . . would be proud."

Kit had no doubts that his mother would be. The hell of it was that for the first time in his life, he realized that he wanted his father to be proud as well.

"Content?" his father asked.

"Yes." Or at least he had been until a few days ago, and he saw no need to raise doubts in his father's mind.

With a look of satisfaction, his father shifted his gaze momentarily to Christopher. "Told you."

Christopher sighed. "So you did. Repeatedly."

Kit placed his father's hand back on his lap and unfolded his body. "I'd like you to meet my wife." He glanced over his shoulder and held out his hand, too late realizing his error. He shoved his hand into his trousers pocket. "Ashton?"

She hesitated before taking a few steps nearer. She offered his father a tremulous smile. "It's a pleasure to meet you."

His father nodded, his eyes narrowing. "Mmm." He looked at Kit. "Interesting."

Kit wasn't certain what to make of that comment. His father had always been too discerning, and he feared the old man might not be as sharp as he once was, but neither was he easily fooled. Kit cleared his throat. "Ashton, why don't you sit in that chair there?"

She sat in the plush chair across from his father. Kit sat on the arm of the chair while Christopher took a seat near their father. Ashton clutched her hands in her lap. Kit desperately wanted to take her hand, to find some comfort in her touch, but he refrained because to give in to his needs would only draw attention to the fact that Mrs. Montgomery had no desire whatsoever to have any portion of her husband's body touch hers.

He had no inclination for either his father or Christopher to see Ashton rebuff him. Perhaps insisting that she come had been a mistake.

Along with a thickening silence, an air of foreboding permeated the room. He hated seeing the deterioration of his father's health, but he was beginning to sense that his father's illness was not the reason his brother had made this journey.

Christopher cleared his throat. "Kit, we need to discuss some matters, but preferably in private."

"I have no secrets from Ashton." Although he desperately wished that he had managed to keep his sins from her.

"You may feel otherwise, once you hear what I have to say."

Kit glared at his brother. "By God, you'd better not tell me that you've lost Ravenleigh."

"No, at least not in the manner you think. Your letters, your advice, and the money you've sent have all served Ravenleigh well."

Kit felt Ashton's gaze come to rest on him. He supposed he should have mentioned that he kept close tabs on all that happened at Ravenleigh, had even at times provided funds if Christopher indicated a need or wanted to expand the family holdings in a way their father might not readily approve.

"Then for God's sake, will you reveal this deep,

dark secret so we can get on with the evening?" he demanded.

Christopher cast a quick glance at their father before turning his attention back to Kit, clasped his hands together, and leaned forward in his chair. "When Father had his first stroke, I assumed complete responsibility for Ravenleigh, which meant I was privy to all the ledgers, drawers, nooks, and crannies in his office. There, I discovered his private journal."

Kit watched his brother retrieve a black book from the table beside his chair and extend it toward him. Kit shook his head. "I have no desire to impose on Father's privacy."

"A pity I did not share your respect for his most intimate thoughts." Christopher turned the book over and carefully stroked the tooled leather. "Father wrote about the night we were born."

Kit shrugged. "I see nothing uncommon in that. As a matter of fact, I should hope the event was monumental enough to deserve mention within his journal."

"You are right, brother. The birth of the heir was cause for jubilation." Christopher smiled sadly. "The first born son was to bear all the burdens that came with the rank and privilege. All the burdens. Including being marked as the first born, once it was discovered that another child was making his entry into the world."

Kit's stomach tightened into a knot, and subconsciously he rubbed his thumb over the shiny scar just below his chin. "I'm not quite certain what you're implying."

Christopher stood and tossed the book into Kit's lap. "Father did not place the flaming red poker against the flesh of his second born son, as legend maintains. He placed it against that of his first born."

Kit shook his head, refusing to believe the implication of his brother's words. "You're not making sense."

"You are the heir apparent. You are the first born. You are the true Viscount Wyndhaven. You are to be the next Earl of Ravenleigh."

Kit lunged to his feet and threw the book onto the chair his brother had just vacated. "You're out of your mind. You've somehow managed to misinterpret what Father wrote."

"I've read it a dozen times, the words emblazoned in my memory. They are clear, precise, and exact. Father has your penchant for detail. Read his journal. Every word I've just spoken is written in his neat, perfect script. I had planned to send word for you to return to England immediately, but when Father seemed to recover, I thought it expedient to bring him here. Unfortunately, he suffered another stroke on the ship. The physician says a third will undoubtedly be his last. I thought you should know while he was still able to verify the truth that Ravenleigh will go to you."

With his heart thundering, Kit walked across the room and knelt before his father. "Why? If what Christopher says is true, why did you deny me my birthright?"

He watched his father swallow and saw his mouth quivering as he stared into the darkness beyond the window. "Because . . . you were weak, mewling like a kitten. I had already branded you when Christopher was born with the lungs of a lion. You were small and spindly. He was robust. I chose the stronger son because Ravenleigh needs a firm hand."

Confusion surrounded Kit. "But there would have been witnesses."

"Only the physician," Christopher explained. "Father paid him a great deal of money to hold his tongue. Mother was in too much pain to notice anything amiss."

"He chose you," Kit said speculatively.

"Apparently so. But now that we know the truth, you shall return to Ravenleigh and take up the mantle you should have worn all along."

"Is that what you want, Father?" Kit asked.

His father held his silence.

"That's what I thought," Kit said quietly.

"What Father wants is not the issue. What is of importance is that we make right a wrong that was committed when we were born. Father has made arrangements for the heir to marry at Christmas—"

"To hell with his arrangements. I have a wife." Kit uncoiled a body that had never known such tenseness.

"For how long? Bainbridge explained why you married Ashton," Christopher said.

"Did he also tell you that I've fallen in love with her?"

"No, unfortunately, I sensed that bit of information on my own, but it does not change the facts." Christopher picked up his father's journal and extended it toward Kit. "Don't turn aside your heritage without giving the circumstances a great deal of thought. You have always placed Ravenleigh first. You cannot tell me that in your heart of hearts you never wanted to be its heir."

Christopher stepped forward until they stood toe to toe. "Remember, brother, I know your thoughts as well as I know my own."

Dressed in the nightgown Kit had purchased from the mercantile, Ashton sat on the bed with her feet tucked beneath her. She studied Kit as he stood beside the window, staring out, one arm raised, his hand pressed to the wall, the other hand holding his father's journal. He didn't seem to notice the night breeze fluttering the curtains around him.

For a while, within the room with his family, she had ceased to exist, forgotten in the corner. It was a role she had played most of her life—present, but not seen.

Tonight she had played it to perfection, giving herself the opportunity to study three men whose lives were interwoven like flawed bits of cloth. She had little doubt that love existed among them all, but there were also deception and lies, things her family had never engaged in.

She knew Christopher had not meant to hurt her when he'd made reference to Kit's reason for marrying her. He'd simply wanted to point out that Kit was young enough to become a widower, marry another woman, and provide an heir for Ravenleigh. Several heirs, as a matter of fact.

Her worry that he would spend the remainder of his life alone no longer held merit, for a marriage would be arranged for him, had already been arranged for the heir. Obligation to Ravenleigh would force him to have what she wanted for him: a family.

Strange, how she was unable to stop herself from caring for him, even though she knew he had taken an innocent life.

Stranger still was to hear him voice his love of her aloud to his brother, to know his feelings toward her had not altered, even though she had been cold and distant on the journey back to Fortune. She had refused to sleep beside him, had spoken to him only when circumstances forced her to. She wondered if Christopher would still insist that Kit should take his place as the rightful heir if he knew that Kit had murdered Clarisse.

"I suppose Christopher's revelations tonight came as quite a surprise," she said quietly.

"You have a gift for understatement, sweetling."

"You never suspected—"

"No."

She wanted him to face her so she could look into his eyes and know exactly what he was feeling. Her head told her not to care, but she couldn't prevent her heart from aching for him and all the torment he must be enduring. His father's deception was crueler than the scar he'd given his son.

"You told me once that you had only regretted not

being the heir apparent the day that Christopher married," she said softly.

"I lied." He gazed at the book clutched in his hand. "I didn't realize I'd lied or that all these years I'd hidden the truth from myself. I only knew that I loved Ravenleigh and put its welfare above all else."

"And now you'll have it along with another wife."

"I don't want a wife." He glanced over his shoulder. "Unless she can be you. And you no longer want a husband if he can only be me." He swung his leg over the window casing. "Goodnight, Ashton. Sleep well."

She sat up straighter. "You're leaving?"

"I'll return in the morning. Per our previous understanding, while Father and Christopher are here, I'd like to keep up the pretense that we are happily wed."

The sadness reflected in his voice brought tears to her eyes. Then he was gone.

And she found herself wishing that he'd stayed.

Kit walked into the saloon, amazed by the familiarity that hit him. He'd never expected to give a damn about this state that he was certain had been built three feet above hell.

"Kit! Thank God you're back."

He turned and smiled at Harrison Bainbridge as he made his way awkwardly toward him. "So you aren't one of the people who confused Christopher with me," Kit said, forcing a lightness into his voice that he did not feel.

Harrison staggered to a stop. "Good God, no. Christopher carries himself like a real nobleman. You, on the other hand, look to be an arrogant yet disreputable nobleman."

"I appreciate the compliment."

"It wasn't a compliment, you bloody idiot."

Kit's smile grew along with a tightening in his chest. "I never thought I'd say these words, but it's good to be back."

"It's even better to have you back. Christopher feared you were dead."

"So I heard, and so I almost was."

Harrison narrowed his eyes as though he detected something was amiss. "Would you like to go to my office for a bit of brandy and some private conversation?"

"No. I feel a need for the chaos created by people. Whiskey and a corner table should do us well enough."

Kit led the way while Harrison signaled for Lorna. Kit sat and glanced around the saloon. Harry had done a remarkable job of sprucing it up. It would never pass as a gentleman's club, but here a man could relax and be himself. Seldom was the case in London.

Even within his own home, a man would have to project a mien of authority and nobility unless he be considered an eccentric fool.

Harry took his chair as Lorna set a bottle of whiskey and two glasses on the table. She studied Kit. "Is this 'un still the marshal's brother?"

"No," Harry said, amusement reflected in his voice.

Lorna's face lit up as she plopped onto Kit's lap. "I sure did miss you."

Kit slipped her a coin and patted her hip. "Be a good girl, then, and leave me alone to talk with Harry."

Her face fell as she stood and looked at the money in her hand. "You're one of them fellas who's faithful to his wife, ain't you?"

"Apparently so."

She lifted a shoulder to her ear. "Reckon I'm glad. I wouldn't have liked you as much iffen you weren't."

He watched her saunter away, flirting with the men she passed. He turned his attention to the full glass of whiskey Harry shoved toward him. He downed it in one swallow and waited patiently while Harry refilled the glass.

"So what did happen?" Harry asked.

Kit wrapped his fingers around the glass. "Remember the man shooting your floor?"

"He wasn't an easy character to forget."

"He's also a thief. Robs stagecoaches. He attempted—succeeded, actually—in robbing the one in which Ashton and I were traveling. A bullet grazed my temple and knocked me unconscious. I don't know how Ashton managed to do it, but she hid me from them and nursed me back to health."

"Quite an accomplishment for a dying woman."

"Indeed. She is remarkable." Kit took a long, slow swallow of whiskey, relishing the burning along his throat. He lowered the glass and met Harry's gaze. "Ashton knows about Clarisse."

In the process of tipping the bottle, Harry stilled. "What exactly does she know?"

"Everything." Harry was the only person Kit had

ever confided in entirely. "It seems the bullet jarred my conscience and loosened my tongue. Unfortunately, she was not the dispassionate confidant that you were. She loathes me."

"Although I can see it troubles you, perhaps her knowing is for the best. You were bound to lose her sooner or later. Sooner is better, before your feelings for her deepened."

Kit shook his head. "I love her, Harry. I never thought it would be possible to love any woman as much as I loved Clarisse." He leaned forward. "The bitter truth is that I love Ashton more, and she looks at me as though she fears at any moment I will take her life."

"Perhaps she doesn't understand the extent to which Clarisse suffered."

"I told her. I tried to explain. How can I expect her to understand when I have regretted my actions these many years all the while knowing that I would do them again."

"I wish I were a man of wisdom who could offer you some sage advice."

Kit chuckled. "You did give me some wise advice. I simply failed to heed it, and you were right. I have dropped more deeply into the bowels of hell."

"Well, if it ain't the marshal that don't wear a gun."

Kit jerked his gaze past Harry to see Jasper and several of his men standing nearby.

"Heard you was back in town," Jasper said with a sneer, his gun leveled at Kit's chest. "We got some unfinished business."

"Harry, move away from the table," Kit said in a

calm voice that did not reflect the turmoil churning within him.

"Not bloody likely. Guns are not allowed in my saloon, gentlemen, as the marshal has told you before."

"Think I give a damn?" Jasper asked.

"You would if you knew my wife."

"I'm getting damned tired of hearing about your wife. Maybe I'll just make her a widow."

Kit held up his hands. "We're both unarmed. Shoot us now and you will have committed coldblooded murder in front of over a dozen witnesses. You *will* hang."

Much to Kit's surprise, Jasper nodded and holstered his gun. "I'm all in favor of a fair fight. Tomorrow at noon. South end of town. You don't show, and we burn every building to the ground."

Kit watched the man saunter across the saloon, his spurs jangling. At the door, he scraped his rowel across the floor, leaving a deep scar. "See how your wife likes that."

He walked out, followed by his men, the door swinging in their wake.

"He's the type of man Jessye would love to kill," Harry said quietly before turning to Kit. "You'll need to send a telegram and get reinforcements—"

"No," Kit said succinctly. "I have no confidence in the abilities of the State Police. Besides, if we call them in, they are liable to put the town under martial law, which was the very reason the citizens asked me to become the marshal. So we would not have to deal with the corruption and ineptitude that often accompanies the State Police."

Kit rose and addressed the slack-jawed customers. "You all heard Mr. Jasper's announcement. I believe his quarrel is more of a personal nature against me rather than against the town. I shall meet him on his terms. No buildings will be burned, but I need you all to get the word out that no one is to be on the streets tomorrow at noon."

Among stares, mumbling, and whispers, Kit sat and picked up his glass of whiskey, surprised to notice the steadiness of his hand. "He said he'd heard that I'd returned. One of his men must have seen Christopher and mistaken him for me. I shudder to think what might have happened had I not returned tonight."

Harry leaned forward. "You are not serious about meeting him tomorrow."

Kit lifted his glass in a mock salute. "Believe it or not, Harry, the man has solved a great many dilemmas for me."

Chapter 22

Unable to sleep, Ashton slipped on the wrap Kit had purchased at the mercantile and walked out of her room. The man had thought of everything, which came as no surprise to her. He was incredibly gifted at taking care of the details.

The boardinghouse was dark. She made her way quietly down the stairs. She saw a pale light spilling out from beneath the kitchen door. Mrs. Gurney always seemed to be cooking, day or night. Little wonder Kit ate here even though he didn't live here.

She stepped into the kitchen and came to an abrupt halt at the sight of burnished hair. Sitting at the table, the man glanced up from the book he was reading, smiled at her, and stood. Her heart settled into its normal pace as she recognized Christopher and shoved aside the immediate disappointment that it wasn't Kit.

She waved her hand. "Please don't get up. I didn't mean to disturb you. I thought Mrs. Gurney was here, and I just wanted some warm milk."

He held up his cup. "I have a weakness for cocoa. I made a bit extra, if you'd care for some."

She gave him a tentative smile. "Yes, thank you."

"But you can't run back to your room with it. You'll have to sit and talk with me."

Obediently, she sat while he poured the cocoa into a cup for her. The resemblance between him and Kit was striking, and yet there were as many differences. He was more slender. Responsibility had carved lines within the noble planes of his face, but they did not run as deep as those within his brother's face. Just like Kit, he carried himself as though he were a man who not only knew, but completely understood, his position in the world.

He placed the china cup in front of her before returning to his chair.

"Kit mentioned that you had a fondness for chocolate." She brought the cup to her lips and sipped the warm brew, savoring the flavor and the mist tickling her nose.

"My brother has a gift for understatement."

"He purchased me a lot of chocolate when we were in Galveston," she said inanely, wishing she'd stayed in her room. "What are you reading?"

He lifted the book. "A dime novel. Not very literary, but extremely entertaining. It helps me to relax. The hero in this particular story reminds me a great deal of Kit."

"He never mentioned that someone was writing a book about him."

"Modesty would prevent his making such an announcement, I'm sure. Perhaps the character isn't based upon him, although I've heard rumors since

I've been here that he doesn't wear a gun, which apparently is quite unusual for a marshal."

She shrugged. "Most men in Texas wear guns whether they're marshals or not."

"So I've noticed. It's still quite the frontier, isn't it?"

"I suppose so." She took another sip of cocoa.

"I take it that your marriage to Kit is in name only," Christopher said quietly.

Ashton's fingers tightened around the cup handle. "Why would you think that?"

"Because Father saw Kit climb down the beam that supports the roof over the porch, and since your room is above ours, we both assumed you weren't sharing a bed."

She felt the heat flame her cheeks. "Currently, we're not sharing a bed. No."

Christopher tilted his head as though to consider possibilities. "But you were for a while? So you've had a quarrel."

Deliberately, she set down the cup. "I don't see that where we sleep or if we've quarreled is any of your business."

"I would agree if I did not love Kit as much as I do."

She wondered how much his love would diminish if he knew what Kit had done to Christopher's wife.

"Kit desperately wanted to hold your hand while he was in our room learning of Father's secret."

Ashton felt her chest tighten. "Why do you think that?"

"Because I could see it in his eyes, in the way he looked at you, wanting, but fearful. Come to think of it, he didn't touch you when he introduced you to me in the foyer, so your quarrel must have occurred before you arrived tonight."

"We did not have a disagreement," she snapped. She didn't like knowing that Kit had wanted to touch her but hadn't because she'd asked him not to. She was always thinking of her needs and not his. She should have realized how hard visiting with his father would be, should have put aside her disgust with him for a short time. Lent him her strength instead of her weakness, after all he'd given her.

"Are you unhappy at the prospect of moving to England?" he asked.

"I will not be going anywhere with Kit. Our marriage is temporary—"

"Because of your health?"

"Yes."

He nodded thoughtfully. "All marriages are temporary. Eventually, one spouse dies. The marriage is over. 'Tis only the love that remains."

She furrowed her brow. "I'm not sure if you're being morbid or romantic."

"Realistic. But I apologize. I'm in a pensive mood. Did Kit mention to you that he loved my wife?"

Her mouth suddenly dry, Ashton could only nod.

"Sometime tonight," Christopher said, "it shall dawn on him that he should have married Clarisse." He lowered his gaze to the table and touched his finger to his mouth. "Life is full of ironies."

"But you loved her, too. And she loved you. Kit told me she died with your name on her lips."

"While lying within his arms."

A secretive smile played upon Christopher's lips as

he pointed his finger at her and raised a brow. "That was a guess upon my part, but the expression in your eyes confirms it. He never told me that, you see. He no doubt told you a great many things that he never confided in me."

"If you have questions about her death, you'll need to ask him." She started to rise.

"Stay."

"I don't think I should."

"Afraid you'll confess my brother's sins? I am well aware of his sins, Ashton."

"Then you don't need me to stay."

"Tell me what you quarreled about."

She slid back into the chair. "I told you that we didn't quarrel."

He nodded his head toward her. "Your cocoa is growing cold."

She brought the cup to her lips. It was cooler, but still enjoyable, if she could just force it past the lump in her throat.

"Clarisse was in such agony," Christopher said as though he'd drifted out of the room. "Her cancerous disease showed her no mercy. Twice, nay, three times, I prepared a brew that would end her suffering for all time, but I could not bring myself to carry it to her lips. So I sent for Kit. He has always been the stronger, you see. Even in the beginning, when he was scrawny, he possessed the strength of spirit that put mine to shame. I knew he would find the will to do what needed to be done. He never told me what had transpired within the room while he was with Clarisse, but when he said, 'It matters not where my body is, *I* shall be in hell,' I knew. I knew he had granted her wish."

Staring at him, she slowly set her cup down. "She wanted to die, and you sent him to her knowing that he would kill her?"

She watched a tear roll down Christopher's face. "Pain was all that remained in her life. Death was the only thing she ever asked of me that I could not give her, but I knew Kit would deny her nothing, regardless of the cost to himself. And he has suffered greatly for it."

Details. So many details to be considered.

Sitting at his desk, Kit glanced momentarily at the room in which he slept. He knew if he were smart, he'd stretch out on the cot and catch a few hours of sleep before his meeting with destiny.

But as he'd learned of late, he was not a smart man.

And the details were staggering.

Jasper had planned that stagecoach robbery so Kit knew he, too, was a man who understood the concept of leaving nothing to chance.

Kit had already oiled and cleaned his rifle and loaded it. He would not need extra bullets. If the fourteen that his Henry rifle held didn't do the job, he seriously doubted he'd be alive to reload and finish the job.

Still . . . he placed spare bullets beside his rifle. Leave nothing to chance.

He had to determine exactly when to step out onto the street. He did not want to seem overeager, but neither did he want to be standing there with the wind whistling by and his palms growing sweaty.

So many damned details, and they were all unimportant. All except the ones he now worked on. Ones that revolved around Ashton.

He had considered climbing to the window of her room and slipping into bed with her. His arms ached to hold her, his shoulder longed to again feel the little nodding motion she made as she worked her way into a comfortable position against him.

He dipped his pen into the inkwell and made a notation on the paper in front of him. He had considered writing her a letter of farewell, but what was there to say? He thought about thanking her for the time she'd shared with him, but the words made what he truly felt seem trite. He contemplated writing a letter of explanation regarding his sin, but if spoken words could not sway her, he doubted that written pleas would.

So the only thing he would work on tonight was a missive that he would hand to Christopher tomorrow. It was best this way.

He picked up the black book that Christopher had given him. He studied the cover and wondered at all his father might have written inside. Thoughts he'd never meant for another soul to read.

He looked up as the door opened, and Christopher stepped in. His brother glanced around. "I have yet to understand why you bothered to lock this dreary place."

"Because I have weapons, and I didn't want anyone to take them."

Christopher nodded thoughtfully. Kit turned over the paper on which he'd been making notations. He didn't know how he was going to explain all that would transpire tomorrow, but he thought doing it on short notice would serve him best, so Christopher would have little time to try and persuade him to travel a different path.

"What are you doing here anyway?" Kit asked.

"I saw you leave the boardinghouse." Christopher raised a brow. "The building does have a front door, you know."

"I'm aware of that fact, but I prefer to live dangerously."

"That explains the reasoning behind your taking this position as marshal then, doesn't it? Your life must be at constant risk."

"Hardly. Mostly I escort drunken cowboys out of Harry's saloon," Kit said.

Christopher looked into the room where Kit slept. "It's a far cry from the grandeur of Ravenleigh."

"It suits me," Kit said quietly.

With a sigh, Christopher sat in the chair that David Robertson had occupied several weeks earlier. A lifetime ago.

"Why didn't you write me when Father had his first stroke?" Kit asked.

"I did," Christopher said. "I assume the letter hasn't arrived."

Kit glanced around his desk. "Not that I've seen, but then, there seems to be no pattern to how long it takes a letter to reach me."

Christopher jerked his head toward the book Kit held. "Have you read it?"

"No."

"Ah, what a tangled web we weave, heh?" Christopher asked, intertwining his fingers and placing them over his flat stomach.

"Father's web seemed fairly straightforward." Kit set the book aside. "You could have kept this discovery to yourself, you know."

Christopher nodded slightly. "I considered it and not because of greed, avarice, or hunger for a title. But who am I if not the heir to Ravenleigh?"

"You're Christopher Montgomery."

He scoffed. "But who is that, Kit? Who I am has always been defined by what I would be. When I read Father's journal, I felt as though someone had tossed me carelessly into a tempest. I have yet to find my anchor in this storm of deceptions."

Kit remembered the vivid dream he'd had the night when the fog rolled in. Now that it made sense, he sympathized immensely with his brother's frustrations. "Under the circumstances, I should think any man would feel doubts and confusion. Still, you could have burned the journal."

Chuckling softly, Christopher shook his head. "I was tempted, so tempted. I even built the fire, but in the end, I knew I could not live with myself, nor would I ever be able to look you in the eye if I were not honest with you, if I did not share my discovery."

Kit leaned forward to voice the concerns that had been bothering him. "You risked Father's life bringing him here. You could have waited—"

"I had not intended to bring him, but he insisted. I did not realize that he wished to come so he could use the time to try to convince me to hold my tongue. I'm angry with him. Furious, in fact. All these years, he deceived us. He made me into someone I was not meant to be."

"He made you into who he *wanted you* to be."

Christopher pounded his fist on the desk, surprising Kit by the unusual display of rage. "English law does not work in that manner. The aristocracy does not select its heirs. God does." Briskly rubbing the side of his hand, Christopher sighed. "I apologize for my outburst."

"No need to apologize. You have every right to be upset."

"You don't seem bothered by this turn of events."

Kit stroked the scar beneath his chin. "I suppose it hasn't all sunk in. Besides, I believe that I've made a small contribution while I've been here. You have to understand, Christopher, that I have found a measure of contentment."

"Father warned me that would be the case, that you would not find this revelation as enticing as I envisioned you would. I'm surprised to discover him right."

"As difficult as it is to admit, Father knows us well—both our strengths and our weaknesses," Kit said, willing to admit to himself at least that his father had done him a service in raising him as he had. By never giving him an inch, he had prepared him to stand on his own.

Christopher held Kit's gaze. "Have you no curiosity as to what brought on Father's first stroke?"

Kit shrugged and gave his brother a grim smile. "I should imagine he was yelling at one of the tenant farmers for not managing his crops to specifications."

"He was yelling at me. He'd found the letters you'd written to me. He was not at all pleased that I had turned to you for advice."

"You were a fool not to burn them as soon as you finished reading them."

"They contained far too much wisdom. I referred to them often . . . had considered making them into a book, actually."

Kit scoffed. "It would be a very short book."

"I realize that, but still I consider a short book of wisdom more useful than a long book of nonsense." Christopher leaned forward. "The overall management of Ravenleigh I understand completely. It's the details that thwart me from time to time. You're so bloody good with details. You always were. That's the reason I suggested we manage Ravenleigh together. I suppose it angered Father to realize he had selected poorly."

Kit studied his brother's dejected mien. To be toppled from an exalted position was much harder to accept than being lifted to one. Christopher's willingness to expose the truth was a testament to his integrity. "Father did not select poorly. You carefully measure every decision, determining where the benefits will be best achieved. You are exactly what Ravenleigh needs."

Christopher laughed, a sound Kit had not heard from his brother in a long time.

"What so funny?" Kit asked.

"You do not see yourself as the lord of the manor?"

Kit shook his head slightly. "In all honesty, no."

"Then what *are* you here, if not lord of the manor?

You are responsible for the welfare of these people. In the short time I've been here, I've had more questions thrust upon me than I have in the whole time since I assumed management at Ravenleigh."

Kit pondered his brother's observation. In an odd way, he was a lord, but he did not have absolute power, only absolute responsibility dictated within the confines of the law. "Interesting. I suppose we could argue that if I am lord here, I have no need of Ravenleigh."

Christopher settled back in his chair. "No, we cannot argue that. Father was wrong to deny you your birthright."

"Who among us is without sin?"

"Perhaps that is true, but that does not change the fact that you are the rightful heir."

Kit held up his father's journal. "It is not as simple as you make it out to be. I shall consider the matter very carefully and let you know my decision on the morrow."

With a heavy sigh, Christopher stood. "Regardless of your decision, my feelings for you will not change. I could not have asked for a finer brother."

Kit swallowed hard, the words incredibly difficult to accept, harder to speak. "I feel the same. You were a blessing in my life."

"You say that as though your life were over. I *am* a blessing in your life and shall continue to be so. I'll be off so you can get some much needed and deserved rest."

Christopher walked to the door, stopped, and turned slightly. "I'll see you at breakfast."

"I have some matters that need my attention in the morning. I'll visit you and Father shortly before noon," Kit said.

"Before noon, then. Arrive with the answer I want, not the one I expect." Christopher stepped outside and closed the door.

Kit set the journal aside. His father had gone to great lengths to ensure that Christopher was the heir apparent. Ironically, tomorrow a stranger named Jasper would unwittingly fulfill his father's deepest wish.

Chapter 23

"I don't know who I am," Christopher said quietly.

"You're Christopher Montgomery."

Chuckling low, he glanced at the woman walking beside him in the moonlight wearing nothing but her nightgown. She had gladdened his heart when she hadn't questioned his disturbing her in the middle of the night, but had simply suggested that they walk so he could talk out whatever was bothering him. Against his better judgment and his earlier resolve not to do so, he'd eaten dinner at her house every night. She possessed a calmness—when her daughters weren't threatened—that drew him like a siren's song. "Kit said the same thing. But who is that, Elizabeth?"

"I don't see that it's any great mystery. You're you."

He stopped walking, turned, and faced her. "My entire life, I have been Viscount Wyndhaven with the knowledge that one day I would become the Earl of Ravenleigh. Now, I'm only Christopher."

She folded her arms beneath her breasts, and he fought not to lower his gaze. "You put too much stock in a name. A name doesn't make you who you are. Until I was seventeen, I was Elizabeth Morgan. Then I got married and was Elizabeth Fairfield." She pressed a hand flat against her chest, above her breasts. "But I was still just Elizabeth, in here where it mattered."

He shook his head, wondering how he could possibly explain to someone who had not grown up in his society how he viewed himself. "You were a daughter, and then a wife."

"Daughter, wife, mother, friend—it doesn't matter *what* I am; *who* I am is Elizabeth. You can be a viscount, an earl, a king, a farmer, and you're still Christopher."

"A farmer?" The thought was incredible enough to make him want to burst out laughing.

"Nothing wrong with being a farmer." He heard the solemnity of her voice and was grateful he hadn't laughed.

"I can't see me as a farmer."

"Don't reckon your brother ever saw himself pickin' cotton or herdin' cattle."

He sighed heavily. "No, I don't suppose he did. A farmer, heh?"

She started to walk and he fell into step beside her.

"I could always use some help around here, if you're of a mind to stay." She darted a quick glance his way.

He smiled. "I'll consider it."

"No you won't."

"You're right. I won't."

"Still feeling lost?" she asked.

"Not as much, although I must apologize for getting you out of bed—"

She interrupted him with a burst of laughter. "You are the most apologizingest man I've ever met. Friends are supposed to be there when you need them no matter what the time or situation."

"But it seems I'm the one always in need of you. I can't see that I've given you anything in return."

"You spared me from having some lonely evenings."

"That hardly suffices to make us even, especially since I benefited from those evenings as well."

She shook her head. "Friends don't keep a tally sheet."

"Perhaps not," he murmured. He walked her to the porch, said goodnight, and watched her disappear into the house. He had not known Elizabeth long, and yet he knew he would always carry the memory of their evenings together with him.

Kit crouched beside the bed and watched his wife sleep, carving her features onto his memory. The past week, returning to Fortune, had been hard on her. She would no doubt sleep the day through, which he preferred.

She would awaken to discover that she was a widow, but at least she would not have to go through the worry of waiting to hear the news.

How ironic that their roles had reversed. He had married her because she was dying, and now he was the one who faced death. He considered waking her, but he did not wish his last memory to be gazing into eyes that no longer sparkled.

He much preferred the memory of her sleeping.

The shooting would no doubt awaken her. He should not have accepted Jasper's terms so readily. He had not considered that meeting these men at the south end of town would give those within the boardinghouse a clear view of the fight. He could only hope they had the sense to keep down and out of the way.

He laid a white rose beside her on the pillow before unfolding his body. For all the hardship and sorrow that had come at the end, he would not trade a single moment of the time he'd spent with her. The joy she had brought him could not be measured, but it would carry him through eternity.

Quietly, he walked out of the room and down the stairs, where another goodbye awaited. Unfortunately, this one would not be silent.

He knocked on the door to his family's room. Christopher flung open the door, worry clearly etched on his face.

"What are these rumors I'm hearing about some ruffians calling you out?" Christopher demanded.

Kit stepped into the room and closed the door. "Good morning to you, as well."

"Damnation, Kit. Mrs. Gurney said that a notorious band of outlaws—"

"Mrs. Gurney tends to exaggerate."

"Perhaps, but she does not lie. I want the truth."

"You heard correctly. There is to be a duel of sorts at noon. The gauntlet was tossed, and I accepted the challenge."

"Why in God's name did you do that?" Christopher asked.

"Because I'm the marshal—"

"Who doesn't wear a gun!" Christopher snatched up a dime novel from the bedside table. *"The Marshal Who Didn't Wear A Gun.* This is you, isn't it?"

"I don't use pistols, but I'm skilled with a rifle."

"A rifle? You're going to engage in a duel with a rifle?"

Kit sighed heavily. "It's not a duel as you envision it. An outlaw has taken offense because I hit him, and later, when he was attempting to rob the stagecoach upon which I was traveling, I killed two of his men. He wants justice."

"Justice? Justice would be him hanging from the nearest gallows."

"Yes, if we were in civilized England, which we are not! He has threatened to burn this town to the ground, and by God, he will do it if I don't meet him and his men at noon."

Christopher straightened his shoulders. "Then I shall stand as your second."

Kit had never loved his brother more. "You bloody well will not. Your doing that would leave Ravenleigh without an heir, and that possibility I will not tolerate."

"Then I shall stand in your stead."

Kit shook his head. "You can best serve Ravenleigh and me by staying here."

Christopher glared at Kit, not only doubting his brother's words, but wondering why he was damned eager to partake in a duel that according to Mrs. Gurney he had little chance of winning. "The whole purpose in our journey was to bring you back to England. Now is as good a time as any for us to take our leave."

"The safety of this town falls upon my shoulders," Kit said with determination. "Granted, I indulged myself for several weeks and left it without a keeper, but that does not lessen my obligation to its citizens. Unfortunately, I have many things yet to finish. I have a list—"

"You don't think you can win?" Christopher asked, dread creeping along his spine.

Kit met his gaze squarely. "Not against six." He smiled cockily. "But I shall take as many into hell with me as I can."

He extended the paper toward Christopher. "I would ask that you see to my plans. Ashton wishes to return to her brother in Dallas. Make certain that she arrives there safely. I've spoken with the banker. My money shall be placed into a trust that you shall oversee. Ashton is to have everything her heart desires, and when she . . ."

Christopher watched his brother swallow as though he fought unbearable emotions.

"I want you to make arrangements for one white rose to be placed upon her grave every day. The remainder of the trust is to be given to St. Mary's infirmary in Galveston for medical research."

Christopher shoved the words past the knot in his throat. "I swear that I shall ensure that all is managed to your satisfaction."

"Thank you." Kit turned to his father. "I realize, sir, that I have been a constant disappointment to you, but I want you to know that you have never been a disappointment to me. A son could not have asked for a better example of a father. I did not read your journal as Christopher suggested, for I saw no need in doing so. You always placed the welfare of Ravenleigh above all else as your duty dictated. And now I shall see to mine."

Christopher watched tears surface within his father's eyes and willed him to say the words that needed to be spoken. Instead, his father simply gave a brusque nod and turned away.

Kit glanced at his watch. "Well, I'd best be off or I'll be putting out fires." He extended his hand toward Christopher. When Christopher took it, Kit pulled him close, hugging him tightly. His voice was low, rife with emotion. "For what it's worth, I understand why you could not be with Clarisse at the end. I will not deny that I loved her, but I know now that my love was not equal to yours. I'm grateful she had you, Christopher."

Christopher felt an ache in his chest that threatened to crush his ribs. Words clogged his throat as Kit abruptly released him. He watched his brother stride to the door, jerk it open, and freeze.

Grayson Rhodes and Harrison Bainbridge stood just beyond the threshold, guns strapped to their thighs.

"What in the bloody hell do you think you're doing here?" Kit demanded.

"You're skilled with a rifle," Harrison said, "but I wager you can only shoot four, which leaves one for Gray and one for me."

"Neither of you has ever killed. Believe me, it's not something you want on your conscience."

"And you think knowing our trusted friend died with no one beside him is something we prefer to have on our conscience?" Harrison asked.

"Bloody hell, Harry. You're right handed. You need that hand to hold a cane, not a gun."

Harrison angled his chin defiantly. "I only need the cane to walk. I can stand for quite some time without it. I can easily release the cane and quickly draw my gun—"

"And leave your wife a widow. Has either of you given any thought to that? Or to the fact that your children will be raised without fathers?"

"We both discussed our decision with our wives through the night," Grayson said.

"And they gave you their blessing?" Kit demanded.

"They gave us their understanding," Grayson said.

Kit shook his head. "Knowing that they would give you a burial?"

"Not if we stand together," Grayson said. "You've stood by us in the past, Kit. You can't expect us to abandon you now. We came here together—"

"No man has ever had truer friends, but this fight is mine and mine alone. I wounded Jasper's pride. I'll not have others pay the price for my actions."

"You also killed two of his men while they were breaking the law attacking a stagecoach with robbery in mind. Now he's threatening our town," Grayson pointed out. "Everyone else may think this is your fight, but not I. I haven't worked as hard as I have these past five years so some arrogant ass can destroy my happiness. I'll not have my wife and children threatened by the likes of men such as him. If he wins, Kit, in the end we all lose, because more of his ilk will follow. I say we stand together now so we won't have to tomorrow."

Kit sighed heavily. "There's not a bloody thing I can say to change your minds on this matter, is there?"

"Not a thing," Grayson and Harrison said at the same time.

"Then I'll need to deputize you so everything is legal."

"By all means," Harrison said. "I don't fancy a hanging shortly after I've become a hero."

Christopher couldn't believe his brother was chuckling as he closed the door behind him. He turned to his father, who was staring at the portal through which his first born son had just disappeared.

"After all you've just heard and witnessed, do you still feel that I shouldn't have told Kit the truth?"

With Gray and Harry flanking him, Kit walked down the center of the dusty street. Now and then, he saw someone peering out a dirty window, but for the most part the citizens had apparently heeded his advice and sought cover far from anyplace where a stray bullet might strike.

"You are not to draw your guns until one of them makes the first move," Kit commanded his comrades.

"I'll wager that little rule ensures that at least one of us gets shot," Harry said caustically.

"It's the law," Kit pointed out. "To do otherwise changes our actions from self-defense to murder. I shall attempt to convince them to turn themselves over to me—"

"You'll be wasting your breath on that endeavor," Gray cut in.

"Still, I shall try."

Six men sauntered out from between two buildings at the far end of town. Kit's mouth went as dry as the dirt his boots were kicking up. "Regardless of how things turn out, I want you both to know that I have always considered it an honor to have the privilege of calling you friend."

"Don't get sentimental. We may make it through this yet," Harry said.

"And if we don't," Gray said, "we shall reign together in hell. I wager it must be cooler there than it is here."

"I'll take you up on that wager," Harry said.

Kit couldn't prevent himself from smiling. No man had truer friends.

They halted a short distance away from Jasper and his five comrades. Kit doubted that they would stand as firmly by Jasper.

Jasper spat tobacco into the street. "Well, Marshal, you ready to meet your Maker?"

"No, actually, I'm here to arrest you."

"Arrest me?"

"Yes. I know you are responsible for the deaths of at least three men. I've written up a detailed account of the stagecoach robbery in which you participated, and I've forwarded it to the stage line, as well as several law enforcement officials in neighboring towns. I've included a sketch so they'll be able to spot you a mile away. Surrender to me now and I shall do all within my power to see that you go to prison and not the gallows."

Jasper scoffed. "Surrender? Are you loco? I'm fixing to put you six feet under."

Kit slowly, steadily moved his gaze from one man to the other until he'd given all six a pointed glare. "Then when you are ready, gentlemen, take your best shot, for I guarantee you that it shall be your last."

Ashton awoke and smiled at the white rose resting beside her on the pillow. Kit had been here, and no doubt left her to sleep. She picked up the flower and inhaled the sweet scent.

Dawn had been easing over the horizon before she'd finally fallen asleep, Christopher's words tumbling through her mind. Her husband wasn't a murderer. He was a savior. Why had she ever thought otherwise?

She sat up in bed and glanced at the clock on the bedside table. A few minutes before noon. Kit had probably already had his breakfast and was now either visiting with his family or working in his office. She needed to talk with him, set things right between them.

She would still go to Dallas, but at least there would be no hard feelings between them. His place was in England, not beside her. But she wanted him to go with a clear conscience and the knowledge that she now understood his actions. She was not completely comfortable with them, but she also realized she was in no position to judge him.

She scrambled out of bed and quickly donned the dress he'd purchased the night before. She smiled as she glanced in the mirror. A perfect fit.

She unbraided her hair, brushed it vigorously, pulled it back, and tied a bright yellow ribbon around it to hold it in place. She would go to greater lengths to make herself attractive later. Right now, all she wanted was to see Kit, to explain that she understood, and to tell him that she loved him.

She opened the door and hurried down the stairs. Mrs. Gurney stood at the window in the front room, staring out.

"Mrs. Gurney, have you seen my husband this morning?" Ashton asked.

Mrs. Gurney spun around, horror reflected on her face. "He didn't tell you?"

"Didn't tell me what?" Ashton asked, foreboding sweeping through her. Had he already left to accept his place at Ravenleigh?

Mrs. Gurney bit her knuckle and shook her head. "Land o'goshen, he should have told you."

Christopher walked out of his room and held his arms out toward her. "Ashton, come here."

She took a step back, afraid for reasons she couldn't understand. If Christopher was still here, then Kit hadn't left, but everyone was too solemn. "Where's Kit?"

"It's them outlaws," Mrs. Gurney blurted. "They called him out, and he's facing them this very minute."

"Outlaws?"

"The men who attacked the stagecoach," Christopher explained. "Apparently, they are to have a duel."

"A duel? You mean a gunfight?"

Christopher looked surprised. "Yes, of course, guns are involved in a duel."

Ashton shook her head, refusing to believe what she was hearing. "No, no. It's not a duel like you think. It's a bloodbath. He'll be killed. We have to stop it!" She began running for the door.

Christopher grabbed her, holding her close, pinning her body against his. "It's too late to stop it."

She fought to break free. "You don't understand. He thinks I hate him. I have to tell him that I understand now. I love—"

She heard exploding thunder, a deafening cacophony as round after round was fired.

"No!" she cried, slumping against Christopher, her body trembling and tears streaming down her face. "No."

But neither her words nor her tears could stop the echo of gunfire.

Chapter 24

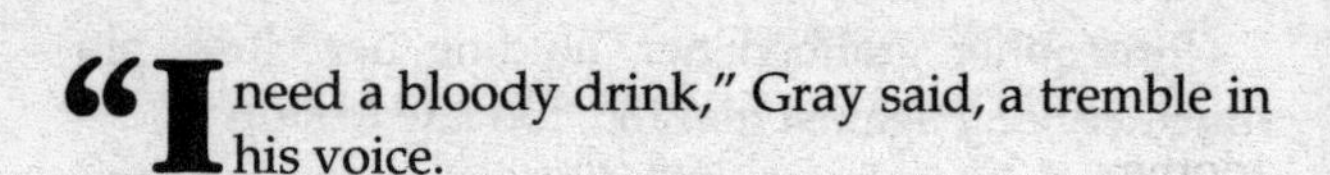

"I need a bloody drink," Gray said, a tremble in his voice.

"I need a bloody bottle," Harry responded, his voice equally shaky. "Two bottles. Three. Three bottles sound quite extraordinary. Shall we each have three bottles of whiskey?"

"None for me," Kit said, as he walked toward the men sprawled over the ground, their blood seeping into the earth. Such a damned waste. But at least the town was safe from this particular group of outlaws. As were stagecoaches and saloon floors.

"Harry!"

Kit glanced over his shoulder and watched Jessye throw her arms around Harry's neck. Harry latched his mouth onto hers with such passion that Kit knew a pang of envy.

Harry leaned back. "I couldn't leave Kit to face them alone."

Tears filled Jessye's eyes as she nodded. "I know." She looked past Harry and held Kit's gaze. "Would have been here myself if I wasn't afraid we might leave our daughters orphans."

"You made the right choice, Jessye," Kit said quietly. "You always did where your daughters are concerned."

She picked up Harry's cane and handed it to him. "Let's go home and give those girls a hug."

Harry slipped his arm around her. "Let's stop by the saloon and pick up a bottle of whiskey on the way, shall we? Then I feel a strong need to practice giving you a daughter."

"I'm already expecting."

"Yes, but I need to stay in practice so I can give you another."

A movement caught Kit's attention, and he turned to see Abbie walking toward Grayson. She stopped within an arm's reach of him. "I lost you once before. Don't know how I would have survived losing you again."

Grayson drew her into his embrace, lifted her off the ground, and kissed her deeply. When he released her, he said, "Let's gather up the children and go on a picnic."

Kit watched them begin to walk away. Grayson turned slightly. "Did you want to join us?"

And witness what he would never possess? He shook his head. "No, I need to finish up here."

Grayson nodded and pulled his wife more snugly against his side as they walked toward the livery stable.

Thank God, his friends had survived unscathed, although he suspected it would be several nights before either of them slept peacefully. Even when the action was justified, taking a life was not an easy burden to carry.

"What do you want me to do with 'em, Marshal?"

Kit turned to the mortician. "Pilfer their pockets, Mr. Dawson. See if you can determine who they are. Then use plain pine boxes and bury them at the back of the church cemetery. Fortune will cover the expenses."

"I'll handle the matter right away."

Kit saw people cautiously leaving their shops. "Make it quick," he said to Dawson. "This sight is not one people need to witness."

He walked toward the boardinghouse, knowing he had other matters that needed his attention. The door swung open and Ashton burst outside, running across the lawn as though the demons of hell nipped at her heels. Tears dampened her cheeks. She flung her arms around him, and he could feel her body trembling violently.

"What's wrong?" he asked.

He gazed over her head to see Christopher standing on the porch. He turned his attention back to Ashton, slipped his finger beneath her chin, and tilted her face up. He captured a falling tear with his thumb. "Why are you crying?"

"You went to face death without even telling me goodbye."

"I'd made arrangements to see that you were well cared for."

She stepped out of his embrace. "Is that all you think I wanted?"

"Quite honestly, yes." She closed her eyes and tears leaked from the corners. "Look beyond me, Ashton. I am Death. I am what you fear above all else."

She opened her eyes to reveal limpid pools of sadness.

"For a while, with you, I was able to forget. You gave me moments of great joy that shall sustain me for the remainder of my life. But you'll never be able to look at me again and not see the darkened shadows that hover inside my soul, and I shall see them reflected in your eyes, and that, sweetling, I cannot bear."

"You can't possibly know how I'll look at you!"

"Yes I can, because you've looked at me in that manner since our first night in the cave."

She looked as though she wanted to say more, but her eyes suddenly widened and she gasped. "You're bleeding."

He glanced at his throbbing shoulder. "Just a nick. Bullet went through."

She grabbed his uninjured arm. "Where's the doctor?"

"The other end of town."

"We need to get your wound taken care of before infection sets in."

The determination in her voice made him want to smile. He looked past her to Christopher. "I have some business to finish up, and then I'll return so we can settle our affairs."

Christopher nodded and walked into the boardinghouse.

"You're shaking," Ashton said as she strolled beside him, clinging to his arm.

"I always do after I've killed someone."

She jerked her gaze to his. "You enjoy reminding me that you kill."

"Not particularly, but it is a fact of my life, and it's suddenly become imperative that you not forget it."

"Do you ever count how many lives you might have saved?"

"No, because the count is inconsequential. I could not save the lives that mattered most."

Ashton walked around the jail, taking note of its stark, drab appearance. Kit had told her that he'd needed to tend to some paperwork so they'd come here after the doctor had stitched up his shoulder.

She had so much to tell him and didn't know where to begin.

She stopped inside a doorway and peered into a desolate room that she was certain had once been used for storage. It held a cot and a carton of books. Clothes hung on the wall beside a shaving stand. It wasn't a place of solitude, but of loneliness. "Is this where you live?" she asked.

Kit glanced up from the papers strewn across his desk and met her gaze. "Yes."

"It's not very fancy."

"I don't need fancy. I only need useful."

The front door opened and a tall, thin man walked in carrying a small box. "I was able to get some identification off a couple of 'em." He set the box on the desk. "I don't think these here things originally belonged to any of them."

Kit pulled a watch out the box.

"The initials on that there watch is CS. I don't think

any of them had a name that matched the initials," the man said.

She watched Kit nod and place the watch carefully back into the box.

"I think I've managed to identify them from the wanted posters." He closed his eyes and sighed. "A shame I didn't check the posters the night they were shooting up Harry's saloon. Three innocent men might still be alive."

"Can't see the death of these outlaws as any great loss."

Kit opened his eyes. "The ending of any life is a loss, Mr. Dawson. Even when that life was not put to good use."

"Iffen you say so. Me, I say good riddance."

Mr. Dawson turned and tipped his hat at Ashton. "We are surely proud to have your husband as our marshal, Mrs. Montgomery."

"So proud that you all stood beside him."

"We was there, we just wasn't visible on account of him telling us—"

"Thank you, Mr. Dawson," Kit cut in.

"It wasn't our fight and we was to stay out of the way."

"I think you've adequately taken care of the business at hand, Mr. Dawson," Kit said. "Once I've finished completing the forms, I'll see that you're reimbursed for expenses."

" 'Preciate it, Marshal."

Mr. Dawson walked out of the office, leaving a deafening silence in his wake. Kit cast Ashton a quick glance before he returned to scribbling on his papers.

"You told the townspeople to stay out of sight?"

Kit continued to write. "Wounded pride brought Jasper back to Fortune. His quarrel was with me."

She studied the room where he lived. "It looks like a prison."

"Of course it looks like a prison. It's a jail."

"I meant the place where you live. There's not an ounce of comfort anywhere here."

"I have my books."

"You're punishing yourself."

She heard the scratching of his pen fall into silence.

"Other than irritating the devil out of me, what are you doing here, Ashton?"

She crossed the room and planted her hands on his desk. "Trying to figure you out. You couldn't save Clarisse, so you try to save everyone else. You feel guilty for taking her life, so you place yourself in situations where you might lose yours."

"Asinine assumptions."

"But true."

He tossed his pen aside, leaned back in his chair, and pinned her with his hardened gaze. "Your point being?"

"I love you."

"You can't possibly, after knowing all that you know." He picked up his pen and began to write fervently. "I have details to which I must attend. So many details. Sometimes I can get lost in them . . . incredibly lost . . . that for a second or two I can forget the feel of her final breath whispering across my flesh. I can forget . . . I need you to leave. I have to fill out reports on the deaths that occurred today. Detailed reports. I can't concentrate on the details with you standing there."

Slowly, quietly, she walked around the desk and knelt beside him. She saw the tears welling in his eyes, and her own eyes began to burn.

"I must concentrate on the details. Will you please leave?" he asked.

"No," she replied softly.

He jerked his head around and within the depths of his eyes, she saw the agony with which he'd lived for so long. Tears rolled along his cheeks. Reaching up, she cradled his face. "Oh, Christian."

"A completely inappropriate name for me. One of life's sick jokes."

"I don't think so."

His fingers came incredibly close to touching her face before he curled them into a fisted ball.

"Giving Clarisse an abundance of pain medication seemed the right thing to do at the moment. She was in so much agony." He released a wretched sob. She rose and slipped her arms around him, pressing his face to her bosom. "Then she was dead and the doubts and regrets slammed into me. And they have plagued me since. It was my suffering that I wanted to end. I could not bear to watch her valiant struggle when I knew the outcome. I wanted her to face death with a measure of dignity before her disease stripped it all away." She felt the shudder rack his body. "Selfish, so incredibly selfish of me. She was not mine to love. Her life was not mine to end."

She pressed a kiss to his neck. "I love you."

"How can you now that you know what I am capable of doing?"

Leaning back, she trailed her fingers along the tears staining his face and held his gaze. "I love you more. You must have known the guilt you would suffer if you granted her wish."

"My suffering is nothing compared to what hers had become."

"But yours is eternal, and you knew it would be when you made your decision."

He slammed his eyes closed. "Yes."

"Will you take my life?"

He opened his eyes and captured her gaze. "If you ask it of me."

She brushed her lips lightly over his. "I won't."

"That is easy enough to say before every second is measured by the depth of your pain."

Standing, she took his hand. "Come with me."

"I have things to which I must attend."

"So do I." She tugged on his hand. "Lie on your cot with me."

He shook his head. "Ashton, bringing you pleasure will not solve our problems."

"I only want you to hold me."

"It is a very narrow cot."

"Then hold me close."

He stood and followed her as she led the way to a room she'd already come to despise. How could he have lived here all these years?

He stretched out on his side on the cot with his back against the wall. Gingerly, she lay down, pressing her body closely against his and wrapping her arm around his waist so she wouldn't fall onto the floor.

"You see? I told you it was narrow," he said.

She lifted her gaze to his. "How do you sleep here?"

A corner of his mouth lifted. "On my side."

"It has to be the most uncomfortable thing I've been on." She unbuttoned the first button on his shirt. "You don't wear a hair shirt, do you?"

"No, but I do give myself mental floggings every morning."

"Why?"

He sighed deeply. "I took an innocent life, Ashton."

"Christopher knows."

His eyes darkened with fury. "You told him?"

"He told me."

He raised up on an elbow. "What do you mean, he told you? He doesn't know I killed Clarisse."

"You told me that you know each other's thoughts."

"Not this one. This one I buried deeply inside myself. He couldn't have found it with a shovel."

She placed her hand over his heart. "He knows you, Kit, as well as you know yourself. Why do you think he sent for you?"

She watched the fury recede to allow in the doubts.

"He wanted me to kill her?"

She nodded. "Because he couldn't bring himself to do it."

He cradled her face. "He told you this?"

"Last night. I couldn't sleep and I went to the kitchen. We shared some cocoa."

Kit gazed at the far wall and nodded. "He has a passion for cocoa."

He lay back down, and she could see within his eyes all the battles he waged. Disbelief, acceptance, understanding. But no anger. She had expected anger.

"He used you," she pointed out, "because he was too weak—"

"Because he loved her too much."

If Kit wasn't going to get mad, she was. "Shouldn't he have loved *you* enough not to ask or expect of you what he did?"

"You have to understand the bond between Christopher and me."

"So if I asked you to end my life you'd send in Christopher to do it?" she snapped.

"No." He shifted his gaze to her and trailed his fingers along her face. The depth of love reflected in his eyes was enough to make her want to weep. "No, I want to be the one to grant all your desires. Taking a life is not an easy task. I cannot fault Christopher for shying away from it. He did not hold a gun to my head. He simply gave me the opportunity to give to Clarisse what I could."

"But at what cost to you?"

"At a price I was willing to pay."

She felt deflated as she studied his face. "I don't think I'll ever understand."

"You don't have to. You only have to know that my love for Christopher is such that I would do anything for him." He trailed his thumb over her lower lip. "Just as I would do anything for you."

He eased his face nearer to hers. "Earlier, you said that you loved me."

She nodded.

"And here we lie with our bodies pressed close."

Again she nodded.

"When it was only last night that you asked me not to touch you."

"Last night I didn't understand," she whispered.

"Why I killed Clarisse?"

She shook her head. "What it would feel like to lose you." Tears welled in her eyes. "When Mrs. Gurney said you were going to face the outlaws—" A sob broke free and a shudder ran through her body. "Oh, Kit, I was so frightened! I didn't want you to die!"

"So the tears you wept earlier were for me?"

"Of course they were," she said.

"And if I were to press my lips to yours, you would welcome my kiss?"

"With all my heart."

His mouth covered hers with a desperation that spoke volumes. She combed her fingers up into his hair, holding him in place, wondering how she had ever managed to doubt his motives, to distrust his actions. He had risked his soul for Clarisse, risked his life for the people of this town, and risked his heart for her.

Chapter 25

"By God, I cannot . . . believe how . . . wrong I was!"

Standing in his father's room with Christopher beside him, Kit listened to his father's slurred words, watched his face contort as he forced himself to speak. Kit felt the unbearable ache in his chest at the sight of his father trying to maintain his dignity.

"You instill loyalty in men . . . understand the true measure of responsibility . . . are willing to make the greatest of all sacrifices to protect those who have entrusted you with their care. Who would have thought it?"

He pointed a trembling finger at Kit. "You were born first for a reason, but I thought I was wiser." His father shook his head. "I was a fool. You are the heir of Ravenleigh, and soon you shall bear its title."

Kit crouched before him. "You have prepared Christopher for the role, and he has always expected to hold the title. It is not fair now to deprive him of it."

"Fair?" his father croaked. "You talk of fair when

you have been cheated since birth?" His father wrinkled his grizzled face and poked his finger, with no strength, into Kit's shoulder. "You see? Again you prove my point."

Kit resisted the urge to scoff. "I was also sent here for a reason. I am not a worthy heir, regardless of what you think. My reputation is scandalous."

His father moved his finger in a circle as though he were stirring tea within a cup. "No one will know. You need only switch names."

Kit glanced up at Christopher. With usual British aplomb, Christopher had shuttered his emotions so his face revealed none of the inner turmoil with which Kit knew he was struggling. Emotions Kit battled as well.

Taking the black book that held his father's sins, Kit stood. "Is this the only evidence we have that mentions what happened the night we were born?"

"Yes," Christopher said succinctly. "The physician has since passed away."

Kit tore a page from the book before placing the journal in the hearth.

"What are you doing?" Christopher asked.

Kit rolled the paper and inserted one end into the lamp until the flame reached up and set the paper alight. He removed it from the lamp, knelt, and placed it against one corner of the book. With fascination, he watched the flames lick greedily at his offering.

"That does not change the truth!" his father spat.

"No, but it removes the evidence."

His father pounded his fist on the arm of the chair. "I want you to be the heir!"

Kit stood and faced his father squarely. Never had words been so difficult to speak.

"When you arranged for Christopher to marry Clarisse, knowing what I felt for her, you asked me to put Ravenleigh first. And I did. I held my silence and I put what I valued most—the heritage of Ravenleigh—above what I treasured most.

"When you feared I did not have the strength of character to keep my hands off my brother's wife, you asked me to put Ravenleigh first and to leave the home that I loved, and I did as you bade.

"Now, you're asking me again to put what I value above what I treasure." He held his father's gaze. "This time, Father, I cannot. I have always loved Ravenleigh. I thought no greater love existed, but I was wrong, for I love Ashton more. I will not leave her—not for all the earldoms in England."

He watched his father's jaws tighten. "Then bring her."

"And condemn her to death? The English winters are harsh, wet, and cold. She might survive one, but I doubt she would survive two. Regardless, this time, I am placing what I treasure most above what I value."

"You can't!"

"I can and I will."

"I am not going to claim what is not mine by right," Christopher said adamantly.

"I will not leave my wife to die alone," Kit insisted.

Christopher met his gaze. "You are overlooking the obvious solution, brother. You shall take my place and return to England with Father, and I shall stand in your stead and hold your wife as you held mine."

"If only it were that simple, Christopher. Unfortunately, it is not."

"You are doing this to spite me," his father grumbled.

"No, Father. My heart is no longer at Ravenleigh. Christopher cannot say the same. Can you, brother?"

"My feelings on this matter are of no consequence."

Kit smiled. "You offered to stand in my stead. Do it at Ravenleigh and not here." He bowed slightly. "Now, if you gentlemen will excuse me, my wife awaits."

Christopher shook his head slightly. "You know you can go out the front door instead of the window."

Kit winked at his brother. "Not tonight."

With the flame burning low within the lamp on the table while she lay in the bed, Ashton stared at the ceiling, Kit's words resounding in her head.

If only it were that simple . . .

Kit had told her that he wanted to speak with his father and brother alone. She'd gone downstairs for some warm milk. She had not intended to eavesdrop, but the door stood slightly ajar and their deep voices carried into the hallway.

If only it were that simple . . .

Again, Kit was sacrificing everything for her. He would not leave her to die alone, regardless of the cost to himself.

The door opened, and she watched her husband stroll in, a lazy smile enhancing his features.

"Still awake?" he asked as though he'd expected nothing different.

She thought she would never love him more than she did at this moment. She nodded slightly, etching into her memory the manner in which he removed his clothes, slowly, seductively, as though he knew how much she enjoyed the sensual performance.

"How did the talk go with your father and brother?"

"It went well. I destroyed Father's journal so there is no evidence to indicate anyone other than Christopher is the rightful heir to Ravenleigh. I think Christopher is much relieved. He can take up the reins now with no guilt."

He sat on the bed and tugged off his boots. "Besides, he's in love."

"How do you know?"

He shrugged. "I sensed it tonight. I suppose it's the woman Father arranged for him to marry. If I accepted Ravenleigh, I would take from him not only the title, but the woman he wants."

She reached over and placed her palm against his warm, bare back.

"What about you?"

He leaned back and threaded his fingers through her hair. "I have what I want."

He kissed her tenderly, sweetly, his lips playing over hers as though they had all night to do so.

"Father and Christopher leave for Galveston tomorrow to hail a ship back to England. I thought we might travel with them, perhaps spend a week at the shore before we go to Dallas."

"We go to Dallas?" she repeated inanely.

"Yes, I thought you might want to tell David in person that you've decided to stay with me," he said as he nuzzled her neck.

"Did I decide that?" she asked quietly.

He drew back and cupped her face between his hands. "I know there are things you want that I cannot give you, but we can still have a meaningful life together."

"For how long?"

"For as long as we breathe. You told me this afternoon that it frightened you to think that I might die. Do you not think I feel the same way each night when I fall off to sleep, hoping every morning when I awake that you'll still be with me?"

"But our staying together is so unfair to you, it deprives you of so much."

"It deprives me of nothing as long as you are with me." He returned his lips to her throat. "Stay with me."

He skimmed his hand along her leg, lifting her nightgown. "Stay with me."

She became powerless when his words were accompanied by the magic of passion. "Pleasure me," she rasped.

His mouth swooped down to cover hers, urgent, needy. She could have this passion every night for the remainder of her life. Desire, strong and powerful, surged through her while his tongue moved within her mouth as his body had once stroked hers. She knew they would never again experience a complete joining, but for tonight it didn't matter.

Tonight she wanted what he offered, even if it fell short of all she desired. She needed the memory of this night, of their giving to each other what they could.

With his hands, he worked to make their clothes disappear, and then they were flesh to flesh, heat to heat, trembling, writhing, touching, exploring. He had always been the aggressor while she had taken what he offered. But not tonight.

Tonight she wanted more, needed more. She wanted to give all that she had taken.

She moaned in wonder as his mouth began its sojourn along her body, tantalizing her breasts, his tongue swirling and circling before his mouth closed around her nipple and he suckled gently. Pleasure spiraled through her.

He moved lower and dipped his tongue into her navel, and lower still until he kissed her most intimately. She gasped as pleasure peaked under the guidance of his relentless, skillful pursuit. He knew her needs and where to find their solace.

She trembled as he carried her to the highest wave of the tempest and lifted her over.

Kit placed his head on the pillow of her stomach and slid his finger inside Ashton. He smiled with pure male satisfaction. "I love the way you throb afterward," he said quietly.

"Could you feel me throbbing the last night when we were together like this?" she asked.

He lifted his gaze to hers. "Yes."

"Couldn't you just . . . for a moment . . ."

"No." He kissed her stomach and shifted upward to kiss her breast. "You have no idea how hard it is for me to hold back. I'm close to bursting now."

She combed her fingers through his hair. "If I can find pleasure without our bodies joined, why can't you?"

She watched his throat work as he swallowed. "I can," he rasped.

"Teach me."

He tangled his fingers in her hair and brought her mouth to his, kissing her deeply, hungrily. He rolled to his back and she levered above him on her elbow, keeping her mouth mated to his, her hand pressed against his chest.

He took her wrist and tore his mouth from hers before kissing her palm and each of her fingers. He captured her gaze. "Are you certain?"

She nodded. "But the rule is that you have to look at me, right?"

He gave her a seductive smile. "Right."

He lowered her hand and she wrapped her fingers tightly around him. He groaned low in his throat, his gaze never leaving hers. He guided her hand until she understood the rhythm, then he cupped her breast, kneading the soft, pliant flesh as she stroked him.

She heard his breathing change into short, gasping breaths as his eyes darkened. The fingers entangled in her hair tightened. He grunted as his body arched and she felt his hot seed spurt into her hand.

He shuddered and his body relaxed beneath hers. She pressed a kiss to his dew-coated throat.

"I love the way you throb," she said huskily.

He laughed low before tracing the outline of her face with his finger. "I love you, Ashton."

"But is it fair to you if this is all we'll ever have?"

He drew her head down to his chest, and she heard the rapid pounding of his heart.

"We can make it be enough," he told her. "I promise."

"He is so bloody obstinate!" Christopher glared at the moon as though it were the source of his anger.

A small, albeit strong, hand covered his where it rested on the arm of the rocker. "You should tell him how you feel."

"Dear God, Elizabeth, he *knows* how I feel! He knows my thoughts as well as I know his. He is well aware that I came here out of a sense of obligation and fairness, that I covet Ravenleigh and its title. He does as well, though he claims to love Ashton more. But she is to die, and then what? He shall spend the remainder of his life alone. At least if he returned to England he could marry."

"Is she pretty?"

He glanced at her. "She is frail, ethereal. She reminds me of a fairy. Have you not met Ashton?"

Elizabeth smiled warmly. "I meant the woman your father has arranged for you to marry."

"Ah." He sighed. "I have yet to meet her." He furrowed his brow. "I can't recall her name. Father mentioned it in passing when he told me that he had made the arrangements, but I did not care. My heart was still on Clarisse." He turned to face her squarely. "That's hardly fair to her, is it? The woman I'm to marry, I mean."

She squeezed his hand. "I wouldn't worry. You're bound to learn her name before you marry her. Besides, once you've met her, maybe she'll help you to stop missing Clarisse."

He cradled her cheek. "Who shall help you to stop missing Daniel?"

He watched her smile wither, and she licked her lips. "I don't thing about Daniel so much anymore. I feel guilty about that sometimes."

He leaned nearer. "I have a confession to make. I haven't thought of Clarisse since the first night I sat on your porch until dawn."

He brushed his thumb over her lips. "I desperately want to kiss you. Do you suppose being in the position I am of being betrothed that it would be an unforgivable offense if I were to give in to temptation just once?"

She shook her head slightly, and he felt her pulse quicken where his palm pressed against her throat. He lowered his mouth to hers, drinking greedily of the sweet nectar she offered, and cursing his brother for condemning him to hell with his act of generosity.

Languidly, Kit awoke and stretched. He had not slept this well in years. He rolled over to draw his wife into his embrace and discovered he was alone. His gaze quickly darted around the empty room. She'd no doubt risen early to relish the sunrise.

He got out of bed and saw to his morning routine of getting ready for the day. Ashton would need to purchase a few more items before they left for Galveston. Whatever else her heart desired, he would purchase for her there.

He walked out of the room and down the stairs

with a sense of well-being. He glanced at the door that led into his father's room. Hopefully by now, his father understood Kit's reasoning and forgave him.

He entered the foyer just as Elizabeth Fairfield strolled through the front door. She came to an abrupt halt and stared at him.

He smiled warmly. "Good morning, Elizabeth."

She shoved a quilt at him. "I brought this for you."

He stepped nearer and examined the intricate stitching. "It's lovely." He lifted his gaze to hers. "A wedding gift?"

She nodded quickly and looked as though she were fighting back tears. "You can call it that if you want. I just thought it might help to keep your bed warm."

Her generosity caught him off guard as he took her gift. "Thank you. All this time I never thought you cared much for me."

"Why would you think that?"

He heard a door open and watched her gaze shift toward the sound.

"Elizabeth, what in the world are you doing here?" Christopher asked.

Elizabeth jerked her gaze back to Kit's, her cheeks flaming red. She snatched the quilt from his arms. "You varmint, I should have realized it was you."

Kit chuckled. "So you're the one who mistook Christopher for me. That must have been an interesting encounter."

"Indeed it was," Christopher said quietly, amusement reflected in his voice as he approached Elizabeth.

She thrust the quilt at him. "I brought this to keep you warm at nights. Made it myself. It's a lone star pattern, and since Texas has a lone star on its flag, I thought you might think of me whenever you used it."

Kit knew a pang of guilt when he saw the wistfulness in his brother's eyes as he took the gift.

"I'll need no reminders of you, but thank you for the gift."

Elizabeth jerked her head up and down. "The girls are in the wagon, so I gotta go."

"I'd like to say goodbye to your daughters," Christopher said quietly.

"They'd like that. I'll meet you outside."

She turned and scurried out, but not before Kit saw the tears welling in her eyes. Christopher set the quilt down on a nearby chair and strode toward the door. Kit grabbed his arm and spun him around. "You neglected to mention that you had a reason why you no longer wanted to be heir."

"The reason didn't exist until I came here."

Kit studied his brother. "Last night I felt that you were in love, but I thought it was with someone in England. It's Elizabeth, isn't it? You love her."

"My feelings and whom I love are of no consequence regarding your decision."

"The hell they aren't."

"Father has made arrangements for a wedding to take place at Christmas. You are quite right that Ashton will die if you take her to England, and you cannot serve as master of the estate from here. You sacrificed your love for a woman once before—a woman who rightfully belonged to you, I might point out—so now it is my turn to make a sacrifice."

"To hell with Father's arrangements. If you love Elizabeth, marry her and take her to England with you," Kit suggested.

"Marshal?"

Kit turned at the sound of Mrs. Gurney's voice. "Yes, Mr. Gurney?"

She held an envelope toward him. "I was told to give you this."

Kit opened the envelope, withdrew its contents, and felt all the blood drain from his face and his knees grow weak. His chest ached, tears stung his eyes, and his entire world ceased to exist. His fingers went limp, and the papers fluttered to the floor.

"What is it?" Christopher asked, concern clearly reflected in his voice. "What's happened?"

His voice strangled with emotion, Kit forced out the words. "Ashton is dead."

Chapter 26

Ignoring the elderly couple sitting across from her, Ashton stared out the window of the stagecoach, the countryside a blur of green leaves, brown soil, and blue sky. She felt as hollow, as dead, as the certificate she'd paid the physician to draw up for her.

The actual date of her death was unimportant. Today. The end of the year. It didn't matter because she knew death's arrival was imminent.

What mattered was that Kit was free to return to England, to take his rightful place at the home of his birth, the estate that he loved and had watched over even from afar. He needed to return with his father and establish his right to inherit.

His father's time was as limited as hers was. Once he died, the new Earl of Ravenleigh would take his place. She wanted that man to be Kit, and her actions had ensured that dream's reality.

True, her record of death was false, but no more false than Kit's record of birth. How could his father have tampered with fate?

A gunshot sounded. The woman sitting across from

Ashton squealed and burrowed her face into her husband's shoulder as he wrapped his arm around her and drew her near. Ashton clenched her hands and squeezed her eyes shut. Another robbery!

Was there no law beyond the boundaries of any towns?

She felt the stagecoach begin to slow and didn't know whether to be relieved that they weren't going to try to outpace the outlaws or fearful for what the thieves might do. She'd had one experience and it was enough to make her fear all lawless men.

The stagecoach rolled to a stop. Ashton's heart beat unmercifully in her chest. She swore that given the opportunity she would never again ride in a stagecoach. She heard the pounding hooves and a horse's neigh.

Then silence that was more frightening, because it left no hint as to what she should expect.

The door burst open. Ashton screeched at the foreboding figure blocking the sunlight. Her fellow female passenger fainted.

"We have no money," the woman's husband blurted out.

"I have no interest in money." The shadowy figure extended his hand toward Ashton. "Mrs. Montgomery."

Relief warred with anger as Ashton stared at her husband. "Didn't you get the letter I left for you?"

"Indeed I did, once my heart returned to normal. Might I suggest that the next time you decide to pull such a fool stunt that you place the letter on *top* of the death certificate instead of beneath it."

"I don't see that it matters where I placed the letter. It explained everything."

"Now I have some things to explain to you." He reached farther into the coach. "Please, come with me."

Reluctantly, she slipped her hand into his, relishing the strength and warmth she'd never thought to feel again. With his assistance, she stepped into the sunlight. She released her hold on him and straightened her skirts before angling her chin.

Bearded stubble shadowed his face and his eyes were red rimmed and swollen. She desperately wanted to touch him and relieve his suffering, but she could not give in to temptation. She had to remain strong. "You'd better talk quickly. These people are in a hurry."

"I intend to take my time in explaining." He glanced up at the driver. "Is my wife's valise up top?"

"Yes, sir," the driver said as he grabbed it and tossed it down.

Kit caught it easily. "Thank you, Mr. Jordan."

"You're welcome, Marshal Montgomery. Good thing I recognized you. Wouldn't have stopped otherwise. Been too many robberies lately."

"What do you think you're doing?" Ashton asked with equal frustration and anger. She'd finally managed to find the gumption to do something on her own and Kit was thwarting her plans.

"Give me a week, and if at the end of that time, you still feel your actions are warranted, then I shall honor the record of your death and return you to Dallas myself."

"And you promise to go back to Ravenleigh?"

"Yes."

The sadness in his eyes tore into her heart, and against her better judgment, she found herself nodding.

"Why would Ashton have her own death certificate drawn up?" Elizabeth asked Christopher as he leaned against the porch railing, one hand stuffed in his pocket, his head bent.

He slowly shook his head. "I can only presume that she thought she was giving Kit what he wanted." He lifted his gaze. "Theirs is a complicated relationship, not unlike ours."

Elizabeth furrowed her brow, pressed her shoulder against the beam that supported the roof over the porch, and crossed her arms beneath her breasts. "I don't see our friendship as being complicated."

Christopher shifted his stance. "It's not complicated here, no, but it would be in England. I am nobility, you aren't. I am well educated, whereas life more than schools educated you. I am expected to project a certain mien, and you are refreshingly adept at revealing your true self."

Elizabeth narrowed her eyes. "Why do I feel like I'm being insulted?"

"Believe me, it is not my intent to insult you. I'm merely striving to realistically and tactfully identify obstacles that we might have to overcome if we were in England."

Elizabeth rolled her eyes, wondering why he was

pursuing this path of conversation. "I don't see the point in identifying anything. We're not in England."

"No, we're not." He held her gaze, and she saw uncertainty reflected in his pale blue eyes. "But we could be."

She furrowed her brow. "I don't see how."

"If we wished it to be so." He took a step closer. "My father arranged both my marriages. The first one worked out splendidly. Clarisse and I were well suited, and until she took ill, I was extremely happy. I have immense doubts regarding the second one. I cannot envision that I shall be content."

She lifted a shoulder. "I know you're feeling guilty because you don't remember her name—"

"My misgivings regarding this second marriage have nothing to do with my inability to remember my intended's name. They reside in the fact that I shall be unable to forget you."

She felt as though the breath had been knocked out of her, and all she could manage to his flattering declaration was a soft, "Oh."

She turned and looked toward the fields that had lain fallow since Daniel had left to fight for the Confederacy.

"I realize that we have not known each other long," he continued, "and perhaps my feelings are premature but I must confess that I've fallen in love with you. I was hoping that you might consent to marry me."

Tears burned her eyes, blurring the fields that her husband had planted and harvested. She pressed a trembling hand to her lips. It had been a good many years since she'd captured a man's fancy, a good many years since she'd wanted to. But lately, the wind whispering through the leaves, her daughters' voices and their laughter, weren't enough to ease the loneliness. "Everything here reminds me of Daniel," she rasped. "It would be like leaving him." The tears rolled down her cheeks as she turned and looked at Christopher. "I know I told you that I haven't thought of him lately . . . and I haven't, but I can't *leave* here, leave what I know." An unexpected sob escaped her.

He drew her into his embrace and pressed her face against his chest. He didn't smell of sweat, horses, soil, or crops. He smelled like lemon, crisp and clean.

"I'm so sorry," she croaked, hating this weakness that made her feel incredibly young and vulnerable.

He closed his arms more securely around her. Oh, Lord, he was sturdy. He would have made a fine farmer.

"The apology is mine to give," he said quietly. "I should not have placed you in this awkward position of having to reject me. My earlier blathering was an attempt to get an idea of how you might feel on the matter. I handled it poorly."

She snapped her head back to meet his sorrowful gaze. Her heart tightened into a painful knot. She didn't want to hurt him, but the thought of leaving what she'd known her entire life scared the living daylights out of her. "It's not you," she reassured him. "I just—"

He shook his head slightly. "It's all right. You don't have to explain. I realize that what I was proposing was selfish on my part. I've enjoyed being with you, and I wanted to prolong our time together, for the remainder of our lives, actually." He smiled warmly, his gaze traveling over her face as though he wanted to memorize every curve and hollow. "I'd even planned to have a porch built around the manor so we could watch the sunset."

She felt more tears surface. Gently he wiped them away.

"Don't weep," he ordered softly. "I don't want my last memory of you to be with tears dampening your lovely face."

She clutched his shirt and pressed her face against his chest. Why was this parting so hard? She twisted her head slightly, and her gaze fell on the long stretch of road, a dirt path she looked down every morning when she woke up. Of late, she hadn't been looking for Daniel. She'd been looking for the man who now held her, and she'd still be looking for him when he left. "I love you," she said quietly.

"Then accept my proposal. I know it won't be easy, and I know it must be as frightening to consider being my wife as it was for me to contemplate being a farmer." He threaded his fingers through her hair and bent her head back until their gazes met. "But I promise that you'll never come to regret your decision if you agree to be my wife. I can't deny that your life will change drastically, and the demands will be many, but I'll gladly teach you all that you need to know, and I rather think you'll enjoy the challenge." He kissed her cheek, her temple, her brow. "Say yes, Elizabeth."

The plea, spoken with such tenderness, melted her

heart. She wrapped her arms around his neck, leaned away from him slightly, and looked into his pale blue eyes. "Yes."

A beautiful, joyous smile eased across his face before he lowered his mouth to hers, his passionate kiss easing aside the doubts until she could readily admit that no other answer had been possible.

Nestled between Kit's thighs as he sat astride Lancelot and guided the horse, Ashton heard the thunder of the waterfalls long before they reached them. Their time here had been short, and in spite of the circumstances that had caused them to discover this small Eden, she'd thought it beautiful and peaceful.

But she had not expected Kit to bring her here.

With the lush green surrounding her so unlike the flatness of Dallas, for a fleeting moment, she felt as though they had returned to paradise. But it was only a beautiful illusion, an elaborate unforgettable tapestry in which explanations could be rendered, understanding could be reached, and a final farewell be exchanged.

She would not allow Kit to return to Dallas with her. She would go alone, for she had no desire to taint Dallas with a memory that she felt certain would break her heart.

This place was appropriate, for its majesty would sustain the most painful moment of her life. Why had Kit not been content with her letter of explanation? What could he possibly say to change her mind?

She knew he loved her, knew she loved him. Love

required sacrifices, and he had made them all for her. Now she wanted to return the favor. How could he not understand?

She saw the falls in which she'd bathed when he'd been injured. The current was not strong as it hit the rocks below and journeyed through cracks and crevices toward destinations she could only imagine.

Kit drew Lancelot to a halt and dismounted. Reaching up, he wrapped his hands on either side of her waist and brought her slowly to the ground, her body brushing against his, causing warm tendrils of pleasure to curl through her. She refused to give into the temptation to wrap her arms around his neck and draw his head down for a kiss.

She must remain dispassionate and project a false image of strength when all she truly wanted was to remain in his embrace forever. She wanted to die within his arms, and for a brief moment, she envied Clarisse.

Perhaps if his father were stronger, Kit could stay with her until the end, but she knew in her heart that if he did not return to Ravenleigh now, he would never return. He would be the one who placed the solitary rose on her grave. He would lead the lonely life he'd always envisioned for himself.

She stepped back. "Is this where we intend to talk?"

He smiled lazily. "I said nothing of talking."

"But you wanted to convince me—"

"With actions, not with words. Let me see to Lancelot's comfort, and then I shall see to yours."

He led the horse away, and she walked to the babbling water. What did he have in mind?

Whatever it was, he would not sway her from her decision or the path she knew she must follow.

His hands came to rest on her shoulders as he pressed his warm mouth against the nape of her neck. If it were not for the coolness of the mist caused by the cascading water, she thought she might melt on the spot. She felt his tongue tease her flesh just before he whispered, " 'Tis a wise dead woman who packs her valise."

She spun around. He had spread a blanket over the ground and her case rested near it. She looked up into his light blue eyes. "Kit—"

"Shh." He cradled her chin and touched his thumb to her lips. "No words, not yet."

He lowered his head and brushed his lips over hers.

"Kit, passion isn't the answer."

"I know that now, but it's a splendid substitute," he rasped, before capturing her mouth totally with his, his tongue seeking entry she could not deny him.

Like a vine seeking purchase, she entwined her arms around his neck and pressed her body flush against his. Regardless of the pleasure he brought her, she would not stay with him; she loved him too much. She'd tried to show him the last night they'd shared a bed. Perhaps that had been her mistake, pleasuring him as he had pleasured her.

But still she had felt the emptiness. It would always be there between them, a chasm they could not fill because he would not give all of himself to her, and damn her heart for understanding and for hurting so painfully. And for wanting so desperately what she could never give him.

With another woman, he would not have to deny himself complete surrender to passion's glory.

As he trailed his mouth along her throat, she tried not to think of his lips touching someone else's neck, igniting another's flesh.

She felt as though her knees were turning into pools of wax, and she would soon melt at his feet. He wrapped one arm sturdily around her waist, holding her upright, while the fingers of his other hand began to deftly unbutton her bodice.

"What are you doing?" she asked on a breathless sigh.

"What I've wanted to do since I first saw you beneath the flowing waters of the fall. Only duty called then, and I had no time to enjoy you."

"As duty should be calling you now." She cradled his face between her hands. "You're only prolonging the inevitable."

"Perhaps that's what I've been doing all along."

He crushed his mouth to hers with a desperation she'd never felt in him before, as though he were clinging to her, fearful of his own demise should she not be within reach. She heard the material of her bodice rip, and quite frankly, she didn't care.

Nothing would change her mind, but she could take this memory with her, hold it near when death hovered close, and smile. Eagerly, she moved her hands over his strong shoulders and along his sturdy chest until her fingers found the buttons on his shirt.

She felt the cool mist touch her bare shoulders and soon her bare back as he removed her clothes with an efficiency that left them in tatters. With only half his buttons free, he stepped back and she stood nude before him, his gaze wandering slowly over her as though he were painting an image in his mind, soft sweeping strokes of the brush.

His gaze left her only momentarily as he pulled his shirt over his head and cast it aside. His boots followed. Then he stripped off his remaining garments, leaving her with the breathtaking sight of his nudity. Always before, shadows had played over him, hiding portions here and there, careful to never reveal the full measure of his magnificence.

A jolt of regret shot through her. She never wanted any woman to gaze upon him as she did now, bathed in the shafts of sunlight filtering through the thick branches and leaves above.

She wanted him forever.

She gave him a tremulous smile as he held out his hand, so much larger than hers. So much stronger. With his hands, he had saved a town, and each time he touched her, she felt as though he spared a portion of her, created a memory that might never fade.

She slipped her hand into his and his fingers closed securely around it. He pulled her close and wound his arm around her as he led her to the falls. The mist grew thicker and a shiver traveled the length of her body. Her nipples puckered.

Kit released his hold on her and nudged her toward the cascading water. She glanced over her shoulder at him. "Aren't you coming?"

He shook his head slightly. "I want to watch you for a while."

Ashton felt the heat of embarrassment suffuse her

body from head to toe. "I feel like you're wanting me to put on a performance."

"I want nothing more than memories, Ashton. Should my power of persuasion be less than I think it is, should you not tear up the death certificate that's in my saddlebag, memories are all I'll have to sustain me through my grief. Is that too much to ask?"

She felt the tears sting her eyes. "Kit, you have to understand—"

"I do understand, sweetling. That's why I need the memories. I have so few of the first woman I loved that I'll not make that mistake again."

With a sigh and a burning desire to give him more than he asked for, she averted her gaze and walked beneath the shower of water. Its strength was as palpable as its gentleness. She allowed it to wash over her, cleansing her heart as well as her body.

She would leave him so he could follow his destiny.

Standing proud, she turned and faced him. Even through the mist, she could see the intensity of his gaze, feel its vibrant heat as he watched her. He stood as still as any statue, as any animal waiting for its prey.

She suddenly felt vulnerable and unprotected. His penetrating gaze never left hers as he stalked across the rocks and ferns, a man with a purpose.

Lord help her, she didn't know if she had the strength to withstand the assault on her heart that she knew he was capable of delivering.

He stepped into the falls, and she watched as the sheets of water washed over him, plastering his hair to his head as they continued on their journey. He drew her to him, and she looked through the droplets into his eyes.

"You are so beautiful," he said in a low voice. He cupped one of her breasts, lifted it slightly as he dipped his head and closed his mouth around her hardened nipple. The fury of passion exploded within her.

"You've gained weight," he said quietly.

She had. She knew each time she put on her clothes, but all the weight in the world would not defeat death.

He cupped her other breast and drew the tip into his mouth, suckling gently. She grabbed his shoulders, seeking to remain standing when all she wanted was to lie beneath him, to have her body a molten pool of wax shaped by his hands into the raging passion that she knew he could bring forth.

He brought his mouth to hers and an insatiable appetite swept through her. She thrust her tongue into his mouth, wanting him as she'd never wanted him before, with fierceness and needs that were almost frightening. More than receiving the pleasure, she wanted to give it to him again, to witness his body's reaction, his eyes darkening as passion consumed him like a fire gone unfettered.

She wanted it all, and God help her, she wanted it for the remainder of her life whether it was measured in hours, days, or weeks.

Kit slid one arm beneath her knees, the other around her back and lifted her into his arms, cradling her against his chest. "Kiss me," he commanded, and she could no more deny him than she could cause the sun to stop shining.

She tasted the purity of the water rushing over them, drenching them, and more she tasted him, a flavor as distinctive as the man himself. Intoxicating. Her arms wound around his neck, and she pressed her body more closely against his as the urgency of his kiss increased.

He carried her from beneath the falls. She shivered and his hold on her tightened as though he wanted to warm her. Carefully, he dropped to one knee and laid her on the quilt. He grabbed one end and began to blot the droplets of water from her skin.

"Bloody hell, I can warm you more quickly," he murmured before laying his body over hers.

Instinctively, she spread her thighs until he was nestled snuggly between them. He covered her completely from hip to chest. Raised up slightly on his elbows, he cradled her face and kissed her forehead, her closed eyes, her cheeks, the tip of her nose, working his way along her body.

"Kit, this won't change anything," she whispered, her argument sounding weak even to her.

"I know," he murmured as his tongue circled her nipple. He moved back up until their gazes were even. He held hers steadily. "I want to be inside you, Ashton. If only once more."

With one palm, she cradled his cheek and nodded.

"Promise me that you won't close your eyes," he rasped. "I want to see the rapture in your eyes when the passion overtakes you."

She swallowed hard. He wanted from her what she could never have from him. Yet she would gladly give him this one last gift, accepting the pain of bereavement that she knew would accompany it when he stilled without giving her what she craved most: his complete surrender. To be so lost in her that he forgot his vow, forgot everything but her.

She slid her hands around to his back and urged him forward. "Come to me."

He kissed her deeply, hungrily before levering himself over her, capturing and holding her gaze. Her hands stroking his back, she noted the tenseness in his muscles as he drove himself into her. Moaning with pleasure, she lifted her hips, meeting his initial thrust, relishing the fullness, the rightness of their joining.

The love she felt for him blossomed more fully as he moved against her, lowering his head now and again to kiss her throat, her breast, her shoulder, her lips. Lifting his head to hold her gaze while his body held her enraptured.

This time would be the last for them and she wanted every memory, every sensation. As though she were a starving woman, she ran her hands over him, every inch she could touch, memorizing the varying textures of his flesh, the hair on his arms, his chest, the thick strands that covered his head, the cords of muscle that rippled with each movement.

Beneath him, she responded in rhythm to the crashing of the waterfalls, cascading sensations that seemed unceasing as they escalated. She wasn't going down the falls, but climbing ever higher, reaching beyond the limits.

She felt the tenseness in his muscles increasing, his thrusts quickening, driving her toward an escalating pinnacle. She cried out as he drove her over the edge into unequaled sensations richer than any she'd ever known. She watched in wonder as his back arched with his final driving thrust, and he released a low, guttural groan.

Glorious. She felt glorious inside and out. Complete. Whole.

Her body quivered, while his trembled violently, his gaze still holding hers, his breathing harsh.

"Oh my God," she whispered, cradling his face. "You didn't—"

He nodded slightly, lowering his body and pressing a kiss to her temple before burying his face within the crook between her neck and shoulder.

She tightened her hold on him. She'd never experienced such joy or such grief. He'd given her what she'd desired most, but at what cost to himself?

The tears rolled along her cheeks.

He kissed the corner of her eyes. "Don't cry."

"But you didn't want this."

"It's exactly what I wanted." He lifted his head and combed his fingers through her hair. "I've wanted it since I saw you standing on the porch that first morning at the boardinghouse."

"But your vow—"

"Was made out of fear, a fear that seemed so insignificant when I opened that envelope and saw your death certificate." He trailed his knuckles along her cheek. "Dear God, Ashton, the regrets that swamped me seemed insurmountable. I thought every moment we've shared would sustain me through the remainder of my life. But as I stared at that damned document I realized that it didn't matter when you died—whether it is tomorrow or a hundred years from now—I shall always want one more moment, one more moment. And to deny either of us anything that we want while you continue to breathe is a sin."

"But what if I get with child?"

"I've thought a lot about that possibility. Everything in life is a risk. Either of us could have died when the outlaws attacked the stagecoach. I could have perished when I faced them in the street of Fortune. No moment is guaranteed. I have always strove to anticipate the unexpected, to plan for it. But I never expected to fall so madly in love with you. If I get you with babe, then you shall simply have to live long enough to give me the chance to hold him."

"I can't control that!" she cried.

He brushed his lips over hers. "I know that, sweetling, but what if the physician were wrong? Instead of six months, you have twelve. 'Tis time enough to make a child. You flourished in Galveston. I spoke with a physician at St. Mary's, and he told me that evidence suggests that a drier climate can prolong the life of a consumptive, and on rare occasion, it can cure. He doesn't know why or what the secret is. I've visited the western part of this state and the air is drier than it is here, and I had thought that perhaps we could move there.

"Right now the area is rampant with outlaws and renegades, but a bill was recently passed allowing the state to reestablish the Rangers in the western part of the state. They need men with experience to lead the way."

Terror seized her. "You're considering being one of the men?"

"Yes."

"You have lost your mind. You could die! Outlaws could kill you!"

"So will you leave me here because that possibility exists? Death awaits us all, Ashton. I am as likely to die from a bullet as you are from consumption. I say we give death a merry chase."

A bubble of laughter burst from her, and she slapped her hand over her mouth. "You're insane. What about Ravenleigh? I know you love it, that you secretly wanted to be its heir all these years."

"I love you more." He held a finger in front of her face. "I will admit this to you and you alone and you are never to tell a soul." He heaved a sigh. "I've grown rather fond of this damnable state."

"But if the physician is right, and I don't survive this winter—"

"Then I shall mourn." He kissed her lightly before capturing her gaze once again. "But if he is wrong and we part company now, I shall mourn all the more for the moments together that we lost."

With the quilt draped around her shoulders, Ashton sat at the edge of the falls watching the cascading water. Like the ocean, its movements never ceased. If only she could be assured that her breathing would not cease before she was ready, before Kit was ready.

Would there ever come a time when she would welcome death's touch? She didn't want to leave all that surrounded her. Most of all, though, she didn't want to leave Kit.

He had asked for a week to convince her to stay with him, yet he had persuaded her with one simple action. He had given her everything. She had seen it in the light blue depths of his eyes and felt it in the straining, shuddering muscles of his body. She'd seen it in the sweat glistening over his flesh and heard it in the harsh breathing and deep groans. She had known it when her body had closed snuggly around his while his seed pulsed into her.

His seed. The possibility that she might carry his child filled her with incredible joy, joy that she'd never experienced.

He had given her what she craved most, and now she was terrified that death would not afford her the opportunity to enjoy everything.

She heard his movements as he dressed while all the doubts in the world plagued her. She had lived her life appreciating each day, fearful that she would have no tomorrow.

Yet, tomorrow always arrived to mock her uncertainty.

Kit knelt beside her and placed her clothing in her lap. "You should get dressed."

She slanted her gaze at him. "I have spent my life waiting for death."

He tucked a strand of hair behind her ear. "Death waits for us. We should not wait for it. When Gray, Harry, and I faced those outlaws in the street of Fortune, just before I fired my first bullet, I thought of a thousand things that I wished I had done before that moment." He smiled. "A few moments ago, I managed to enjoy the first thing on my list, which leaves me with nine hundred and ninety-nine things left to do."

Irrational anger shot through her. "So making love to me fully was an item on a list?"

His smile warmed. "Every item on my list revolved around doing something with you. I want to watch the sun rise with you. And watch it set. I want to watch storms roll over the land. I want to inhale your fragrance when I awaken and hear your breathing as I drift off to sleep."

She clutched his shirt and buried her face against his chest. "Oh, Kit, what if you give up Ravenleigh and I die tomorrow?"

"What if I don't give it up and *I* die tomorrow?"

She jerked her head up and met his gaze.

"Twice in the past month, I've come nearer to death than you are at this very moment. You told me once that tomorrow is a gift, and we take for granted that it will be there. So we've both held back, fearful that if we gave too much we would lose what we treasured and our grief would increase. I say to hell with living only for today. Let's live as though we have a thousand tomorrows."

She combed her fingers through his hair before trailing them along the strong cut of his jaw. "I don't want you to have regrets, to give up something that you cherish."

"You are all that I cherish. All that I hold dear." He

slipped his hand inside the blanket and splayed his fingers over her bare stomach. "If what passed between us a few moments ago wasn't enough, tell me what I must do to convince you that all I shall ever regret are the moments that I don't have with you as long as you live."

Tears burned her eyes and clogged her throat. "I love you so much."

"Then grow old with me."

"And if I can't?"

He released a wistful sigh. "Grow a moment older with me. An hour older. A day. A week. Just don't leave me until you absolutely must."

"You broke your vow. Your child could die with me."

He shook his head. "You're stronger than you realize, not nearly as frail as you once were. I'll risk giving you a dozen children if you'll but fight death."

She placed her hand over his where it rested against her stomach. "I've never been more afraid than I am at this moment. I've always faced death. I don't know how to face life."

He entwined his fingers through hers. " 'Tis simple, sweetling. Just hold my hand."

Chapter 27

Sitting on the sofa, Ashton nestled against his side, her fingers threaded through his, Kit studied the man standing before the window, gazing out. He had welcomed his visitors, but Kit doubted that he would welcome their news.

"I love Ashton, David," Kit said quietly and felt Ashton's fingers tighten their hold on his.

David slowly nodded. "I was afraid that might happen if you spent much time alone together." He glanced over his shoulder, sorrow etched in the lines of his face. "I won't ask how you feel about him, Ashton. Your love for Kit is reflected clearly in your eyes."

With a sigh, he shook his head. "I'm sorry, Kit. I don't know why I thought everything could stay simple and uncomplicated. You're welcome to stay here"—he darted a quick glance at Ashton—"for as long as you want."

"Actually, Ashton and I are going to move to the western part of the state."

David took a step toward them. "You can't be serious."

"Deadly serious."

"She isn't strong enough—"

"She is," Kit insisted. "She's stronger now than she was when we married, and I have hope that a drier climate will serve her well."

David looked at his sister. "I suppose you want to go."

She smiled warmly. "I want to be with Kit."

He held out his arms. Tears welled in Ashton's eyes as she rose to her feet and walked into her brother's embrace. "I love you, David."

Kit saw tears fill David's eyes as he touched his sister's cheek. "I love you, too, and I just want you to be happy. If going wherever this Englishman decides to take you is what will make you happy, then go with my blessing."

"Thank you, David."

Kit stood, placed his arm around Ashton as she joined him, and drew her close against his side.

"So when will you leave?" David asked.

"Christopher is in Fortune now, arranging his own wedding," Kit explained. "Once that happy event takes place, we plan to spend a month in Galveston with my father and Christopher's new family. When they set sail, we'll begin our journey west."

Ashton stood on the dock as Kit bade his brother and father farewell. As a new bride, Elizabeth glowed. Her three daughters were jumping, skipping, and talking excitedly about their journey. Ashton wanted to ask them to be still. She wanted to ask everyone to quickly get aboard the ship or leave the dock.

It was too crowded. She was having a hard time drawing in air and the more she fought to breathe, the harder it became. She could feel the August heat suffocating her.

Too many people. They were blocking the breeze. She desperately needed the breeze.

Ashton felt the beads of sweat pop out on her brow and the bile rise in her throat. Something was wrong, terribly wrong.

She heard Kit's laughter from a great distance as he talked with Christopher.

Kit glanced over his shoulder, and she saw his brow furrow. He took her arm, concern clearly etched in his features. She hoped she didn't look as bad as she felt.

"Are you all right?" he asked.

She nodded, her tongue thickening. "I'm fine."

"You look pale."

Tears stung her eyes as she cradled his face with trembling hands. She wasn't fine, and she knew it. Symptoms had been arriving daily, and today they were the worst. "Please, go with them. Return to England."

"Why?"

She felt the tear roll along her cheek. "Death is here."

"The bloody hell it is. Ashton, listen to me—"

She desperately wanted to, but his voice faded as she sank into a darkened abyss.

At St. Mary's, Kit stared out the window. He felt like a ship without an anchor caught in a tempest at sea. He couldn't remember the last time Ashton had coughed. She had seemed so much stronger that he'd almost forgotten that she was ill.

Today's episode on the dock had been a sudden and frightening reminder that all was not well with her. He wanted to rant and rail and curse, but he didn't know at whom he should direct his anger.

His thoughts were as scattered as promises on the wind, unable to take hold.

"The physicians in England would not keep us waiting like this," his father grumbled. "Do they not realize who I am here?"

A smile tugged at the corner of Kit's mouth. His father had grown rather fond of Ashton in the past month and, in the end, had accepted with grace Kit's decision to stay in Texas.

"Your ship will sail without you if you don't leave now," Kit said quietly.

"There will be another," Christopher replied.

Kit nodded. Yes, there would be another. A hundred more would follow this one. How many more moments would he have with Ashton?

A door opened and a man stepped through. Kit recognized him as the physician he'd spoken with before, Dr. Stewart. "Mr. Montgomery?"

Kit turned to see Christopher take a step forward and his father struggle to get out of his chair. If his heart weren't breaking, he would have laughed. He placed his hand on his father's shoulder to still him. "He only means me."

"We all bloody well care," his father snapped.

Kit squeezed his shoulder. "I know you do. I'll let you know what he says."

Kit followed Dr. Stewart into the room. His chest tightened at the sight of Ashton sitting in front of a desk, her hands clasped together. She was still so incredibly pale. He sat in the chair beside her and placed his hand over hers.

She shifted her gaze to him and gave him a tremulous smile. How he wanted to pull her onto his lap, into his arms, and reassure her that all would be well.

The physician sat behind his desk and smiled. "I always like to begin with the good news first."

Kit's heart sank. "I prefer the bad news first."

Dr. Stewart gave a brisk nod. "All right." He crossed his arms across the top of his desk and leaned forward slightly. "Your wife tells me that last winter a physician diagnosed her with pulmonary consumption." He pursed his lips and held Ashton's gaze. "I see no evidence that the disease has spread beyond your lungs. As a matter of fact, I see very little evidence of lesions in your lungs. You mentioned that you were coughing up blood last winter."

Ashton nodded. "Occasionally. It was frightening."

"I imagine it was." Dr. Stewart held up a palm as though he hoped to find an answer there. "When the lesions burst, the patient may cough up blood. Sometimes the lesions heal. Unfortunately, most of the doctors in this state are self-taught. They can misread symptoms or jump to conclusions based on limited knowledge. Because I did not examine you last winter, I have nothing by which to compare the examination I just gave you. But if his diagnosis was correct, then you show a remarkable improvement in health that is not unheard of. Diet, rest, activities that force the lungs to work harder than they have before can make a difference."

Ashton intertwined her fingers with Kit's. Kit shifted his attention away from the doctor, his heart gladdened by the adoration in Ashton's eyes.

"My husband forces me to eat and take long walks with him." She smiled. "We're going to move to a drier climate."

"Based upon what we've been able to ascertain, that should help as well," Dr. Stewart said. "I'd like to recommend one more thing. The town of Mineral Wells has a medical well that has been known to cure a variety of illnesses. I would suggest a visit once or twice a year."

Kit leaned forward to make certain he had not misunderstood. "Once or twice a year? You say that as though you expect my wife to live beyond Christmas."

"I do, Mr. Montgomery. I have read of documented cases where a patient was given a month to live and lived fifty years. Consumption is a baffling disease. Unfortunately, as is the way with many diseases, we don't know all we need to know."

Squeezing Ashton's hand, Kit settled back in the chair. "That is good news, Dr. Stewart. I should have let you begin there."

Dr. Stewart grinned broadly. "Oh, that wasn't my good news, Mr. Montgomery. My good news is that your wife is with child."

Kit felt as though he'd taken a blow to his chest. Ashton gasped and pressed both their hands against her stomach. Such joy radiated from her face that Kit felt a lump rise in his throat. Leaning over, he kissed the beautiful smile on her face.

He glanced back at the doctor. "You're certain?"

"It's an easy diagnosis, Mr. Montgomery. I've never been mistaken yet."

Unease settled in. "She fainted on the dock—"

"Probably too many people. She's breathing for two now. She needs more air, more food, more rest, more attention."

Kit looked back at his adoring wife. "I'd give her more *love* if it were possible."

Epilogue

October 1871

My dearest Kit,

It is with heavy heart that I write to tell you that Father passed away. He went peacefully with a smile and mother's name upon his lips.

And so damned much pride. Your letter had arrived announcing the birth of your son. He proclaimed that Damon Montgomery would be the next earl of Ravenleigh.

I have a feeling in my heart of hearts that he was correct in his assumption, and I am glad of it. I have a fondness for daughters, and Elizabeth has just blessed me with one who looks very much like a Montgomery as I hold her while I pen this letter.

I believe Clarisse smiles down on us from heaven and shares in our happiness. I also think she would heartily approve of your decision to put your funds toward medical research rather than flowers.

With love,
Christopher
Earl of Ravenleigh

Kit bowed his head, his throat tightening and his chest aching. Even when death was expected, grief was overpowering and came without warning. He was grateful that he had reconciled any differences he had with his father, more grateful that in the end his father had respected his decision.

Kit heard the soft footfalls and glanced up as Ashton knelt beside him.

"Your father's gone," she said quietly, resting a hand on his arm.

He nodded as his eyes filled with tears. "I had not expected to miss him. He was an ocean away, for God's sake. When I saw him off in Galveston, I knew I would never see him again, but I did not weep."

She placed her palm on his chest, right over his heart. "Grief knows nothing of distances measured in miles. Love dictates its depths."

He pulled her onto his lap and nestled her head within the crook of his shoulder. "My wife has become a philosopher. Whatever shall I do with you?"

"Grow old."

He gazed into her penetrating blue eyes that dared him to deny her words. She was stronger than she'd ever been with a glow to her face that he hoped would never fade. In the farthest recesses of his heart, he knew he would watch her hair turn silver and wrinkles form across her brow.

He wiped the tears from his eyes. "Christopher says Father proclaimed Damon to be the next Earl of Ravenleigh."

Ashton smiled. "It seems appropriate that our son would be, since his father should have been."

"We shall have to see that he receives a proper education and is well mannered. None of this spitting tobacco and cursing that these Texans are so fond of! We shall have to endeavor to bring culture to this state."

She laughed lightly. "First you bring law to the western part of the state, and now you want to bring culture to Texas. Whatever am I to do with you?"

"Grow old," he murmured, before he gathered her into his arms, stood, and carried her to the bedroom where he planned for them to grow old together.

Author's Note

Several years ago as I was browsing through a bookstore, a book caught my attention. I long ago stopped questioning why certain books stood out on the shelf and simply got into the habit of purchasing them when they did, certain there would come a time when I was glad that I had.

Doc Susie, written by Virginia Cornell, is the biography of a physician diagnosed with consumption who traveled west to die at the age of thirty-seven. Incredibly weak and occasionally coughing up blood, she had to be carried to the train. When she arrived at her destination and word spread that she was a physician, she found herself called upon to walk to the homes of people in poor health to offer what medical assistance she could. No one knows if it was the air, an improved diet, her brisk walks, or simply a determination not to die, but Susan Anderson, M.D., soon discovered that her health was improving, and in time, no signs of consumption remained. She lived another fifty-three years.

Her story served as the inspiration for my character,

Ashton. Although Ashton is not a physician, she does eventually recover from her illness. As the author, I should know if the air, the improved diet, or the brisk daily walks improved her health. As a romantic, however, I have to believe it was the very special love of Christian Montgomery.

I hope you enjoyed Kit and Ashton's story and find it possible to accept that sometimes miracles do happen.

Coming next month

A Breath of Scandal

by *USA Today* bestselling author

Connie Mason

Julian Thornton, Earl of Mansfield and secret agent to the Crown, is rescued by Lara, a beguiling Gypsy he takes as his bride. But when seeds of betrayal are planted, will their love survive?

An Avon Romantic Treasure

"Connie Mason writes the stuff dreams are made of."
Romantic Times

And don't miss these other unforgettable Avon romances next month
Sweethearts of the Twilight Lanes by Luanne Jones
The Lawman's Surrender by Debra Mullins
His Forbidden Kiss by Margaret Moore